Dear Jacqui,
Much love
enjoy.
Love,
2019

THE NEW FLESH

A Literary Tribute to David Cronenberg

Edited by Sam Richard & Brendan Vidito

Weird Punk Books

Front cover art and design by Michael Bukowski and lastchanceillustration.wordpress.com

Back cover art by Sarah Seember Huisken

Back cover/spine layout and formatting by Don Noble

Internal illustration by Jim Agpalza

Photo of the editors courtesy of Leza Cantoral

TABLE OF CONTENTS

INTRODUCING THE NEW FLESH - KATHE KOJA

We've all got the disease, the disease of being finite.

The body as wunderkammer. The body as nightmare. The body as playground. The body as vehicle. The body as master. The body as meat. The body as metastatic riot. The body as mystery.

Everybody's a mad scientist, and life is their lab.

Fetish technology. Pleasure technology. Sinister technology. Incomprehensible technology. Inhuman technology. Technology plus velocity, velocity plus death, death plus technology.

Everybody has antennae. Some people mute them.

The songs of Trent Reznor, Robyn Hitchcock, and Scott Walker. The photographs of Joel-Peter Witkin. The couture of Alexander McQueen. The performance machines of Survival Research Labs. The poetry of Lautréamont. The menus of Carsten Höller.

Do you remember when you found out you wouldn't live forever?

The sound of hard rain on dry concrete. The sound of a ventilator malfunctioning in the ICU. The sound of blood trickling into a floor drain. The sound of an electric gate opening and closing. The smell of brake fluid. The smell of carefully collected human bile. The smell of wet flowers at the bottom of a vase. The smell of a drained gymnasium pool. The smell of used gauze.

I'm really happy not to be in any of my movies.

Dead Ringers. The Fly. Crash. Scanners. Videodrome. eXistenz. A History of Violence. Maps to the Stars. Cosmopolis. A Dangerous Method. Naked Lunch. Eastern Promises. M Butterfly. The Dead Zone. The Brood. Rabid. Shivers. Fast Company.

To feel that you were really beginning to understand the form of life...that was exciting. That's not horror to me, that's pure ecstasy actually.

Brian Evenson. Sara Century. C.M. Muller. Leo X. Robertson. Max D. Stanton. Emma Alice Johnson. Cody Goodfellow. Bruno Lombardi. Katy Michlle Quinn. Jack Lothian. Mona Swan LeSueur & Fiona Maeve Geist. Madeleine Swann. Charles Austin Muir. Ryan Harding. Alex Smith. Gwendolyn Kiste. Brendan Vidito. Sam Richard.

Welcome to the New Flesh.

[All quotes: David Cronenberg.]

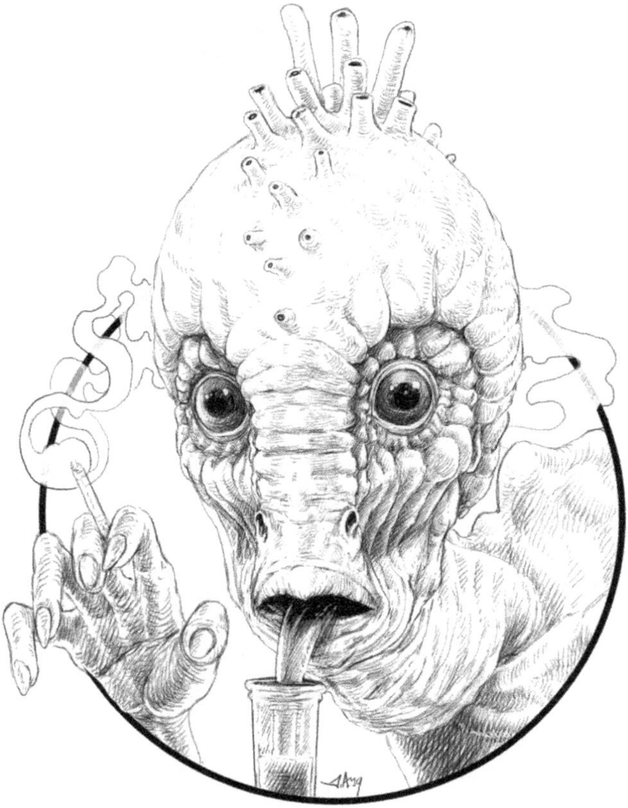

A BAD PATCH - BRIAN EVENSON

In January, I began to have difficulties with my stomach and intestines. I could hardly keep any food down, but despite this my belly began to bloat and swell. It was sore, tender to the touch, and soon I could no longer wear any of my pants: the pressure of the waistline against my belly caused cramps and acute pain and made it impossible for me to walk. Instead, I began to wear the housedresses my wife had left behind when she died. These were billowing and voluminous and put no pressure on my belly at all.

The first week, unsure of what was happening, I called in sick to work. In retrospect, I should have gone to see a doctor, but I kept thinking it would pass. As the second week began, I found my thoughts sufficiently muddled and confused that I somehow no longer even thought of a doctor as a possibility. I was not, in a manner of speaking, myself. I didn't leave the house, did very little beyond sit on the couch, staring down, watching my stomach rippling gently beneath my wife's housedress.

I still had enough presence of mind to call in each morning and report myself ill to the Corporation. But as the third week began, I was told by the Corporation's health auditor that I needed a certification from a medical professional if this was to continue. If I did not submit one in four days, he regretted to inform me, I would be terminated.

And so, the morning of the fourth day, I put on my favorite of my wife's housedresses—which, by now, I had begun to think of as *my* housedresses—and put a trench coat over it. I found a pair of my wife's leggings and snipped the legs off mid-thigh with a pair of shears. These snipped-off leggings legs I slid over my own legs, affixing the top of them to the inside of the dress with safety pins to keep them in place. I pinned up the hem of the dress too so it wouldn't show below the trench coat. When I regarded myself in the mirror, forcibly holding the trench coat closed with my hands since my belly was too distended for me to belt it, I approved of what I saw. From a distance, it looked like I was wearing pants, like there was nothing wrong with me beyond the fact that I was wearing a trench coat in summer. With my protruding belly I looked a little strange, perhaps, but I did not judge myself to be alarming.

My wife's brother was a pathologist. He was, technically speaking, a medical professional, though he was currently employed as a coroner by the police. Since the corporation had not specified that I must see a particular kind of medical professional, I decided he would do.

My belly roiled as I walked. Several times my stomach clenched hard and I had to hold to a light pole or lean against a building wall or a parked car until the pain passed, sweat beading on my forehead. Something, I realized briefly, was very wrong with me, but almost as soon as I thought this, the thought swirled away and was gone. As long as I had stayed at home, in my wife's housedresses, moving little, I could pretend I was experiencing a transient illness, that it would soon pass, but now, out and walking, there was no denying how ill I was. I was almost tempted to go see an actual doctor, but since I had almost reached the police station, I simply continued as planned.

My brother-in-law was not at his desk. *Has he perhaps taken a very late lunch?* I wondered aloud. One of his colleagues was looking at me with a certain amount of what I interpreted to be anxiety. I asked him if he knew where my brother-in-law was.

"Morgue," he said, and turned away, a look of disgust crossing over his face.

And so I thanked him and made my way to the morgue.

He had a body laid out on the table. It looked fresh, but perhaps it was not all that fresh and had merely been kept cold in a refrigerated drawer. It was very pale, no doubt exsanguinated. He had cut open the breastbone and spread the ribs. He appeared to be removing and examining the organs one by one, occasionally speaking into a portable tape recorder. He was wearing a mask and gloves, a smock. After a few moments he noticed me out of the corner of his eye.

"You can't be in here, miss," he said. And then, "Oh, it's you, Peter." And then, "Is that Helen's dress?"

"Hello, Magnus," I said, and tugged the trench coat closed again.

"Hello," he said warily.

"It's nice to see you," I said.

"It's nice to see you too," he claimed, but he sounded less than certain of this. "You look awful. What's wrong with you?"

"That's what I came to see you about," I said. "I need a doctor's note."

"A doctor's note?"

"Saying I'm ill. To give to the Corporation. Otherwise, I'll be terminated."

"You want me to recommend a doctor?"

"No," I said patiently. "I want you to write the note for me."

"I'm not that kind of doctor. I only deal with corpses."

"It doesn't matter," I said. "You're a medical professional. They'll accept a note from you."

He stripped off his gloves and deposited them in a bin. He kept his mask and smock on. He came closer. His brow furrowed.

"What's the matter with your stomach?" he asked. He reached out to open my trench coat, then thought better of it. Instead he went over to the dispenser and took a new set of nitrile gloves, wriggled them on. Only then did he coax my hands away and pull the trench coat open.

"Jesus," he said.

When he pushed against my belly, I groaned. I had to grab hold of a table to keep from collapsing.

"You've got to get to the hospital, Peter," he said. "Right away."

"It'll go away," I said. "I'm just going through a bad patch." Even as I said this I realized that I mostly didn't believe it, but something compelled me to say it anyway.

"Remember what happened to your wife," he said. "You need to go to the hospital. I'll call an ambulance."

"I can make it," I said. "I'll walk there."

He looked at me a long moment, then shook his head. "No," he said.

"No?"

"You'll die on the way over. Come on. I'll drive you. We're going now."

He turned and picked up his tape recorder, slipping it into the pocket of his smock. While he was turned, I pocketed the scalpel he had been using. *You never know when you are going need a good scalpel,* a part of my mind thought. The rest of my mind was puzzled as to what I was doing stealing a scalpel, though not sufficiently so to stop myself from doing it.

He wore his mask and gloves as he drove. He kept glancing over at me nervously. The funny thing was that on the way over to the hospital I realized I *didn't* remember what had happened to my wife, to Helen. It was at that moment that I began to suspect my mind was not entirely my own. I knew she was dead, but the specifics of her death had grown vague to me. It was as if there was a curtain in my mind, gray and fibrous, and behind it were things I was not allowed to remember. What else was to be found behind it?

"You should have gone to the hospital days ago," my brother-in-law was saying. "Lord knows how advanced you are."

"Like Helen did," I said, trying to get some information from him.

"Like Helen should have," he said. "It's the same damned thing all over again."

"It was terrible what happened to Helen," I claimed.

"Yes," he said, keeping his eyes on the road. "Terrible. But you look even worse."

When we pulled into the emergency drive, my brother-in-law said, "Stay here. I'll go get help. Don't move."

"All right," I said.

He ran inside. Then he ran back out and removed the key from the ignition, and ran back in again.

You should leave, a part of my mind told me. I have since

come to understand that it was not part of my mind at all, but something quite different. *You can't stay here.*

I need to stay here, I told myself. *My brother-in-law told me to stay here. He's getting me help.* But even as I thought this, I felt my body getting out of the car. It was like I was watching it, riding in a little chamber behind the eyes as it moved, jerky and swaying, across the drive and over the curb and through a stretch of ground strewn with woodchips, finally pushing its way into the bushes before collapsing there. Someone was groaning. With surprise, I realized it was me.

From where I was I could see Magnus's car. After a moment two men wearing protective suits came out of the hospital, my brother-in-law following them. They stopped at the open door of the car, looked around.

"He can't have gotten far," my brother-in-law said, and they began to search for me.

Quickly, my mind that was not my mind said, *you don't have much time.*

I did not know what this meant. But as the men in protective suits ran to the opposite end of the drive searching for me, my hand fumbled in my pocket until it closed upon the scalpel. In a moment I had cut open the dress over my belly. I could see my brother-in-law's legs; they weren't far from me. He would find me soon. And then I felt a prickling and looked down to see my hand push the scalpel into my belly and draw the blade quickly down.

There was a kind of whoosh of fetid air and an uprush of yellow fluid. The smell was awful, as of something dead. There was very little blood, but yes, there was some blood too. There was little pain, or rather what pain was there seemed to be muffled, as if hidden behind the gray curtain and beating its wings against it.

I reached in and let my fingers travel over the slick dampness within myself. I did not know what I was looking for or why I was doing it. After a moment, something slid through my fingers and wrapped around my wrist. I tried to withdraw my hand, but could not. I tugged hard, then harder still, until, with a sudden pop, it came free.

Pain came roaring over me and I cried out. Suddenly the gray curtain parted and I remembered how my wife had died, of the same bloating, and how in the emergency room, short-staffed, they had needed me to immobilize her hands as, with an insanely long needle, they had injected her belly, or rather the thing within her belly, with poison. But since the thing was attached to her spine, the poison took her along with it. And in her struggles to break away as I held her, she had managed to bite me and had broken the skin.

Around my hand was something that seemed like a lamprey, slick and dark, strangely ridged along its spine.

"Jesus," said my brother-in-law.

At the sound of his voice, the thing released my hand and flowed quickly toward him and up his boot. He cried out and shook it off. This time it flowed instead the other way, away from him, wriggling into the bushes. He followed it, stomping, trying to crush it. I was in so much pain that all I could do was lie there and wait to die. The two men in protective suits suddenly appeared, peering down at me. Somewhere out of sight my brother-in-law was screaming, screaming. I passed out.

When I came to, days later, I was not the same person. I was in an isolation chamber, lying in a hospital bed. I could not move my legs. A nurse was there, beside me. At least I assume it was a nurse; she was in a protective suit with a mirrored faceplate. In it, I could see reflected an image of an emaciated man on the verge of death. It took me some time to realize this was me.

The person in the suit could have been a doctor, I suppose. To be honest, I'm not even sure if the suit contained a man or a woman.

"How are you feeling?" a voice asked. It came from a box on the neck of the suit and was electronically processed, flat.

"I…" I said. "Am I going to be okay?"

"No," said the box. "You are going to die. We would like to have permission to study you, both before and after your death."

"Study me?"

"We want to understand what happened to you. So we can keep it from happening to other people."

"I… Where's Magnus? My brother-in-law? Did he kill it?"

"He killed it, but not in time."

"Not in time for what?"

Instead of answering, the faceless figure pressed a button on the side of my bed. Slowly the head of the bed lifted until I was sitting upright. At that height, I could see through the window and into the isolation chamber next to mine. There was a bed in it, and in this bed was my brother-in-law. His belly was swollen, though not to the extent mine had been. A respirator was strapped over his face.

"Will he die too?" I asked.

"We are seeing what we can do," the box on the neck of the suit said. "We might be able to save him. We have refined our procedure since your wife underwent it."

I leaned back. I closed my eyes.

"Do we have your permission to study you?" asked the box.

"No," I said.

I opened my eyes. The suited figure remained motionless. I did not, I realized, have any idea who was in it at all. For all I knew, it might have been empty.

"To clarify," said the box. "Technically we do not need your permission. We ask only as a courtesy."

I chose not to respond. After a time, the being in the protective suit left and entered an adjacent decontamination chamber. Later, I saw both a doctor and a nurse on the outside of the wall, looking in through the glass at me and at my brother-in-law. I do not know which one of them, if either, had been in the suit.

I do not know how much time I have left. I am weak, and the way the creature was separated from my spine left me paralyzed from the waist down. My belly, now flat and crisscrossed with stitches, feels empty. My stomach no longer functions as a stomach, and I take my nourishment by drip. They will study me whether I want to them to or not.

All I can do is elevate the head of my bed and sit there, waiting, looking through the glass at my brother-in-law. Despite the distance I can see his belly roiling. It swells bigger every day. At first, from what the box on the neck of the suit said, I thought they had plans to try to remove the creature, but I have come to believe these are no longer their plans at all. They are more interested in studying it, in seeing what happens once the creature is allowed to mature. There are individuals in protective suits in with Magnus day and night now, two at a time, monitoring him, measuring him. Sometimes he struggles or resists, but so far the straps have held him in place.

That could be me, I sometimes think. I know the creature convinced me not to go to the hospital for its own purposes, but, still, had I gone, what good would it have done me? I would have spent the rest of my brief life in isolation under bright lights as a group of individuals in protective suits watched my creature kill me.

Soon, it will burst out, of its own accord. These suits think they have the situation under control, but I know better. It was part of me for long enough that I can still sense it, its impulses, behind the tattered gray curtain within my mind. From this, I know that we have seen nothing yet. The suits have never seen one that is full grown, one that leaves the host not prematurely out of fear but because, simply, it is ready to unfurl.

I watch. I wait. When it finally happens, the creature opening and spreading redly in the window before me, the suits disposed of quickly one by one, I will not look away.

RED LIPS IN A BLUE LIGHT - SARA CENTURY

One thing she appreciated was that the studio was dimly lit. She'd lost her taste for bright lights as a young girl. They gave her a headache. On her third day of work, she had nervously asked the men behind the mirror to dim them and they had complied. Now, when she entered the studio, the lights were off, and she could set them herself. They had changed the color from glaring white to a soothing blue.

They were nearly done for the day. She had two stacks of paper, the one on the right was the things she had already read and the one on the left was the pages she had left. The left had dwindled until she was down to just one. She lifted it with both hands and scanned it, waiting for them to speak.

"So, what do you do for fun?" one of the men asked.

She set the paper down on top of the others. "It's actually really funny." She smiled. "I'm really a very private person. Despite the popularity I have experienced this last year with you all, in my regular life, I'm... well, I'm painfully shy. My favorite activity is just to curl up and read a book. Or, more often than not, a catalog."

The men chuckled, and she nodded and bowed to them, even though she couldn't see them from her side of the glass. She could just see herself, basking in a blue glow.

There was some minor discussion after this, but eventually, they said it would be fine for her to go home. She was relieved. It might have been just another script, but she did get so anxious when she had to be out of her house for more than a few hours.

She was used to seeing herself on screens. Everywhere she looked, there she was, the recordings of the previous Sunday morning flashing across the landscape of the city. She had to walk around in scarves and long coats and wide-brimmed hats to avoid being noticed when she left her 15th-floor apartment. One blessing of the job is that she didn't have to be outside for long.

Only Sundays and Wednesdays did she really have to go out to sit in front of the cameras and microphones in Studio 31. There, she would record pages of disconnected dialogue that sometimes sounded like nothing more than incoherent rambling as she tripped over her own tongue trying to say it all. She would read straight from the teleprompter, stare into the camera, pout or smile depending on what she felt was appropriate, and after several hours, she would leave. Some days, it was easy. Other days, it was hard.

She had gotten the job only a year before, but it had long since become a monotonous grind. She imagined anything would eventually be that way. The job also happened to be all she had. She had been struggling desperately when she'd been hired and it was a godsend. Who wouldn't want to be one of the most famous women in the city? They took care of everything. All of her expenses. They sent her food in little boxes so she didn't have to shop. They paid for her apartment with only one window, dimly lit and secluded at the end of the hall.

They offered her a car, but she preferred the train. The drivers of the cars would always talk too much, too freely, in that way that she had never quite mastered. She had been raised all alone, with doctors and nurses and teachers and therapists, but no friends, and it had stuck with her. She'd never really had a friend to this day, although she had tried. Most people were raised alongside other people, and it was obvious that this difference alienated her. She had been raised by people that always left by 5 p.m. In the night, if she wanted company, she had to scream and make a racket, but she learned quickly that they didn't like it when she did that. They punished her by tying her to her bed only one time, and she never did it again.

She waited patiently for the train she needed. She had agreed she would meet the man tonight, but she was already regretting it. The man had shown up quite valiantly one day a few months ago, helping her across the street when she was having an anxiety attack, soothing her. He worked in the same building as her, she realized and was disturbed to be recognized in public by anyone, let alone a man. He had invited her to dinner, and she had gone. It felt like the correct thing to do. He was charming, and she knew that other women found him attractive and funny. It just didn't quite click for her. Then again, nothing ever really seemed to.

She would continue seeing him if he wanted to. She didn't have anything better to do. She would stay inside under a blanket and watch herself on TV, or watch brooding melodramas, and exercise sometimes. Usually, she remembered to eat. She had thought about getting a cat but was afraid that something would happen to it. Besides, she wasn't sure quite what to do with a cat. The same she did with the man, she would sit and observe it with mild terror, she assumed.

A young girl and her mother were next to her on the train.

She tried not to stare, but she couldn't help it. They touched each other's hands and smiled so warmly. She wanted to join them, but she wouldn't know how to be a mother, or a daughter, really. They hadn't offered her any classes on that.

She paused for a moment, considering. Mother. This was a word she knew. Why had she never wondered about its meanings? Nobody she knew talked about their mothers in this grey city under the black and red sky. All she remembered before it was a sterile, cold, clinical youth spent within the blank walls of a building no one ever really explained to her.

Of course, she had a mother, but it wasn't like this. It wasn't warm. It was the woman in the white room, surrounded by gauzy curtains, tubes running out of her into machines flanking her on either side, perpetually pregnant. Not a mother, really, so much as a distant goddess. She was happy to see her for the few moments that were allowed, but these were only brief, fleeting memories in between a childhood that was wrapped in cellophane and lit by overhead fluorescent bulbs.

Still, she missed her. Once she had heard someone say, "you can't miss something you never had," but she was certain that wasn't true. Her heart had grown only increasingly, desperately hungry for it. For anyone to smile at her the way the mother smiled at the daughter on the train.

She had never spoken to her mother, but once she had held her for an extra few seconds and kissed her forehead before she was carried out of the room by staff. It was the only time someone had held onto her. She still remembered. She would always remember.

On television, she saw herself say the words, "my mother passed away when I was only a child. We buried her on the hill in the cemetery overlooking the sea."

She paused. She had never said that. She was sure of it. More and more, quips and phrases that she distinctly knew she would have disagreed with were popping up in the transmissions. "Are they doctoring the footage?" she wondered, "but why would they?" There had only been a handful of phrases in all this time that she'd declined. One card said, "I remember how my father would kiss my mother's forehead before sitting down with us for dinner every night." One had said, "My mother is the most beautiful woman I've ever seen."

The whole point of her was that she didn't know her parents well enough to say anything about them at all. Her father may never have existed. She wasn't totally sure how childbirth worked now, but it didn't seem anything like what she'd read in books. In the city, sometimes people had fathers, but she had no idea who or what had been hers. She wanted to, though. It was another thing she kept in her mind to ask her mother if she ever saw her again.

The line itself had been true. Her mother was truly beautiful, that was undeniable. Like an angry God in the sky, she was serving a terrible, necessary purpose. She represented one view of truth that was elemental and unsettling. It had been true in a way that had made her too uncomfortable to say out loud. Her mother really was the most beautiful woman she'd ever seen. She just couldn't say the words.

She had agreed to meet the man in front of the cafe where they always met. It was raining, so she had backed up to wait under the awning. Immediately, the restaurant workers had demanded to know why she was dallying, so she explained, and they reluctantly agreed to allow her to wait. He appeared in the crowd of people walking down the street, and broke into a jog, rushing up to her. He kissed her cheek and brushed some of the rain off them both.

"Did you get your work done?"

She nodded. "Yes, I..." she thought about it. "I did."

"Great! So you can come with me tonight."

She nodded even more slowly, almost smiling, deciding against it, then going for it, perhaps too great a smile, perhaps too enthusiastically. "Yes!"

"Is there something the matter?"

She shook her head, thought about it, then nodded. "I just think... maybe they're getting angry with me, or... maybe I'm not saying the lines correctly, anymore."

"You're the It Girl, aren't you?" he smirked, somewhat cruel, then becoming self-aware of the cruelty. His smirk faded and he glanced away and back again. He raised his eyebrows as if he'd asked an honest question that warranted a serious response.

"What does that even mean?" She wondered. "We're all constantly using phrases when we have no clue what they mean. Where did that term come from? Even the reporter that called me that had no idea. I asked. I wrote to her. She didn't know."

He sighed, seeming bored. "If you wear yourself out asking pointless questions, you'll be too tired to do anything else," he warned without realizing what a relief it would be to her not to have to go with him tonight.

She smiled with superficial tolerance, suddenly angry with him. "I'm actually not feeling well. Do you mind if I don't go?"

He rolled his eyes. "I knew you were going to cancel. You always cancel."

"I never agreed to begin with. I said..."

"Wait and see," he finished in a sing-song tone, mocking her. "It's what you always say. Well, go on, I don't want to catch whatever you've got, anyway." They still ate dinner with each other. When it was over, he kissed her cheek, and they walked away from one another. He tried to light his cigarette in the rain and ended up losing it to the wind while she walked evenly and gracefully with no jacket and no umbrella through the black raindrops that fell heavily from the sky.

She began wandering, uncertain of where exactly she intended to go. Surprising even herself, she darted into the subway tunnel and scanned the pending trains. There was one bus she hadn't caught in years, not since it had brought her here, to the city. One specific bus, that only went to a single place, with only a few stops along the way. The bus that could take her to her mother, and where she'd come from.

It didn't make sense. She wouldn't be allowed to see her mother. She hadn't been allowed before when they lived under the same roof and it would be worse now. She was fairly convinced she could even get in trouble for it.

Still, she couldn't stop thinking of her mother. She just couldn't. There wasn't anything else in her life. There wasn't anyone. She had bounced from room to room and building to building for years. It was all she knew. To her, other people had always seemed intrusive and loud. It gave her nausea and headaches to be around too many of them. Stepping off the train into the square gave her a panic attack. It had become familiar with time, but never comfortable.

She wondered if her mother had viewed her like that, another braying interruption in what would be an otherwise peaceful day. It was likely that her mother wouldn't even remember her. They hadn't allowed visits between them at all in the last few years of her living there. The worse, more terrible possibility was that her mother might have died without anyone mentioning it.

The train ride out of town took forever, nearly two hours, during which time she nervously tapped on the window and shifted in her seat. She couldn't think of a clever lie, so she simply stated her case. "I'd like to see my mother." She gave them the information they needed. It was the same receptionist that had always worked there, but the woman didn't recognize her.

Still, they acted like this sort of thing happened all the time. There was a short wait, but ultimately she was waved through. The guard didn't even wait on her. He just showed her the door and allowed her to go.

Her heart began to pound in her chest as she walked in, stunned by how lucky she felt to be let through. The thunderous noise of her own excitement stopped dead the moment she saw the inside of her mother's room.

It was the same room that she'd always been in. It was all-white, white furniture and walls, no windows, with her mother positioned on the bed in the middle of the room. It was the same as it ever was, except her mother had changed. Instead of a beautiful woman reclined luxuriously while machines whirred all around her, she had become gray and tired. She was breathing laboriously, her hands draped almost lifelessly over her lap.

Her senses struggled to make sense of what was happening. There was something on the floor and the walls, something not white but grayish pink. She scanned it and scanned her mother, again and again, trying to understand. When it finally clicked, her stomach lurched.

It was her mother. Her mother had grown around the room. The crawling threads were her skin. She was turning the room into some kind of cocoon of her own flesh.

She burst into tears, retching, her body unable to choose whether sorrow or revulsion was its priority. She stepped slowly forward, the skin shifting and sliding under her shoes. Pieces of her mother fell from the ceiling with wet, slopping noises. She wept. She reached for her mother, but when her hand landed on her wrist, the skin began to slide, and she couldn't stop screaming.

The guard led her out, and somehow the staff all managed to push her to the train. The ride home was a blur, horrible and obscured, with her routinely bursting into ragged bouts of weeping despair. There were still bits of her mother stuck in the tread of her shoes, under her fingernails, in her hair. She rubbed her arms and face, but couldn't get the slime off.

She made it home very late, walked into her apartment, and closed the door behind her.

The worst thing wasn't that her mother might die, it was that she herself might live through all the same trauma and horror, pinned to the bed and fed upon by children like little worms stuck to her belly, who she could no longer bring herself to see as her own. Who she no longer saw as children at all. The worst thing wasn't life or death, it was the potential she felt in her own body to become her mother. She touched her skin, mortified by its elasticity. She rubbed it and rubbed it and when that didn't work she just began clawing at herself, scratching and bleeding and finally falling asleep.

She went to work that Wednesday the same as always and acted as though nothing had changed. The speech for today began, "I remember the last time I saw my mother, she told me she loved me . . ." She winced, and flipped the piece of paper face down. The set-up was all the same, but when they told her it was time to start recording, she shook her head. "Actually, I've prepared something I'd like to read," she smiled, pushed the papers off to the side. There was a charged silence, but no voices came.

"I was thinking of last year when I saw a spider eat another spider, and why I couldn't forget it. It appeared to me and my dreams again and again. I couldn't understand why I was so interested in it. Obsessed, maybe. I watched TV all day and all night trying to forget, but it kept appearing in my mind."

She glanced upwards at the mirror. "It's because I viewed it as an analogy for my life." She smiled, triumphant to finally understand. "The point is, the more of myself I lost, the more we all become one. What is death, but a final and sudden erosion of our identities into nothingness?"

She paused. She had memorized the next line, but she still needed a moment to take a breath. "It's just that some basic truths still come as a shock. Nobody likes to think of it, but we've all started rotting well before we die."

The studio was silent. She lit a cigarette in the no-smoking studio and used it to burn the papers they had given her. She calmly reapplied her lipstick and waited for someone to come drag her to the final pit they would throw her in, whatever it might be.

Yet nothing happened. No one came. She waited and waited, but the voices never returned. After a while, the lights began to shut off. She eventually left, uncertain, and more afraid than she'd been before. The streets were emptying in the lateness of the day, and she was afraid she'd missed the bus, catching the last one only by seconds. The speakers were droning, as always. When she made it home, she walked calmly down the dirty green carpeted halls, flanked by the faded yellow walls that made her feel so claustrophobic here. Her door was locked, and her key would no longer work. She tried for a while, then gave up, returning to the streets.

It was dark, now. The streets, where she'd been warned again and again not to be caught out in at night, were empty. The bright blue lights of the police shone as they flashed down the alleys, but even with no one around, the speakers were still present. The voices loomed as ominously as the sky. It wasn't long before she heard her own voice, the voice that sounded just like her but said things she had never said.

"I remember the last time I saw my mother, she told me she loved me . . ."

DESCRAMBLER - C.M. MULLER

Max heard the van well before it turned onto his street. The low drone of its damaged exhaust always reminded him of the opening credits to some unproduced grade-Z video. Clamshell-encased cassettes in hand, he wended his way through the hoard his mother had made of their home during his father's long (and likely permanent) absence. Once outside, Max crossed the cluttered lawn to the weed-blighted boulevard where he awaited the arrival of the video dealer.

In time, Ryshpan's van lumbered around the bend and crept exhaustedly to the curb. It idled there, engine ticking, exhaust fouling the air. An off-center logo filled the upper quadrant of the sliding door, with RYSHPAN VIDEO crammed into a space trying its best to resemble a VHS tape. Max had never asked, but he assumed the design was the video dealer's handiwork. Crude as it was, Max loved everything about it.

The sliding door unlocked, popping from its seal like a pressurized lid. As the panel clattered along its corroded, chain-driven track, Max moved closer to the illuminated interior. A wire display rack spanned the length of the far wall, each row filled to capacity with videocassettes held in place by frayed bungee cords. The majority of Ryshpan's merchandise, however, resided in genre-labeled plastic bins on the floor of the gutted van.

To Max, the organized chaos of this mobile video outlet contained a charm and comfort he could not fully express. He deposited his returns into the bin housed in the space where a passenger seat had once been. Ryshpan, half turned in the driver's seat, offered his standard greeting: the broad, fixed smile of the Cheshire Cat. Dark-framed glasses (containing the thickest lenses Max had ever seen) refashioned the video dealer's eyes into shifting peppercorns, and his shock of wavy auburn hair seemed to move of its own accord in the breezeless space.

"Enjoy the flicks this week?" Ryshpan said without losing the smile.

Max nodded briefly and turned his attention to the bungee-restrained wall of cassettes. Taken collectively, their covers (all of which were displayed face-out) represented the most darkly exquisite mural Max had ever laid eyes upon. His dream was to someday fashion a similar mural along one of the walls of his room, if and when he acquired enough cassettes to do so.

"*Network of Blood* was cool," he said, lifting a cassette from the bin labeled BODY HORROR. "The rest were okay, not too bad."

Ryshpan's smile wavered, though only for a moment.

"Got anything else by the director?" Max bent deeper into the van and selected two additional clamshelled horrors from the wall.

"You're in luck," Ryshpan said, leaning toward the glove compartment. The darkened, rectangular space resembled the front of a VCR, from which the video dealer withdrew a cassette. "Here's his latest." He held the tape aloft with reverence. "This one's special."

Max hesitated but eventually grabbed the cassette (which was not encased in clamshell), and then turned his attention to another bin, where he made his final selection: *Tales From the Quadead Zone*. He reached into his pocket, withdrew a few crumpled bills, and deposited them into the burlap sack affixed to the side of Ryshpan's seat.

"Don't forget your magazine," the video dealer said, his arm resting casually on the dash, finger ready to depress the custom-made switch that activated the sliding door.

Max reached into the cardboard box next to the returns-bin and withdrew a back issue of *Fangoria* with Pinhead gracing its cover. He gazed at the lurid details for a bit too long, forgetting about the sliding door. It was on the verge of pinning him to the threshold as he leapt back.

"Until next week, my friend," Ryshpan said before the door locked in place.

The van slammed into gear and lumbered down the street, its damaged soundtrack accompanying Max all the way to his room, where it eventually faded to black.

Max's initial encounter with the video dealer had been outside the local Blockbuster. The van had shown up there two months ago, idling defiantly in the parking lot as Max exited the store with his bag of videos. The logo on the van immediately drew his attention and, after yanking his Kuwahara from the steel corral, he wheeled in for a closer look. Ryshpan was grinning from the open window, elbows resting on the sill, a tattered clipboard in hand.

"First week of seven is free," he proclaimed, tossing the clipboard near the balding front tire of the Kuwahara. Dumbfounded, Max bent to retrieve it, scanning the names and addresses that filled its sheets. He recognized a few on the list, mostly classmates from school.

As much as he wanted to subscribe, Max returned the clipboard that night and pedaled casually from the parking lot, looking over his shoulder more times than he cared to admit. Two weeks later, after having grown weary of Blockbuster's popular and predictable fare, he again approached the van, setting his apprehension aside to add his name and address to the list. The idea of a mobile video store appealed to him on so many levels, and he was excited to begin this new phase of his video existence.

Before Max ventured home, Ryshpan gifted him his first complimentary back issue of *Fangoria*.

In his room, Max had a closer look at the mystery cassette. The majority of the video dealer's stock was protected by clamshell casings (all of which were nearing the end of their life cycle), but not this one. There were no identifying labels, and its overall pristine condition had Max wondering if it was a blank cassette. The longer he held it, the more he noticed that its texture seemed a bit off, as though it had been produced using material other than plastic. It felt nearly as pliant as the grips of his Kuwahara.

Max squeezed another cassette from its case and held the pair beneath the ceiling light, searching for textural differences. His mind had obviously been playing tricks, for they both looked and felt like any other mass-produced VHS. He knocked the cassettes together, their inner spools clattering in a familiar way, and then inserted the unmarked one into the VCR. As internal mechanisms began to whirr, Max retreated to the edge of his bed. Static-infused darkness infested the TV screen, the image rippling for half a minute before transitioning to a full-on stream of static. Max waited (and then waited some more) for the opening credits, but nothing came.

He rose to eject the tape, wondering why Ryshpan had deceived him in such a way.

Midway to the TV, he stopped. The screen was expanding exponentially as if the static-stream could no longer be contained within its plastic reservoir. This sentient-like static continued to spill outside the frame, the accompanying audio growing in intensity like a swarm of gnats. Max remained paralyzed in disbelief, mesmerized by the…hallucination? He wondered if he had the courage to step into its midst to hit the STOP button, but by the time the decision was made the impossible swarm had eclipsed the whole of the VCR and was now advancing toward him like industrial smoke. The mass curled when it met floor and ceiling, and as it crept across the latter, Max backstepped until he lost his equilibrium and collapsed onto the bed. As though sensing his vulnerability, the static rained down like particles drawn to a magnet.

They enveloped Max in a buzzing cocoon before he lost consciousness.

When he came to, it felt as though little time had passed. The only difference was that the impossible swarm no longer dominated his room. He rose from his bed, arms outstretched with typical early-morning grogginess, feeling as though he'd experienced a full night's sleep. His clock told otherwise. Only ninety minutes had passed. He surveyed his room, expecting to find lingering traces of static, but everything looked normal. The TV was on, its bright blue screen putting Max momentarily on edge as he imagined it filling the room with another illusion.

He cautiously approached the VCR and, with a trembling finger, tapped the EJECT button. After an interminable wait, the machine finally spat out the cassette. Max yanked it from the slot and peered at the inner spool, surprised to find that it had played out in its entirety. More than likely, the run-time had been ninety minutes, the same span he'd been out. At his desk, he slipped the cassette under the stack of those he had yet to view and grabbed the topmost clamshell. He pinched its lower quadrant and jerked the cassette free, a sense of normalcy returning. It was nearly midnight, but Max wasn't tired in the least; maybe viewing another offering would help.

He inserted *Tales From the Quadead Zone,* turned off the overhead light, and slipped into bed. The TV blipped from black to an explosion of static, remaining in this state for longer than it should have. Max tore the bedspread aside and lunged for the STOP button, not wishing to repeat his earlier experience. So far, the static remained contained, cordoned off by the thick plastic walls of the TV. Nevertheless, Max did not hesitate to eject the cassette. After a moment of contemplation, he tried another of Ryshpan's videos.

Each of the seven turned out to be defective, containing nothing but bands of static. Curious, Max checked a few tapes from his personal library…and was met with the same result. Every VHS in his possession had been infected by Ryshpan's viral video. As disheartening and devastating as this was, Max knew he needed to get some sleep. Sensing that he would not be able to do so, he located his back issues of *Fangoria* from beneath the bed and curled up to read.

In the silence of the room, the sound of static still echoed in his ears.

Nothing was right the following morning. To Max, it appeared as if reality was double-exposed, though not in the sense of familiar objects being duplicated. Instead, there seemed to be an overlay of sorts, one that grew more prominent with each passing hour.

How he made it through the school day was beyond him. The ride home had seen him hiding in the rear seat of the bus, eyes closed for the majority of the ride. Horrors existed here as well, though not to the extent of what he had witnessed on the streets of his hometown. The scuttling skinless things appeared vaguely humanoid, but only in the manner of their head, torso, and limbs. Their long, emaciated appendages and distended bellies bespoke of perpetual starvation, and their movement was at its most frantic when they drew near unsuspecting townsfolk going about their daily business. As they circled certain individuals, these monstrosities would thrust their elongated heads mongrel-like to the ground, seeming to feast on something Max could not readily see.

When he could no longer stomach the sight outside, Max shifted his attention to the interior of the bus. From the center aisle, one of the eyeless things was observing him. Its long desiccated fingers clasped the edge of the vinyl seat, and it "looked" at him with what felt like clinical detachment. Its nose, which now existed as a hollow cavity, sniffed at the air, and what appeared to be its mouth opened as though on the verge of communication...but, as the lips parted, the toothless maw produced no words. Instead, a thin tongue curled outward from the lipless mouth and seemed to test the air. The creature dipped its head to the seat and shifted uncomfortably close, forcing Max to retreat as far as he could, until the cold metal of the bus's hull gouged at his side. The creature worked frantically, silently, and Max felt trapped. The only sound, besides chattering classmates, was the diesel-rumbling of the bus itself.

Eventually, the thing completed its weird feast, drifting back to a more observational stance. There was clearly an intelligence there, and it was easy for Max to imagine that in some prior life this monster had been human. As the mouth appendage slowly retracted into its parched lips, Max noticed all the dust collected about its mouth.

More than anything, Max wished he had his wrist-rocket. That could certainly do some damage at this close range. He reached out a trembling hand, wanting—and yet not—to determine the corporality of the thing, or if it was mere illusion. Before he could make contact, however, the creature disappeared down the aisle, the fast-forward motion reminiscent of a VCR tuned exclusively to the thing itself.

During the remainder of the journey home, Max could not shake an insight that one of his teachers had expressed earlier in the year: that the majority of dust in the world was composed of flakes of dead human skin.

Whatever the things were—Max's only theory at this point was that their population consisted of the long dead residing in some kind of purgatorial overlay, their only means of contact with this world being the very dust it produced. *Bottom Feeders From the Fifth Dimension*...this struck Max as the perfect title for a film, and he grew excited by the possibilities. In the last year or so he'd been drawn to the idea of filmmaking, and maybe this Z-grade experience would prove the impetus he needed to begin his journey. He could even get Ryshpan involved, distributing the film to the underground market. Indeed, he was inspired enough to brave the depths of the basement to retrieve the high-end "cats-eye" camcorder his father had left behind. As Max loaded the machine with a blank cassette, he imagined some future interview with *Fangoria* in which the question of origins was posed: "Tell us more about the inspiration behind your award-winning debut?"

Since returning home from school, Max had not crossed paths with any more of the Feeders. Nevertheless, he had gone through each room (after retrieving his wrist-rocket and a few smooth stones from the jar he kept on his desk), just to make certain none of the Feeders were hiding in any of the dusty corners of the house. When his mother asked him what he was doing, he continued his search without a word, and before long she went back to watching her show. She was used to him roaming about the house in such a state, his quirky imagination leading the way.

Eventually retreating to his room, Max charged the camcorder for half an hour before venturing outside, hopeful that he might capture one of the Feeders on tape. He could either use the footage in *Bottom Feeders* or turn it over to the local media. Would they believe such evidence, or tag it as an elaborate hoax staged by his costumed friends? Probably the latter. Nevertheless, Max wandered for six blocks, encountering dozens of people—none of whom were accompanied by parasites. His reality, it seemed, had been cleansed. But for how long?

Max was anxious to question Ryshpan about the time-released delusion he had undergone. Was it some new manner of filmmaking—an immersive leap in technology that the video dealer had been paid to test on unsuspecting patrons? The greater question was whether the experience was real or composed merely of imagery culled from Max's imagination. Had being exposed to the mystery tape allowed him a glimpse into another dimension normally invisible to the naked eye?

Later that evening, Max had his answer. After inserting one of Ryshpan's cassettes in the VCR, fully expecting to encounter the same static-filled erasure, he instead sat on the edge of his bed and watched the movie (as advertised) play through its designated run-time, unblemished and picture perfect. Encouraged, he viewed each of the rentals, in turn, savoring every minute.

It was nearly three a.m. when he finished, and as much as he wanted to give the mystery cassette another try, he held off and continued to do so for the entirety of the week…until Ryshpan's return.

Stack of clamshells in hand, Max scanned the area as though expecting to encounter a stray Feeder or two. But the neighborhood was as quiet and unassuming as it had ever been. In time—*right* on time, in fact—Ryshpan's van pulled to the curb, its sliding door retracting like a beetle's elytra before flight. Per usual, the video dealer was half turned in his seat, showcasing his all-consuming smile and bespectacled eyes.

"So, what's the verdict? Pretty trippy, right?"

Max stared at the video dealer, dropping his returns into the bin without saying a word. Ryshpan reached toward the glove compartment and withdrew another cassette. He held it out to Max.

"I guarantee you'll like this one even better. It's a bit more…*interactive*."

Max eyed the cassette and considered taking it, but in the end declined the offer, selecting seven standard videos from the bins before him. He wasn't sure he was ready to experience this even newer format, at least not this week—and besides, he had more than enough inspiration to begin early production work on *Bottom Feeders*. He planned to start the script tonight on his mother's old Olivetti, a machine that, once his fingers began depressing keys, never failed to remind him of a clattering bug.

"Your loss, my friend," Ryshpan said after Max paid for his rentals. "This is the future. Total immersion and that ain't the half of it…this new stuff'll completely blow your mind."

As the door slid shut, Max could still hear the video dealer's voice going on about the future of video, but it was so layered with static that he could not make out the words. The van pulled away, its hull and the reality around it glitching like the blemished image on an overplayed VHS tape.

This visual glitch occurred twice more as Max made his way back to his room—once while reaching for the front door, and the other upon glimpsing his mother in her TV chair—but in the end, the reality of things tracked back into focus and continued to play along its eternal plastic spool.

LACKERS - LEO X. ROBERTSON

Bodies pulse on velvet throws, plastic lilos, picnic blankets, sodden-looking pillows, and even on the bare concrete floor. Skin glows beneath a string of technicolor LEDs taped across the generator room's goliath metal structures, across their rusting steel wheels and flaking valves.

Even at an orgy, with all these naked people around him, Neil feels underdressed in his crumpled white shirt and jeans. He smooths his lank brown hair and redirects his gaze to anything but the people. Cables stream out to two-bar heaters in the room's corners, which poorly stem the winter chill. Bluetooth speakers, strewn across the floor, ooze some slow and sultry song that resounds around the room.

When Neil musters the courage to look again, more details of the flesh-pile reveal themselves. Large birthmarks. Cleft lips. Missing eyes, digits, and limbs.

By his feet, a half-naked man crawls over a woman. He licks down her neck and across her mastectomy scars, his tongue covering their scaly surface. A prosthetic nose languishes on the floor beside the pair, its metal snap fasteners glinting in the colored light.

The man turns to Neil. There's a red raw hole in his face where his nose once was.

Should Neil keep watching? What's the etiquette here?

Before he can decide what to do, Luka hooks an arm around him from behind.

"I only want to watch," Neil says, startled.

Luka laughs. "I only want to talk."

Luka guides Neil to a room at the back of the power station. Plastic limbs, with tags on them, form a flesh-colored pyramid in the room's corner. Protective masks hang on the wall.

"You can relax." Luka's voice is honeyed, his accent ambiguously European.

Neil takes the time to look at him now. His olive skin, slicked-back black hair, dark brooding eyes. He wears a purple silk kimono with a pattern of robot hands all over it. A long towel covers his legs, much like those dotted all over the generator room floor.

"Sorry for being lame." Neil examines the stained tag on a plastic knee socket. "Shit."

"What?"

"I shouldn't have said 'lame.' In this room."

Luka grins. Moonlight reveals his perfect teeth.

"So you store everything here for afterwards," Neil says.

"We cast off prostheses first, inhibitions second." Luka gestures towards the generator room, his silk sleeve falling across the stump of his left arm. "Here, we are our true selves. Lackers." He looks at the ghost of his missing hand as if to recognize it there in the air.

Neil imagines the hand gesturing. It's even more conspicuous by its non-existence.

"So you'll only observe."

Neil grips the hair at his crown. "I have a husband, for one. Maybe that doesn't stop the others, but it's enough for me. And, well, I've honestly never felt very sexual."

"Why not?"

He bites his inner cheek. "I didn't think events like this were for people like me."

"Before you knew about our mission, you mean?" Luka folds his arm and phantom arm.

"Yeah. I always have to brace people for what they're going to see when I take off my clothes."

"Speaking of which," Luka says, "it's time for me to see. The part of you that isn't whole."

This is the same wording from the lackers' illicit website, where Neil had uploaded the photo of himself that granted him entry to the club tonight.

He knew this was coming. A chill in the room announces itself. He unbuttons his shirt and moves over to the light so Luka can see.

Luka gasps. "Can I touch it?"

"I-I guess so."

With a warm finger, Luka traces the concavity of skin over Neil's heart. The caress sends tingles across Neil's skin.

"But how?" Luka asks.

Neil shrugs. "The ribs just never grew there. I came out of the womb holding a fist over my heart."

"I'll bet you did." Luka flattens his palm over the skin crater.

"Kids used to bully me about it."

"Oh yeah?"

"They saw it one time after gym." A strange, contorted grin takes over Neil's face. "They called me Marilyn. Like Marilyn Manson? They asked if I'd had the ribs removed so I could suck my own dick."

Luka laughs through his nose. "And after that?"

"No one's brought it up since."

"Sometimes what's left unsaid is the most important." Luka feels Neil's heart pounding against his hand. "Does it hurt?"

"No pain at all. It just looks different."

"'Just'? Oh but darling, appearance is everything." With Neil stunned into silence, Luka sends his hand wandering down. "By the way, I'd kill for your legs."

"Enough." Neil pushes the hand away.

"Sorry. I went too far." Luka steps back, pressing his palm to his chest. He seems to savor Neil's warmth.

"It's not just that. Look, I'm a journalist."

Luka's eyes freeze. "Huh?"

"I'm doing a feature. I only sent the photo so I could track you down." Neil buttons his shirt again.

"I appreciate your honesty," Luka says, though his cold expression betrays him. "So, you just came here to gawk at the freak show."

Neil flicks one of the masks. It dangles on a nail and throws shadows across the wall. "You know it's more serious than that. Barb Russ. Alex Tillman. Christian Simmons. These names mean anything to you?"

"No." Luka looks insulted. "People aren't too keen to admit they come here. Some are return customers, others aren't. And everyone has a code name."

Neil holds his gaze, waiting for him to falter.

"They're rumors," Luka continues, walking over to the door. "Obviously. People badly want to believe we're harmful. Undeserving of affection. Get back to me when the gossip dies to nothing. Then we won't need a club anymore."

A well of guilt forms in Neil's chest. Then again, Luka's air of having been offended could be a ploy.

Luka clasps his invisible hand in the other. "You exposed yourself to me, so I'll return the favor. I won't kick you out, and you can interview who you want. Just be upfront with them about your intent. Oh—and no photos."

When Neil returns to the generator room, the lust has cooled down.

Club members wrap blankets over their shoulders and prop themselves against the metal housings. They drape themselves across the cold concrete walls. Some smoke from short glass pipes, thick bongs, and vapes. Others lick substances from stumps.

Neil approaches "Viper", a man whose open leather waistcoat shows the plastic mesh holding in his abdominal organs.

"Industrial thresher accident," Viper says. "Stripped off the skin and muscle. And my right arm, of course." He puffs from a joint stuck in a metal pincer that juts from his shoulder.

"Queenie", a middle-aged woman in a black slip, says she always felt like her right leg belonged to someone else. "Last time I checked, the term for it was Body Integrity Identity Disorder. This one time, I filled a bathtub with dry ice and stuck my leg in it, I had a tourniquet over my thigh and I was biting on a towel to stifle my screams. My parents rumbled me in the act." She dabs her eyes with a delicate finger. "They rushed me to the hospital. Surgeons did nothing but remove the frostbitten flesh while I pleaded with them to take the whole leg with it."

Neil examines her stump. "How did you finally get the leg removed?"

She winks. "Don't worry about it."

Neil speaks to victims of acid attacks, house fires, childhood cancers, and auto accidents. Their tragedies soak into him, his heart cooled as if by the ghosts of so many missing body parts. No one will talk about the missing people and besides, he can't handle hearing more about their everyday realities. He eventually heads for the front door.

The noseless man stands close, with Luka beside him. He taps white powder onto the face of Luka's iPhone.

Luka stops Neil as he passes. "Before you go, we'd better exchange numbers. In case you have any more questions." He enunciates the last word with masterful disdain.

Neil swallows hard. "Of course."

"Adam and Eve were already 'of God', so to speak." JP's biblical pontifications echo through his and Neil's little Hackney flat. "They didn't need to eat the forbidden fruit. That was the snake's trick."

Neil bites at a thumbnail in thought. What's JP doing? He doesn't usually stay up this late making videos.

"Well, that's my interpretation anyway, doofus-face!" JP adds.

Oh. He's livestreaming on Twitch for platinum-rank Patreon subscribers.

Neil peeks into the gaming room.

Controller in hand, JP splays out on his gamer chair, which gathers sweat on his periphery. Boxes of his "merch"—crucifixes and plush toys of Jesus—surround him. He wears an old hoody and pajama bottoms. Wireless headphones sit askew on his head.

When JP turns and sees Neil standing there, he gets up and joins Neil in the hallway, kissing him on the cheek.

"You have that look on your face," JP says.

Neil acts nonchalant. "What look?"

"Distant eyes, sour mouth. You know something you don't wanna tell me."

Neil grins and stays silent.

"So you had a good time, then?"

"I wouldn't say—"

"By the way, while you were out, I googled 'amputee support groups.' Wouldn't you know, they're a thing."

Neil scoffs. "They're not just amputees, they're—"

"Lackers," JP drawls. "Wow, they sure get to people fast."

Neil walks off to the bedroom. JP follows and stops him at the foot of the hallway. Light from the restaurant signs outside casts an ethereal glow across the pair.

JP takes a deep breath, considering how to proceed. "Isn't it harmful to tell people they need to go to a special club for affection?"

"What would you have them do? Stay at home and cross their fingers that they wake up in a—" Neil looks around. "Can your subscribers hear us?"

JP pouts. "Maybe. So what was Luka like? How about that missing arm? I heard he chopped it off himself."

In response, Neil puts on his pajama bottoms, lies on the bed and pulls his laptop out the side table.

"Whatever," JP says on his way out the bedroom. "I'll be done by three."

JP makes YouTube videos on Bible interpretations, a passion that turned into a living. The pair tell each other that happiness is most important, that money isn't everything. Some days it's as if JP grants Neil permission to think that way just because JP makes more money.

Has JP so soon forgotten the years when his subscribers numbered only in the hundreds? The consolations Neil offered him as he cried on the couch? Does JP look back on that time and think of himself as a temporarily inconvenienced famous person? Isn't that the most compassionate way for him to think of Neil now?

Neil tuts and tries to tap these thoughts out his head with a fist. He reaches for his jeans on the floor, takes the phone out of the pocket and scrolls through his contacts.

Luka Novák.

Luka gave his real name?

He opens a new browser tab and searches for the name on Facebook.

Luka grins back at him, wearing wraparound sunglasses and Lycra. Behind him is a summery vista: mountains, winding dirt roads, and a clear blue sea.

Investment banker. Liver of life. Proud cat parent of two.

When JP walks into the bedroom again, Neil closes the Facebook tab.

"I was insensitive earlier," JP says.

Neil feigns confusion.

"I didn't mean to disparage anyone. I just think Luka's attitude is poisonous."

Neil looks at the time. It's three a.m. He isn't getting into it.

JP smiles bleakly, taking Neil's silence as an admission that he has a point. He comes to bed and puts his head on the fully ribbed side of Neil's chest.

They peruse Netflix together and start watching some series that supposedly takes place in a superhero universe, but no superheroes ever show up. At least not while JP is awake. He falls asleep on Neil about half an hour after Neil has lost interest.

Neil lowers the volume and opens Facebook again, clicking on Luka's picture.

Luka stands on two springy black sports prostheses.

I'd kill for your legs. Because he doesn't have his own?

When JP rolls over in bed, Neil slams the laptop shut and puts it back on the side table.

JP places a hand on Neil's chest concavity, quickly withdrawing it again, as if he'd just touched a hot iron. "Sorry," he whispers.

Neil frowns at him, then lies back and closes his eyes.

It's almost light outside when he finally falls asleep.

He dreams of a decade-old hook-up. It was after some club night out with the other waiters at the restaurant he worked at back then. He'd gone back to some stranger's shitty early-twenties apartment. They'd kissed on a couch, surrounded by empty bowls with crusted spaghetti or dried-up cereal. There was a heap of underwear in the middle of the living room carpet and a roll of toilet paper over by the TV, for some reason.

It was dark that evening, the guy was a good kisser and they were both hammered, so Neil only noticed the problem when he felt warm drops fall on his bare chest.

Blood. The guy was slicing his own forearms with a straight razor.

After all these years, Neil still remembered the sound of blood dripping on his skin.

At the time, Neil had gotten up and left without a word. But in the dream, the stranger is Luka. Luka with two arms and hands.

Instead of a straight razor, Luka wields an ornate boning knife with a mother-of-pearl handle. He doesn't just slice the skin but dig into it, into the vessels, muscle, and bone.

Blood ejaculates from the dream wound.

Squirt, squirt, squirt.

Neil wakes up in the thick sweat of nightmares, his come leaking through the sheets.

As I walked around the generator room, taking in all its carnal glory, I thought about how lackers sneaked around this city, relegating themselves to abandoned buildings out of some internalized sense of inferiority. How we were complicit in making this the case, with dating app bigotry and associated contemporary prejudice. But I was also inspired. The lackers drew attention to their imperfections. They didn't cower, didn't lust after one another despite *their flaws. They celebrated those differences and used them to fuel their desire.*

Neil lies in bed, trying to will assignments into his inbox and ignore JP's guffaws from the gaming room when he gets a message from Luka.

Tonight.

There's an address, a train station outside the city. Not quite abandoned, but according to the results on Google Maps, it's so poorly maintained and has so few trains that it might as well be.

"You have that look on your face again." It's JP, standing in the bedroom doorway.

Neil places the laptop to one side.

"Off to see your friend Mr. Novák?"

Neil snorts. "You went through my phone? Used my laptop?"

"What does it matter? Don't lie to me. I know you too well."

Neil stands up, heads to the wardrobe and pulls out some clothes. He shuffles into a pair of jeans.

"When is it?" JP looks at him in the wardrobe's inner mirror.

Neil stops buttoning the shirt. "This evening."

"Right then."

Neil pushes past JP and goes to the front door, trying to find his shoes.

"Don't," JP says. "Please."

Neil looks down at his ribless concavity, which pulses fiercely. He turns to JP. "Touch it."

JP winces and holds out a hand. He stops. "Why are you obsessed with the one thing I can't—?"

"Touch it!"

JP forces his eyes shut and reaches out again. But his hand seems to push against an invisible barrier.

Without another word, Neil puts on his shoes, does up his shirt and leaves.

Viper stands by the train station, wearing a leather jacket and scarf. Glass shards from smashed windows litter the concrete around him. A bashed brass lock lies there, glinting in sickly streetlight.

"Good to see you again," Viper says as Neil approaches.

Neil keeps his head low and nods, walking straight to the door.

Viper holds out a pincer and stops him. "There's a protocol."

"Oh."

"It's no big deal. Can you show me the message Luka sent you? With the address?"

Neil scrolls through his phone and finds the message. When he looks back up, Viper sprays him in the face with a bitter tasting chemical. A black fog consumes his vision.

When Neil comes to, he's lying by the train tracks. Up above, stars peek through a thick canopy of clouds made blue by the night.

He sits up. His jeans are torn above the knee. Cable ties loop around the track and over his legs, securing him in place. Tight rubber tourniquets squeeze at his thighs, his flesh bulging and red.

He tries to move his arms but they're bound behind his back. He tries to scream but a dirty towel gags his mouth.

"After I read your article, I had my doubts that you would show tonight."

Neil tilts his head back and sees an upside-down Luka.

Luka walks closer, pulling the kimono over himself. This one is pink and covered in silk-screened eyeballs. Their long cords of vessels and nerves run across the fabric like bloody snakes.

"You made it sound like you aren't one of us."

Neil shakes his head, trying to protest. Drips of sweat sting coldly in his eyes.

The lackers assemble in a circle around him. Viper, Queenie, the noseless man, the mastectomy-scarred woman and the rest—they're all here, all holding candles that drip big white gobs of wax.

"You redeemed yourself towards the end," Luka continues. "That part about letting imperfections fuel desire. I thought, 'Yes, he has potential. And if he comes back to us, I won't make him disappear.'" He bends down and strokes Neil's hair. "So you can join us. But not yet. Not as you are. Because what we do, it's about more than desire. It's about true beauty." He plants a gentle kiss on Neil's forehead. "You still don't know just how beautiful you could be. But with our help, you'll see."

Horns blare through the night. A train barrels towards them, its ghostly white headlights cutting through the darkness.

HEKATI YOGA - MAX D. STANTON

Barbara gazed upon the brilliant Monterey sunset, tense and annoyed in the face of its beauty. She sipped expensive wine without tasting it. A headache brewed at the base of her skull. *Goddamnit, I don't have time for this,* she thought, scanning the cafe's patio for the old friend she'd come to reconnect with. *There's a million things I should be doing right now, and I let fucking Margie talk me into drinks.*

Barbara sucked down more merlot and checked her phone again. Nothing. Just like Margie not to say that she was running late. In college Margie's hippie, scatterbrained, rules-are-for-other-people nature had been endearing—charming, even—but they'd been out of college for twelve years now. They hadn't even spoken until a few days ago when Margie connected on social media out of the blue and asked to meet up. *Insisted* that they meet up. At the time, Barbara had been curious to find out how the pot-dealing, boy-crazy, New Age madwoman of Epsilon Zeta Tau was doing. Now she regretted that curiosity. She checked her phone yet again, and her furrowed brow pulled itself in even tighter when she saw that her boss had sent her yet another batch of analyst reports to look over in connection with the latest deal he'd schemed up. *Jesus, so many words and so little insight,* Barbara thought. *I'll go through these tomorrow after the Tokyo call and before the meeting with the lawyers. Wait, though, what if Harry wants to discuss them on the Tokyo call? I'd better review them tonight, just to be sure…*

Just as Barbara felt sorely tempted to cut her losses and make her escape, her long-lost friend reappeared. Barbara's first impression was that Margie had made the transition from weed to meth. Her sorority sister's bright, unblinking eyes burned with weird intensity. When Margie spotted Barbara, her lips curled up over her teeth in a chimpanzee grin. But she dressed like an Instagram model and was disgustingly tan and fit, so Barbara guessed that her friend's strange expression was simply the result of bad plastic surgery.

"Baaaaaaaaarb!" Margie squealed, throwing her arms around Barbara.

"Margie, it's so good to see you again!" Barbara said, bringing all of her finely-honed chipperness to bear. "Epsilons forever!"

Margie ordered a gin and tonic and another glass of wine for Barbara, and the two sisters settled in for their reunion. "So how *are* you?" Margie asked, staring intently into Barbara's eyes.

"I'm doing all right," Barbara said. "I've been working at a VC firm specializing in tech. It's a lot of work, but I love it." Margie continued to stare, expectantly. Barbara groped for something else she could say about her life, finding nothing. The backs of her ears burned with embarrassment as she shifted in her chair.

"What about that big rock on your finger?" Margie asked. "Who's the lucky guy?"

Barbara held the too-tight ring up for inspection. "Do you remember Jason Merchant?"

"Your senior year boyfriend, right? With the red hair and glasses? What's he up to?"

"Jason got his Ph.D in English literature, he's a professor now." *An adjunct professor. Who sponges off me for everything and always has his nose buried in a book and who can't ever be bothered to fuck me or even just ask how my goddamn day has gone.* Barbara's gut knotted up, the way it often did when she thought about her husband. She drank some more wine.

"Barb, don't take this the wrong way, but you seem super-stressed," Margie said. "You're giving off a lot of negative energy—your aura is, like, crimson, and your chakras are thundering. I know I haven't seen you in forever, and maybe I'm being presumptuous. Or maybe because I haven't seen you in forever, I'm in a better spot to notice what's going right and what's going wrong. So tell me, *really* tell me...*how are you?*"

Something about Margie's wide-eyed, insistent sincerity forced an opening in Barbara's steely emotional defenses. "It's been tough," she admitted. "I never expected to get anything for free. I knew I'd have to work hard. But sometimes it feels like it's all too much. Like I'm stretched *so damn tight* and can't relax for a minute, not even when I'm exhausted. Especially not when I'm exhausted."

"You know what you need?" Margie asked solemnly. "You need Hekati Yoga. It's this new yoga practice I started a few weeks ago, and it has *changed my whole life*. It's totally amazing. Makes you feel like a whole new person. No, scratch that. It makes you into a whole new person. I used to be anxious and miserable, and look at me now." She flashed that wild, chimpanzee grin again. Her eyes bulged alarmingly.

"I don't know . . . I used to do yoga, but I don't really have the time for it these days."

The smile abruptly dropped from Margie's face. She stared into Barbara with a grim-faced seriousness that took Barbara aback—perhaps even frightened her a little. "Barbara, time is devouring you. With each passing second, entropy takes another bite. Don't you need to make the most of your life before it's consumed?"

In their sorority days, Margie had been more into karma and pyramids than entropic devourers, but the point was well-taken nonetheless, and Barbara had no rebuttal. They made a yoga date for a late afternoon class early next week and spent the rest of their time together trading reminiscences and gossiping about their sisters. On the drive home, Barbara realized that she'd never actually found out what Margie had been doing since college.

Barbara drove past the yoga studio three times, cursing her cell phone's GPS before she realized that the gated beachfront compound to her left was not, in fact, a billionaire's home or a country club, but rather, her destination. She announced herself to the intercom at the entrance, sheepishly mentioning that she'd come at Margie's invitation.

"We've been waiting for you, Barbara," the intercom crackled. "Please, enter. The studio is the white building at the end of the drive." The iron gates buzzed and then slowly swung open.

The view from the road was misleading—the compound was even vaster and more beautiful than it had appeared. Barbara drove through in a state of covetous awe. The palatial grounds were impeccably manicured, with vast lawns and tastefully arranged gardens overflowing with spiky, bulbous greenery, plants exotic even in the botanist's playground of California. It was good that the gatekeeper had specified to look for the white building, for many sleek, ultra-modern structures occupied the grounds. Barbara tried to imagine how much it all could have cost, and her imagination failed her. This place made Harry's mansion look like a pauper's hovel. The yoga studio itself was a smallish, cube-like building on a low cliff directly overlooking the water, its walls the color of polished bone in the sunset. As Barbara emerged from her car, the Pacific wafted a cool, salty breeze over her. *Margie didn't say anything about this,* she thought.

The reception area of the yoga studio was as minimalist as the exterior. A young, pretty receptionist in white manned a desk at the entrance. In the center of the space stood a waist-high marble sculpture of three cloaked women standing back-to-back-to-back. Where their bodies contacted they merged into one like Siamese triplets. The room was otherwise bare. "We're so happy you've come," the beaming receptionist said. "Welcome to Hekati Yoga."

"This place is amazing," Barbara said as she filled out the (suspiciously comprehensive) liability waivers. "I'm surprised I hadn't heard of it earlier. How long have you been here?"

"Oh, we have always been here," the receptionist said dreamily. "Even before the Indians, we were here."

Space cadet, thought Barbara. "What else do you offer besides yoga?"

"This is a full-service spa and healing center. We have all sorts of therapeutic treatments available to our advanced students."

"Ooh, what about massage? I haven't had a good massage in ages."

The receptionist's demeanor turned unexpectedly stern. "Spa appointments are for advanced students. Beginners would only harm themselves." In any case, after seeing what a single yoga class cost, Barbara wasn't sure that she could afford to ever return. *You need to treat yourself once in a while,* she thought, trying to convince herself. *You deserve the occasional splurge on something luxurious.* She paid for the class, and the receptionist directed her deeper into the building.

Margie was in the mat room, chatting with a few of her

fellow students when Barbara arrived. Margie's face lit up like an anglerfish's lure. "Baaaaaaaarb, I'm so glad you could make it!" she chirped. "Let me make a few introductions…" A shuddering wave of revulsion swept through Barbara as she caught her first glimpse of Margie's yoga friends. On just a moment's further inspection, however, they were astonishingly attractive, fit, and fashionable. Her initial reaction did not fade entirely, but she could not put her finger on whatever could have provoked it. She made a few brisk pleasantries, then gathered up a mat and some blocks and headed for the practice space.

A gust of ferocious heat like the breath of some vast animal greeted Barbara as she opened the studio door. Sweat beaded on her forehead and soaked into her clothes almost immediately. "You didn't mention that this was hot yoga," she complained to Margie.

"Trust me, it's worth it. I know it seems a little kooky at first. Soon you'll understand."

The practice space's western wall was glass, offering a staggering view of the ocean. Waves pounded against the rocky shoreline, suicide attackers in the endless war between sea and land. The dying sun set the water and sky ablaze and suffused the room with blood-red light. The odor of brine was even stronger here than it had been outside. Barbara laid out her mat next to Margie's and sat down, assuming the lotus position. Her knees creaked painfully, and her spine complained. *Too long sitting at a desk,* Barbara thought. *I hope the instructor takes it easy on us.*

A door towards the rear of the practice space opened, and the instructor entered, a slender, long-limbed woman as pale and unearthly as the moon without a hair on her head, not so much as an eyelash. The teacher took up her place at the head of the class, eclipsing the sun. It cast a crimson halo around her, shrouding her round face in darkness. "Namaste, my friends," she said, in a still, monotone voice as soft as baby skin. "My name is Ana Poil. Welcome to Hekati Yoga. I see a number of new faces. That makes me very happy. I promise this class will transform you."

She looks and talks like a crazy person, Barbara thought. *I should have known Margie would be mixed up in something weird.*

"Let us begin with our mantra," Poil said. "Iä."

"Iä," the class responded in one voice.

"Iä , iä, iä!"

"Iä , iä, iä!" *Kind of catchy,* Barbara thought, chanting along with her fellow students.

"Breathe deep, and hold," Poil said. "The whole of the universe is negative space surrounding you. Allow it to enter your core. Let the not-you suffuse every cell, till all distinction between you and not-you is erased. And exhale. Iä , iä, iä!"

"Iä , iä, iä!"

"Breathe deep…and exhale. The negative space defines us, gives us form and meaning like a key defines a lock. Let it inside you to unlock your treasure. Breathe deep, to bring the great emptiness into yourself…now exhale, and discard yourself into the great emptiness. All is nothing, and nothingness is all. Iä , iä, iä!""

"Iä , iä, iä!"

Despite herself, Barbara was having a good time.

The class was unlike any that Barbara had attended before. Poil led her students through a series of esoteric poses —the Worm, the Gorgon, the Hydra, the Broken Circle, the Dying King—strenuously exercising muscles Barbara barely knew she possessed. Many times she thought that she couldn't go on, that only a circus contortionist could move the way these people did, but every time she was close to failing Poil's damp, yogurt-white hands grasped her and gently twisted her into position. The tension she'd been carrying throughout her whole frame gradually evaporated, leaving her loose and free. It felt as if she were melting in the heat; as if she were experiencing the pleasure that a rigid block of ice feels when it softens into cool, flowing water. By the end of the session she was panting, red-faced, and dripping with sweat, yet she couldn't remember the last time she'd felt so relaxed. On her way out, she made an appointment to return the following week.

Jason was dozing shirtless in the living room when Barbara returned home, a half-finished book and a half-finished beer resting on the arm of the sofa. Barbara paused in the doorway, watching his thick, furry chest rise and fall. A warm flush rose in her cheeks. The intensity of her breathing increased. *The negative space is coming inside me like a key into a lock.* To her surprise, she wanted something else to come inside her. She pulled off her sweat-drenched yoga clothes and dove atop her husband, ravenous with a long-forgotten hunger.

"What was that all about?" Jason asked during the cuddles afterward. "I'm not complaining, mind you, it just seemed . . . unlike you."

"I went to a superb yoga class today," Barbara said, running her fingers through her husband's chest hair and down along the curves of his stomach. "God, I feel *alive* again. Invigorated. You should try it with me sometime."

"Nah, not really my thing. I'm glad you had a nice time, though."

Barbara idly grasped one of her fingers and pulled it backwards, twisting the digit until its fingernail touched the back of her wrist.

"Jesus, cut it out!" Jason yelped, averting his eyes. "Gross."

"But it feels so good," Barbara purred. "Like a nice stretch."

"I never even knew that you were double-jointed."

"Neither did I. I guess I just never tried before."

Barbara awoke the next morning sore all over, so stiff that she could barely get to her feet. A headache throbbed behind her eyes; her limbs felt like they had been broken one by one and inexpertly set. Even Jason noticed, and he hardly ever noticed her suffering. "Think you might have overdone it on the yoga, babe?" he asked.

"Maybe," she grudgingly admitted. Later that day, she called Hekati Yoga to move up her appointment.

Barbara began doing Hekati Yoga multiple times a week, and then, multiple times a day. She found a little-used wellness room at the office and turned it into her own private yoga studio, slipping into it at every opportunity to practice the Dying King, the Hydra, and all of the other sinuous maneuvers that Poil had taught her. Soon she could twist her head like an owl, and coil herself like a serpent. Once she had learned how to twist her knees and elbows backward at a 90-degree angle she graduated from the beginners' classes and into the intermediate ranks. At night she would stay up late and imagine the wonders of the advanced sessions. Her mantra was never far from her mind. *Iä , iä, iä.*

To fall behind was to endure agony. Falling behind in her practice meant reverting to a clenched carcass of knotted muscle and exposed nerves, and so she dedicated herself to her practice as one pursued by furies. Jason said that he knew what it was like to be married to a drug addict. Nonsense. Drugs were bad for you, whereas Hekati Yoga was the most healthful thing that a person could do.

On the other hand, it *was* about as expensive as a high-end drug habit. Intermediate classes were even costlier than beginners' lessons had been, and then there were the artifacts to consider. Poil offered a wide variety of crystals, lotions, tinctures, sculptures, amulets, pyramids, and other such occult bric-a-brac intended for healing and wellness. Barbara quietly cleaned out the retirement accounts and took out some new credit cards. Fortunately, Jason trusted her to manage the money. One day after class, Poil took Barbara aside and showed her a black marble orb the size of a pigeon's egg, veined with blue and purple. According to Poil, the orb was intended to sit inside Barbara's vagina, where it would infuse her root chakra with vaguely-defined cosmic power. It was available for sale, at a price that would require a second mortgage to afford. Barbara went back to the office and put in a call to her bank.

The orb made her feverish. Her mouth broke out in a red, sore rash that blistered and peeled. She believed it to have been worth every dime that she paid.

Hekati Yoga made Barbara's body pulse with life, drawing up a wellspring of desperate, consuming lust. She put all of her newfound strength and flexibility into her lovemaking, sometimes delighting Jason and sometimes traumatizing him and sometimes both. He began closing his eyes during sex, since seeing her boneless throes of passion alarmed him. "Like fucking a tangle of snakes," he remarked once as he sat on the edge of the bed, bloodless and distant. "You're going to be the death of me." And he was correct.

It happened during a torrential thunderstorm that sent sheets of water crashing against the roof and rattled the air with thunder. Barbara was riding Jason hard, the way a warrior might ride a horse on a suicide charge, while simultaneously flexing the core muscles she'd developed through countless repetitions of the Broken Circle. Exquisite sensations flooded her from her clit to her collarbone. She was lost in a world of her own. Suddenly her husband yelped underneath her.

"Jesus Christ!" he screamed. "Barb, what's happening?"

His shrieks broke Barbara out of her erotic fugue. She glanced downwards and realized that her flesh was running like hot wax. Lumpy rivulets of molten skin trickled down her torso; her breasts sagged almost to her belly button and headed further south. Jason tried to pull out, with no success. When he tried to push his lover away his hands sank into her chest up to the wrists. Barbara quivered with joy like a tower of human gelatin.

"Get off me, get off me!" Jason cried. "We've got to get you to a doctor. We've got—"

"Hush," Barbara murmured, as lightning crashed outside. She thrust her hand into his open mouth and shoved it down his throat all the way to her elbow, enjoying the tickle of his frantic tongue on her slackening skin. Then she began to double and redouble her thrusting, each lunge pressing him deeper inside of her soft, loose body. Jason's increasingly desperate struggles to free himself brought Barbara satisfaction that his meager missionary work had never approached. Every kick and thrash sent warm, honey-sweet waves through her moist flesh. Jason bit down hard on her rubbery arm, and Barbara gasped with delight at the feeling of his teeth sinking into her. Her moans of pleasure turned into shrieks of ecstasy, and then into a low, gurgling roar. She felt a little queasy when one of his flailing hands got tangled up in her viscera. No matter, flexing the muscles she'd developed practicing the Worm pose pulled those inconvenient organs into a ball, freeing up more room inside her for her lover, her prey. A tempest raged outside the bedroom, and a tempest raged within it.

Oh God, I'm so wet, she thought. *I'm a geyser, I'm a tidal wave, I'm an unstoppable tide.* Jason's doomed struggles brought her towards orgasm like cracks racing along a dam, crumbling everything that kept her tremendous sexual power contained within her, until at last she climaxed in a cataclysmic torrent of passion that annihilated everything before it. Barbara shrieked as the dam collapsed and then her whole body exploded into liquid, covering Jason head to toe in her devouring jelly. Lost in a delirious post-coital haze, she felt his struggles for air slow and then cease...she felt him twitching inside her as his oxygen-starved brain gave up the ghost. Together they slipped away into darkness. Barbara fell into a sleep as deep as death, and Jason fell into the genuine article.

Barbara regained consciousness in agony, as swollen as a blood-gorged tick. Her body was beginning to regain its usual solidity, except that now she carried all of Jason's mass within her bloated torso. Painful spasms pierced her to her core as her innards tightened around the man-sized teratoma within her. It was as if a two hundred pound fetus had died in her belly. Slick, cool, pungent-smelling human grease soaked her skin, the sheets, and doubtless the mattress underneath. She was sweating Jason out. It wasn't enough though; it wasn't fast enough. Searing, invisible knives stabbed Barbara from every angle. *Oh God, I'll die if I can't save myself somehow,* she thought.

Barbara was too heavy to sit up outright, so she painfully rocked her clenching, spasming body back and forth—the bed creaking beneath her in protest—until she'd built enough momentum to get herself upright and into the lotus position. Folding her legs into place with her belly so grotesquely distended was a challenge. However, it was a challenge that Hekati Yoga had prepared her to meet. Barbara closed her eyes, concentrated on her breathing, fought through the pain, and stretched herself into the Gorgon pose. She began to recite her mantra. *Iä , iä, iä.*

Once she got started, it was all astoundingly easy. Exercises that had previously struck her as pointless now revealed themselves as valuable preparation for a situation she could never have anticipated. Grease beaded on Barbara's flesh and poured off of her in cool waves. She switched things up, assuming the Hydra pose, and dozens of toothless mouths opened all over her slick torso. Barbara pushed, and the mouths vomited hairy pink sludge studded with teeth and fragments of bone. She groaned with relief from all of her mouths as she pushed Jason's offal out of herself. At one point she passed a wedding ring.

Once the pain had subsided Barbara rotated to the bedside table to look at her phone. She'd been passed out for two days. Despite her gruesome ordeal she felt well-rested and refreshed. Work had lit up her email and voicemail with escalating fury. Reluctantly, Barbara put the phone to her oily cheek and called her boss. "Harry?" she said. "This is Barbara. I just wanted to let you know that I'm never coming in again. Fuck right off." Without giving him a chance to respond she ended the call and tossed the phone away. Even that was more of a courtesy than she felt he deserved, however, the very last thing that she wanted was for some busybody to report her as a missing person. She wasn't missing at all. She was exactly where she was supposed to be.

It took Barbara two more days to finish processing Jason. Once she'd excreted the last of him she left the fetid swamp of the bedroom and treated herself to a scalding-hot, hour-long shower, washing away the last reeking, slimy remnants of her husband. She couldn't stop looking in the mirror as she toweled herself off. She'd never imagined that she could be this lithe, this strong, this beautiful. Her skin literally glowed. She looked human again but knew that she was so much more than that.

Barbara retrieved her phone from the bedroom and called Poil. "I want to come in for an advanced class," she said. "I'm ready for it."

"I know you are," Poil replied coolly. "We start at midnight." Barbara checked the time. It was already 11:40.

Barbara drove to her yoga class with the reckless intensity of a demon except that she was utterly serene, passing trucks on blind curves at 90 mph in a state of Zen bliss. At the studio, a garbage can in the mat room overflowed with discarded clothes. Barbara stripped and threw away her own.

Eight men and women waited for her in the chamber, Margie amongst them, and a few others whom Barbara recognized as well. Poil sat in her usual spot at the front of the class, gleaming white in the moonlight. Lunar reflections from the waves bathed the hot room in shimmering silver light.

"Namaste, my friends," Poil murmured. "Let's start with our warm-up exercises."

Poil showed her students how to twist themselves into hideous, unthinkable forms, violating the laws of anatomy and geometry alike. The strains of the ghastly contortions, the hypnotic drone of the guru's voice, and the hot, damp, body-temperature atmosphere brought Barbara into a state of relaxation so profound that her body and soul collapsed. Her eyelids melted—they trickled down her cheeks like tears made of skin—and as they dripped away and exposed her eyeballs she saw the rest of the class likewise transforming. Flesh sloughed away and pooled upon the mats in wrinkled mounds. At the front of the studio, Poil blossomed into a milk-white meat orchid, beautiful and utterly alien.

"Stretch yourselves further," Poil said, speaking through an uncanny multitude of toothy mouths that had sprouted around what used to be her torso, her voice soft and mild as ever, even though now it spoke in a chorus. "Grasp your fellow students and become one with them. Grow extra windpipes if you need help with your breathing. And remember your mantra."

Iä , iä, iä.

Barbara extended her body to form a half-dozen tentacles that radiated from her core like the spokes of a wheel. This pose was very difficult to achieve, and even more rewarding to obtain. She shuddered with ecstasy as one of her tendrils came into contact with another student's appendage and they intertwined. More and more joined in. Warm, damp flesh coiled around Barbara and into her, forming an impenetrable tangle of impossible bodies. Barbara could not tell where she ended and the other students began, she could not even tell if such a boundary existed anymore. Her fellow students' heartbeats raced within her veins as their circulatory systems merged. Nervous systems intermingled like kudzu vines.

Iä , iä, iä. Many voices recited the mantra inside Barbara's mind. She could not distinguish them from her own. She felt muscles not her own extend beyond human tolerance and burst into jelly. Strange voices cried out from her many throats in pleasure, relief, terror. All boundaries between Barbara and not-Barbara collapsed—the key turned and everything that made her a person was sucked away into the great emptiness.

Barbara's consciousness dissolved in a solution of infinite intimacy and devastating sensation.

"You're doing wonderfully," Poil told the superorganism that writhed and groaned before her. "Now that we've done our warm-up exercises, we can begin."

CONVEX - EMMA ALICE JOHNSON

"Well you know me," Sherry Convex said, wishing she had prepared a speech instead of forcing herself to ad lib in front of a banquet hall full of people she needed to convince to stock her wares, "and I sure as heck know all of you!"

They cheered. Perhaps she had assumed correctly that what she said didn't matter as long as the booze kept flowing into her guests' cups. Besides, the new product line sold itself. Nonetheless, here she was, selling it.

Five pedestals stood behind her, each a miniature column plucked from a Roman coliseum, shrunk to waist height and topped with a purple velvet pillow. Slowly, dramatically, as if picking up the most fragile, valuable item in existence, she lifted a pair of eyeglasses from one of the pillows.

Calling it a pair of glasses was ridiculous, of course. Technically, the label was accurate, but that was like calling a Maserati a car. The design and performance of this particular piece of hardware put it in an entirely different category.

These frames were feather light, baby pink ice carvings that beautified every face she had seen them on. She slipped them on now, precisely, making a show of it, swimming through the crowd's waiting silence. Then she moved her hands away from her face, held them out to her side, model-like, and the applause began, with the men at the closest tables rising for a standing ovation. She gestured them back in their seats. She hadn't even gotten to the good stuff yet, though part of her wanted the ovation now. Having seen what the glasses did to mitigate her crow's feet and laugh lines, she felt it was well deserved.

When the cheers died down, she added, "But wait until you see…"

"Convex!" someone in the crowd shouted.

"That's me!" She chuckled. A late cheer from one of her more drunken customers, she assumed.

But then it came again, louder this time. "Convex!"

Then screams, and people ran from their tables.

A woman emerged from the swirl of chaos. She looked familiar, but Sherry couldn't place her immediately. A former employee? A competitor? Sweaty and disheveled, the woman came at the stage, pointing her finger accusingly.

Except, when the woman got closer, Sherry realized it wasn't a finger she was pointing, not really. What was it? A twist of flesh and metal, a barely decipherable glob of dripping and shiny matter. Whatever it was, the woman jabbed it aggressively toward Sherry, and Sherry did not like the looks of it at all.

Sherry fled toward one side of the stage, but the woman tracked her movement. Sherry backed up as the woman took a big awkward step onto the stage, never faltering in aiming that glob right between Sherry's eyes, right at the nosepiece of one of the most sophisticated pieces of eyewear ever developed.

"All!"

The woman screamed in a whirlwind of saliva.

"Hail!"

Blood dripped from her nostrils, collecting on her cupid's bow.

"The!"

Veins reconfigured themselves on her forehead, bulging, testing the strength of her skin, desperate to be unsheathed.

"Future!"

Her matted brown locks of hair caught fire and the meat around her skull sloughed lower and lower.

"Meat!"

The glob at the end of the woman's wrist exploded, causing a chain reaction that moved up her arm, her shoulder, blowing up her chest and her head in quick succession, blasting a confetti of muscle fiber and bone particles throughout the room and finally setting off the fire sprinklers to douse the tottering, torso-less legs she left behind.

Sherry cowered at the rear of the stage. The woman's legs flopped dead to the ground, and Sherry found the strength in hers again to stand up straight. Cautiously, she moved to the front of the stage. Her eyes wouldn't focus, and she remembered she still wore the glasses. She pulled them off unceremoniously and dropped them on the stage.

There were no legs now, no body, no fire, no water raining from the ceiling. The crowd was still there, standing, but not in ovation. A buzz of confusion and concern fluttered amidst the tuxedo-clad heads of the eyewear industry.

"Ms. Convex, are you alright?" Todd, her secretary, stood in front of the stage, where the woman had been.

Sherry tried to say "Yes," but instead issued a barely audible peep as she nodded her head a little too frantically.

Todd picked up the glasses and reached them up to her. Instinctively, she slapped them back down to the stage. The crowd grumbled in disapproval.

"I think we're done here," a nasally man called from the back of the room.

Sherry glanced down at Todd. "That woman."

"What woman?" Todd turned to scan the dissipating crowd.

"The one who just ran in here?"

Todd bit his lower lip, looking concerned, legitimately concerned. She didn't like the look on him. She had hired him because he was a robotic, emotionless helper who retrieved lattes and researched investors in competing companies with equal precision. "I didn't see a woman run in here."

"What happened?" she asked, deciding to keep it more general.

"I think you might have blown this year's line."

She squinted at him. There was something in his voice now, not concern, but maybe, delight? Why would he be delighted? What would he get out of this? She had treated him well, bought him suits well above his pay grade, dinners, first class seats beside her on flights. Had he instigated this? Had he hired the woman? Was that why he was pretending he hadn't seen her?

She stepped closer to the edge of the stage.

"Wait!" He swiped the glasses from under her high heel. "The glasses!"

The glasses. "Put them on," she ordered.

"They're not really my style, Ms. Convex."

"Put them on now, Todd!"

She caught an eye roll as he slid them onto his face. They looked good. They looked good on anyone. "What do you see?"

"My boss, completely losing her shit."

She awoke on her office floor, still in the blazer and pencil skirt she'd worn onstage last night. She had come here, unwilling to take whatever she had experienced home with her, afraid of it tainting her house. And what had she experienced? Had she experienced it at all? She refused to believe she hadn't.

The glasses lay beside her. Her hands trembled as she picked them up. They were brilliant, not just in their aesthetic design, but in what they could do. In all fairness, it was merely refinement of what many businesses before hers had failed to do properly, in large part because those businesses were tech businesses made up of computer people, people who failed to recognize the realities of how people interacted with technology. These were the sort of people who built programs that required the user to click "Are you sure?" buttons three times before deleting something inconsequential but also failed to incorporate a means of updating an employee's name after a name change.

As the owner of the company that made the most desirable glasses frames, if not the most popular, she simply gathered her top designers, recruited those who had left the tech companies after their awkward glasses products had failed, and forced them to work together. And this was what they had come up with.

She could put these glasses on her face, where her body heat activated them and a swipe of her pupils brought her online, presenting her with an interface that interacted with and seamlessly integrated into the physical world around her. That was the best way she could describe it. Even that didn't do the experience justice.

She had forced her marketing people to write and rewrite the product description. Somehow though, integrating the physical and online worlds in words was more difficult than doing so in her product, which she found endlessly amusing and terribly frustrating. Part of her wanted to simply say, "Oh, you can go online with these glasses," which her age group would understand, but which her marketing people explained would sound boring to younger demographics, which was ultimately who she needed to appeal to.

Obviously, they did much more than bring her online, as she had experienced, or at least seen, last night.

She scanned the floor and found her phone beside her heels in the corner of the room. Without thinking, she crawled on hands and knees over to it, plopping down on her belly when she reached it. She scrolled through her texts, mostly from concerned attendees of last night's show, and one from Todd, outlining his strategy of explaining to attendees that she had put in "blood, sweat, tears and far too many hours in the weeks prior to the event, leading to a minor bout of exhaustion." He suggested that she would have to go to visit them, one-by-one, to give personal demonstrations, if she had any hope of trying to sell them on the line.

First though, she needed to decide if she wanted to sell them on the line.

She called the lab and Hubie picked up immediately. "Sounds like you had quite the night, Mon Sherry."

"You heard?"

"Everyone heard."

She sighed. "I'm sorry."

"We'll figure it out," Hubie said. "You and I have spent nearly 30 years building Convex Eyewear. I'm not about to let one bad night ruin all that work."

She rolled over and sat up, cross-legged. "It was the glasses, Hubie."

"Sure."

"Hubie."

"Bring them down. We'll figure it out."

After straightening herself out as best she could, she made her way down to the lab, thankful that Hubie was the only employee who came in on the weekends, always tinkering on his personal projects in his off time.

"You look horrible, Mon Sherry."

"Thanks, Hubie." She handed him the glasses.

He took them to his workstation, inspecting them superficially. "The left lens is scratched. The bridge looks compromised. That's where the hardware is."

"Possibly from when I threw them."

He looked at her as if she had drowned a baby. "You threw them?"

She nodded. "Twice, I think."

"What happened last night?"

"I saw something. A woman who wasn't there. She was going to kill me. She was pointing something at me. Her hand. A gun. I don't know. Then she exploded."

"Who was this woman?" Hubie asked, pretending to look at the glasses now, as if he couldn't look at her while she said these things. She couldn't blame him. She realized how it sounded. She almost wished there had been a corpse, that the woman's charred legs were still in that ballroom.

"I recognized her, but I don't know. She said something. About future meat."

Hubie looked up now, started to say something, stopped.

"Was it a virus?" she asked.

"These are virus-proof." He slid the glasses on and looked at her through them. They lifted every sag on his face, brightened him. "I'd stake my life on it."

Darius Engle, CEO of Vision Center Ltd, the largest and longest running mall-based eyewear retailer in the eastern half of the United States, scowled at her. "Frankly, Ms. Convex, after Friday night's production, you should feel lucky that I'm even allowing you to sit in that chair."

"And I appreciate you giving me this opportunity. I…"

"Vision Center is not a brand that takes chances. We are not edgy. Our frames are on-trend, but safe. They are for everyday people who are concerned about going about their lives and raising their families, not being the height of fashion. Or technology, for that matter. Our customers rarely even have the latest phone."

"My research indicates that your stocks…"

"Go up and down, as they have for decades. Ms. Convex, my family has been in this business since before malls even existed. You are not new yourself, and I'm surprised that you would come with this approach."

Sherry tried to regroup. She could not walk out of this office without at least a verbal commitment. She needed to get Vision Center in her corner. After that, the rest of the industry would fall in line. If she failed, Convex Eyewear would be dead.

"Mr. Engle, you mentioned that your customers do not have the latest phones, but they do have cellphones. They certainly want the latest technology. It is simply out of their reach. Previous companies that have attempted to take glasses like these to market have come with a price point that was unrealistic, not to mention that they had not refined the technology and completely ignored the fact that people want to look good in their glasses."

"I don't see your price point as being much more realistic."

"Look again," she said, her voice cracking slightly. "Yes, they are more expensive than your current options, but not by a significant amount, especially when taking into account the amount even your customers spend on phones and other tech, some of which may become completely unnecessary with these glasses."

"Put them on," he replied, squaring up to his desk.

"What?" she asked, deflated.

"Prove to me that Friday night's events won't repeat themselves."

"That was exhaustion."

"You were reacting to something you saw in that ballroom, Ms. Convex."

"I hadn't slept."

"Put them on."

With trembling hands, she reached toward the open case on the desk that served as a barrier between her and Mr. Engle. Inside, on a sheet of black velvet, sat the frames, the exact same pair from Friday night. She should have known she'd be asked to do this. She should have brought a different pair. That might have made it easier. It might have been easier if she could have convinced herself that she had experienced exhaustion, and not something else entirely.

She looked up at the man in front of her, his five o'clock shadow fully formed eight hours ahead of schedule. Beneath it, the edges of his lips crept further toward the sides of his face. They were so wet, his lips. And pink. His mouth slit grew wider, wetter, until thick saliva dripped to his chin, from his chin to his desk.

It was happening again. It felt so real. Frantically, she grabbed at the glasses on her face, only to realize they weren't there. They still sat in their case in front of her. She hadn't yet picked them up.

"Ms. Convex?" The words came out of his expanding maw, not as sounds, but as physical words, shaped from glistening intestines, one letter at a time to pile on his desk, a cushion for his face to fall on as the meat of it separated from his skull.

On the sidewalk outside, she panted, catching her breath from running down four flights of stairs as fast as her high heels could take her. All she wanted to see was sidewalk, but she chanced to look up at a passerby, only to see the woman's skin and fascia and muscle weaving together in ways it should not, forming new expressions of hatred toward her. So she ran.

As she pumped her arms and strained her legs, the click of her heels on concrete softened. She felt the meat of her feet weaving through the leather of the shoes, cradling them, until the clicking became the sound of flesh on sidewalk.

Around her, pedestrians melted. Eyes slid down faces, elongating on the way, until they were no longer eyes, but streams of white and green and black swirling through the quickly dripping rivers of pink skin.

One man reached out for her, desperate for help, as if she could simply pull him free from his meltdown. And she tried, but before their hands could touch there was nothing left of his but bone and that too slurped to the ground, joining the mass of disintegrated bodies cascading up to her ankles, her waist.

Soon, running turned to swimming. She paddled desperately through the melted flesh. It was so thick she could hardly move. The thought crossed her mind, what if it all hardened like cement, turned back to a solid with her still trying to move through it? But it didn't, and she kicked and paddled until her muscles burned, catching on wrongly twisted limbs like staunch seaweed, kicking to break free.

Then she was running again.

She was changing, the meat of her moving in ways it shouldn't. Her breasts no longer bounced painfully in her bra. She felt them there still, but wetter now, different. She refused to look down at herself, at her hands. She didn't want to see, so she kept running.

She made her way to the skate park, the one with the graffiti, in the neighborhood one ex-husband had told her she shouldn't go to. There was nobody there. She weaved the liquefying meat of her through spray painted two-by-fours, hunkering into a corner under a ramp. In the light that made its way through the cracks between sheets of plywood above her, she saw dirty mattresses, soiled blankets, hypodermic needles, a gallon milk jug half filled with yellow liquid.

Hesitantly, she glanced down at her hands. One was a knot of muscle fibers and strained skin around a black barrel.

The remnants of her pointer finger twisted around a trigger that hid somewhere under her skin, near the inside of a knucklebone, perhaps built from a knucklebone. Even in the dim light, even crisscrossed with bubbling flesh, bits of the metal gleamed.

She realized why the woman at the conference had looked so familiar. The woman had been her.

With her other hand, she struggled her cellphone out of her purse.

"Call Hubie," she told it, and it did.

"Mon Sherry?"

Her response was undecipherable sobs. She felt like she was crying, but when she tried to wipe away the tears with the back of her gun hand, it slipped through her cheek, pulling liquefied skin with it, exposing cheekbone.

"Where are you?"

She managed to gurgle out the words.

"I'll come to you."

She awoke to Hubie's voice. He stood over her, smiling.

"You're a real mess. I didn't expect the virus to manifest this way. Physically."

She tried to sit up but her back had become one with the beam she was leaning against. "You said it wasn't a virus?"

He shrugged.

"Why didn't Todd get it?

"One time use, Mon Sherry. Just for you."

The betrayal felt physical in her newly reformed body, a clenching fist around her trust gland, around the physically manifested history she had shared with this man growing and nurturing this company side by side.

"Why would you do this?"

"I built this company, Mon Sherry. Your pretty little legs

did the legwork, I'll give you that, but I did the real work. And you put me in the basement?

"I thought that's what you wanted?"

"You take home ten times what you give to me."

"I'm the CEO."

"Not anymore."

Out of the corner of her eye, she saw her gun hand moving up, turning the barrel toward her face. Instinctively, she pulled her head back, straining the lashes of skin that had wrapped around the wooden beam. She couldn't move far enough fast enough to evade her own hand.

The muzzle chilled the warm swirl of flesh at her temple as it sunk into her head, not content to simply shoot her, needing to penetrate her, to get right up against her brain, right into the weeds of her thoughts to ensure that everything there would die with her.

In gritting her teeth, she felt the top row sink into the bottom row, dissolve into each other, building big masses of white enamel that floated on the wavy surface of her lip ocean like buoys.

I'm going to kill myself, she thought, a thought she had never considered before today. She could see it happening so clearly, the explosion, the mess. Because she had seen it, in that ballroom. This was not a thought; it was a program.

And then came another thought she had never thought before, this one stronger, this one real: No, I am not going to kill myself.

She moved her mind. She pushed it out of her head, through her jelly veins, down her neck, into her arm, to her hand, until her consciousness existed in every dripping cell of it, in the wet folds of the knuckles, in the shards of nails jutting out like the fins of sharks, in the barrel of the gun. And then she pulled. She pulled her gun hand out of the wet meat of her temple, where the barrel emerged with a pop. She pulled it away from her, watching it carefully as it found a new aim.

Hubie raised his arms nervously. "It was a joke, Mon Sherry."

Her arm stretched, long, rigid. Bones inside reformed, but not the right way, not the right shapes, the right angles. Instead, they poked out through her skin, jagged, gnarled, a quick growing tree of flesh and muscle and ivory, until the barrel was right in front of Hubie's nose.

Then she pulled the trigger.

A wet bang brought no bullet, but a sloppy gurgitation of tendons and skin to slide up Hubie's nostrils, press through clenched lips into his mouth, muffling his screams. They wrapped around his head and then they wrapped around his head again. She felt them tugging out of her, out of her belly, out of her legs that shriveled up from the loss of what should have been in them.

Hubie tried to pry free, but his arms quickly went limp and dropped to his sides against his seizing body. She expected some sort of bang, a noise to indicate she had accomplished her task, but none came, and after minutes of squeezing, she unraveled from his head and brought all of her back into her through the barrel of her gun hand, revealing all that was left of Hubie: a clean rod of condensed skull poking up from a bleeding fleshy neck, as if he was an action figure that someone had popped the head off of and he could be fixed by popping it right back onto this skull knob. She felt thankful that couldn't happen.

He crumpled to the ground.

She tried to move, but her body was still stuck. Again, she pushed her thoughts out through the whole of her, shepherding her flesh back where it was supposed to be. She was herself again, more or less. Perhaps she had taken some liberties removing the wrinkles around her eyes, the sag behind her thighs.

She had lost her clothes somewhere along the way. She riffled through the detritus that surrounded her under the skate ramp, settling on an only barely urine-stained pair of men's sweatpants and a surprisingly clean pink blazer that was a size too small to fully conceal her chest.

Stepping barefoot into the sunlight, she noticed her gun hand. No matter how hard she tried, she could not put it back to how it should have been. Maybe that was for the best. Maybe this was how it should be now. She tucked it into the front of her pants and started walking, wondering just how far this virus could spread.

SEMINAR - CODY GOODFELLOW

Millie Gordon was standing over my bed, fully clothed, when I woke up in the middle of the night.

"My cover is blown," she said, smiling apologetically, reveling in her intrigue. Hair disheveled, eyes swollen and runny, flickering like a faulty night-light. "They're coming for me, so I thought you should know. They're going to say I pulled out of the program, but that's not true . . ."

"I don't understand . . ." I tried to find my phone, then remembered they'd all been confiscated.

"You having weird dreams?" Millie stood up and shouldered her bag. "Me too, but this isn't one. They found me out and they think I'm a security risk, and they're right. They don't want anyone knowing what we're doing here until it's too late."

"I still don't believe I'm awake . . ." I mumbled. It was the first night of the three-day seminar, and we'd been paired up and assigned this room only a few hours before, but she was likeable. Unlike the rest of our group, she didn't seem like a dysfunctional corporate drone, but a whole, well-rounded human being. Naturally, they all hated her.

"I'm sorry about your training getting disrupted," Millie said, moving to the door. "I like you. You're a really good person. You shouldn't be here."

I liked her, too. She's the kind of person who makes a group feel like a family. How comfortable she was with her size, like her body was for herself, not anyone else. During the initial "exercise," when they had us "take each other's inventory," and Megan asked her how she felt about her "weight problem," Millie shot back, "My weight is my own, the problem is yours."

I must've fallen asleep before she went out the door, if any of it happened, but she was gone when I woke up, the bed neatly made, the room purged of any evidence. I wonder if I should make a stink, or just go along. Everything is some kind of test or teaching game here, but I don't think the thumb drive under my pillow is part of it . . .

Not that there was any shortage of intrigue before Millie Gordon's disappearance. The Seminar is an intensive course in Executive Mindfulness Techniques. But from the moment of our arrival, they've been fucking with us.

"I see some nervous faces today," the trainer said as she watched us file off the bus. "Make no mistake, we're not here to hurt you... We're here to kill you."

A few of us laughed, but this obese outside sales type and a steakhead ex-jock stepped on me trying to get back on the bus.

"Relax!" the trainer shouted. "The old you, the reactive you that wants to take control to sabotage you when it fears change, it's time to say goodbye. We resist change because we think we're no more than the sum of our bad habits and weaknesses. When they're in control, changing feels like dying. That version of you that's just skated along in the middle of the bell curve is going to die a gruesome death this weekend, and the you that arises from the carnage will thank us. Don't make a sacred cow of your worst self. We have a saying around here: Sacred cows make the best burgers."

I'd heard edgier and worse over the years. Team-building retreats, Outward Bound-style survival exercises and every conceivable variety of corporate boot camp. This place only stood out because none of us had any idea what to expect, and they didn't tell us. All we knew was that our beloved CEO, CFO, and COO were all proud alumni of the three-day program, and if we wanted to stay ahead of the next mid-level purge, we would follow in their footsteps.

The first exercise, at least, dispelled any lingering illusions they don't know what they're doing, even if they gave us no idea what it is.

The eight of us—four men and four women, including the now-exited Ms. Gordon, all from XXXXXX, LLC—took our seats in a conference room and were provided briefing papers on a simulated merger negotiation. We had half an hour to prepare before meeting our opposition.

None of us was ready for this. Those who hadn't napped on the three-hour bus ride out here were irritable and tired, and the ones who didn't complain of migraines were probably just holding back. The four folders covered administrative, HR, legal and technical issues. Naturally, Millie and I took the folder on the technology issues in the deal—incompatible data management systems, massive personnel redundancies. I quickly doped out the situation, but couldn't grasp what winning would look like. Was the objective to foist as much of our own infrastructure on them, or was there some ideal synthesis they hoped we'd hash out? Knowing what we know about our company culture and the people who run it, we opted to go for broke and eat their lunch.

They ate our lunch.

The trainer who welcomed us introduced herself as Rebecca Snowden, and her partner, a wiry man with features too small for his face, as Lorne Shigeta. We were still looking at the door, waiting for more people to come in, when they started talking.

They never stopped, that any of us could recall. I remember Snowden running through figures and proposals faster than I could follow. Whenever I tried to get a word in, she interrupted with my own words, then dropped a wall of arguments that threw me back on my notes, just trying to cover my head and wait for it to be over. The sound of her voice was like a maxed-out fax machine. The others seemed to be in the same position, bulldozed by an opposition we outnumbered by six. Whenever I looked to the others, Snowden impatiently demanded my attention and I felt like I'd nodded off, I thought I was naked, and I smelled this stringent herbal aroma seeping into the room, and I vomited all over the table.

That was bad enough, but I saw things in it.

I saw my own face, chewed up in pieces as if I'd eaten it.

I got up and ran from the room. I wasn't the only one. Tom Milsapp, the tubby salesman, complained of chest pains; Portia Kulick, bleach-blonde HR bimbo in a miniskirt, had a panic attack and wet her chair a little. Megan Nguyen, an efficiency expert who specializes in firing people, called it pop psychology voodoo, which prompted a pointless argument about psychoplasmics, which Milsapp evangelized foolishly for.

Snowden came in and apologized for the rough treatment. They promised us that, by the time we left, we could do the things that were demonstrated in the simulation, to others.

None of us opted to leave.

We were issued "self-mentoring" exercises to refine our goals and own our vulnerabilities before sleep. A recipe for insomnia, but I nodded off before Millie came back from the shower. I remember fragments of a nightmare. Running through an endless cubicle farm. Stepping over bodies. Sirens and gunshots and screams. Crawling under desks, tripping over snaking cables, running for the exit and running into a thin woman with copper hair spilling into bright eyes in a pinched, disbelieving face… It's difficult to recognize yourself from outside. Not so difficult, it turns out, to shoot yourself from outside.

Millie woke me up and told me what she told me, and here we are…

The next morning, when they told us to pair up, Snowden put me with Louis Wiggins. Snowden insisted that Millie left because she had doubts about the program after the demonstration. Because of her withdrawal, only three more of us would be sent home early without finishing the program. Quietly shouting over our complaints, they explained that the key to acquiring the disciplines they were teaching was wanting it more than anyone else. Today's exercises would cut the group in half.

We paired up and proceeded to interview each other for what seemed like an hour, but before we knew it, they called lunch.

Wiggins was a very polite, retiring junior exec who, like myself, had been promoted out of his comfort zone in the technical trenches. He was nervous and avoided eye contact, favoring me with a wooden look whenever I successfully trapped his gaze. In the middle of asking him to list his trouble spots in his last performance evaluation, I caught a glimpse of something.

You know that funny movie, they remade it just recently, where a man can suddenly hear what women are thinking? If they reboot it so every woman can hear what the man is thinking, it would be a very short horror movie.

Imagine putting your mouth over a garden hose, and catching a face-full of raw sewage.

I felt sweaty hands holding me down. I felt teeth clicking against mine, a cold, pasty tongue. I felt a boneless, crooked finger boring into me. His eyes left a snail-trail on my skin, blinking, quite unaware of what was gushing out of him.

I could've stood up and called out his disgusting behavior, but what had he done? What had he said? Could he be blamed if I could… read… his mind?

The enormity of what they were offering us hit me, just then. The treatment we'd suffered the day before. The weird tunnel-vision torture those two trainers put the eight of us through, the secrecy around the program, the weird rumors about our CEO…

It took all my willpower to stay in my seat.

I let him have his fantasy, but I turned it back on him. I let him ravish my body, but when he opened his eyes, he was balls-deep in himself and I, and all our coworkers and the trainers and his friends and family and the cast and crew of his favorite TV show were all watching.

Louis scooted back in his chair and tried to get up, but he couldn't see the room. He beat on his own head and raked his eyes. The trainers swooped in to assist him leaving the room. He didn't come back.

Ten minutes later, Portia Kulick broke down crying, repeatedly insisting that she didn't want to die.

Five minutes later, Nate Radford, the ex-jock, came out of his chair and tried to throttle his partner, the amiable Mr. Milsapp. Security had to escort Radford from the room. In the corner, Adan Margolis and Megan Nguyen sat staring into each other's bloodshot, unblinking eyes for another half hour before the trainers sent us to our meal break and a private mentorship session.

We spent the afternoon doing more busy-work, but alone, which was nice. I laughed when they sat me down before the stacked files and left the room. Some mentoring. I was told that I'd have four hours to review and make recommendations on a massively complicated renegotiation of an employee pension plan that would take a team at least a week to sort out. I did the focus exercises, visualizing whipping through all this bullshit in a matter of hours, and just plowed in.

Skimming the documents, I noticed how the signature of the senior attorney representing the union dripped with what I intuited to be pedophilic tendencies and a crabbed quality to his punctuation that betrayed deep fiduciary misconduct. I could see it like you can tell food is spoiled, could almost smell it. I wrote a memo advising that an ex officio contact with said lawyer might yield a plan more in line with our projected figures, which the aforementioned child pornography buff had dismissed as unworkable in his own enclosed memo.

Other things jumped out at me that would normally have stopped me in my tracks, but I made notes and drafted a summary and signed off on it before looking at the clock and realizing only three hours had passed.

It's weird, to say the least, to realize such an enormous boost in productivity due to "mindfulness techniques" I am not consciously aware of having learned.

Tonight's exercise, we've been promised, will be very special.

After dinner, they told us to get dressed for a field trip. We're going to pair up and rob convenience stores.

What do you wear for something like that?

I was paired with Megan Nguyen. Adan Margolis and Tom Milsapp got into a cargo van just like the one that picked us up. They put hoods on our heads, which seemed like unnecessary drama, but must've been another exercise, because I could follow where we were going, looking out through the driver's eyes.

We drive into the nearest exurban business zone and they drop us off out front of a Circle K. The van pulls up in front of the gas pumps. It's after 10 on a Sunday night, and no other customers parked in the lot, hardly any traffic on the two-lane highway.

We were told nothing, but we work out a plan as we walk to the door and don thick rubber gardening gloves. We tell ourselves that we have big guns and no faces as Megan opens the door. I walk in pointing a finger at the clerk. He's a husky older man in a Sikh turban, probably the franchise owner. He's looking at my finger like he's seeing exactly what I want him to see—a Glock 9mm, the dull gray matte finish almost oily under the harsh fluorescent light in the hands of a faceless black man. Megan closes the door and comes around to flank him in the counter area, pointing her own finger. It looks like a James Bond gun, an elegant little automatic.

He looks at the guns as we shout at him to empty the cash register, but he doesn't comply. We push harder. Put our guns in his face, voices raised into hooks digging in his brain and pulling out every ugly thing we can find. He staggers backwards into the cigarette display, but he picks up a baseball bat and comes over the counter at us.

Megan points her finger and shouts, "Bang!" He stumbles and sprawls across the counter, knocking the paperback novels and the take-a-penny dish on the floor at our feet.

We look at each other. I'd seen the hole in his chest, just below his sternum. Megan goes around the counter to the register, orders me to go in the back and find the computer. To my dumbfounded stare, she points at the cameras mounted in every corner of the store.

I go in the back, past stacked cases of soda and beer to the manager's office, a hutch just large enough for a swaybacked chair and a monitor showing, naturally, a compound view of a young black man, his complexion too dark to register as more than a dancing inkspot in a hoodie and track pants.

I see no need to delete it, but I open a new window and scroll back to see two young black men pointing guns at the cashier, who comes over the counter and collapses. No shots were fired and when I pause it, can I really say for sure that either of the two criminals are holding guns, and not just pointing at the cashier? It's like one of those pictures of a dress or a shoe, and you see green and gray, but they tell you the color of the dress varies depending on which hemisphere of the brain is dominant, only now it's pink…

Well played, Megan, I think to myself. Then, looking over my shoulder, I plug Millie Gordon's thumb drive into the computer.

It opens a menu of text files and a single video file, created two days ago. I open a bunch of files and skim them as the video plays.

"I've been researching them for over three years," Millie says in a husky whisper, "but I had no idea what it was about until I got inside. And now… I can't get it out of my head. And oh God, how I've tried . . ."

The files trace past attendees of the Seminar, many of whom were subsequently let go by the companies they worked for after failing to complete the program. Eleven suicides, two workplace shootings, and none of the eighteen Seminar washouts she approached willing to go on record. When three killed themselves shortly after being approached for an interview, she stopped trying.

"They call what they offer mentorship, but the . . . technique they put into you… it's the Thought Without A Thinker, it's a living idea. A separate intelligence without a body, until it has yours. That's who this program is for, that's who they're talking to. They're not mentoring *you*. They're talking to the thing they put into our heads, teaching it how to operate us . . ."

Of those who completed the program, only stellar career milestones. Fast-track promotions into upper management, lateral moves into affiliated companies. Not one willing to go on record with what they learned at the Seminar.

"I didn't believe it, but now it's in me, I can feel it... It's not a physical presence, but it inhabits the brain like a hermit crab, grows into it, replaces it. I have a theory that disrupting the bioelectric field renders it partially material... but there's only one way to find out."

Megan's shouting at me from out front. I rip out the thumb drive and run for the door. Megan asks, "Are we good?" and I nod, then say yes, because she stands over the clerk, poking him like roadkill. Her eyes are another pair of mouths, brimming with gleaming teeth. "Some motherfuckers need a gun to do this," she says. "Can you imagine being that weak?"

We jump in the van as it pulls out of the gas station. They put the hoods back on us. Megan complains, but nobody speaks. I can tell we're not going the same way. We stop in the parking lot of a diner. They remove my hood and lead me across the parking lot by my arm, into the diner, which is all but empty, with two people sitting at the counter and a man eating alone in the far corner booth. It's Lorne Shigeta.

They lead me to the booth and seat me before removing my hood. Nobody looks askance at this, as if everybody eating here tonight is a hostage.

"Did I do something wrong?" Not, *What's wrong with all of you?* Not, *What happened to Millie Gordon?*

"You did what we expected you to," he answered. "You're a promising candidate, so we wanted to step in before you make a serious mistake."

He holds out his hand and I watch in sick fascination as I reach out and put Millie's drive into it. "More serious than murder?"

"Authorities will discover the cashier suffered a fatal

stroke during the robbery. But even a mistake is profitable if you learn from it."

"You put something inside us."

"Intelligence." He sighs. "Was that wrong? Wasn't that what you came here for? Maybe you feel threatened, but consider. You must think the world of your own intelligence because it's the only one you've ever had, but from an objective viewpoint, you're a rudimentary batch of reaction formations to stimuli. What you think of as you is really just a bunch of reflexes keeping you from success.

"And naturally, you're going to resist what we're offering, because any significant change will be the end of those primitive responses. For all intents and purposes, you will cease to exist, but a better, more efficient you will go on in your place. It's natural for you to feel that way, but we're here to help you get over it."

"What are they?"

His eyes swivel around, and for just a moment, they're mouths lined with mirrors, like Megan's. "I could make up an explanation, if that would satisfy you. Tell you they came from inner space, or outer space, or they're artifacts of a management philosophy so effective that it became self-aware and began reproducing like any other organism... But you're smart enough to know it doesn't matter. You've experienced it. I personally like to think it's the company itself, alive inside us, making us whole. A horse is a beautiful, useless thing, without a rider, don't you think?"

"I'm more—we're all a lot more than animals... machines that do a job."

"Are you, though? Tell me, then, how much of your identity is shaped by one traumatic event in your life."

I knew what he was talking about, even before I smelled the smell. It enveloped me, poisoned the ice water in front of me, so I spit it back into the glass.

It was at a conference, four years back.

Our group was staying at a Comfort Inn that felt like a lazy minimum-security prison. I remember the broken waffle maker at the breakfast "buffet" and the pungent, oddly exotic shampoo in the shower caddy. I looked at the label after using it, the stringent herbal aroma blocking my sinuses, already bringing a rash all over my scalp. The shampoo was from a local business, a weird half-ass luxury to offset the generic blandness of the lodgings, and included "essential oils of ylang-ylang and bergamot." I threw it out and bought a travel-size Johnson's Baby Shampoo at the corner drugstore, but I could still smell it throughout the weekend.

I remember going off by myself the last night of the conference, tired of my team's bad breath and worse jokes and hearing my own complaints about the company echoed back at me. It was a slow Saturday night, but I found a nice restaurant and took a walk on the riverfront, then called for a Lyft to return to the hotel. I was assaulted while I was waiting. He forced me off the street into an alley and knocked my head off a wall so I was too dizzy to stop him tearing my tights and forcing my skirt up around my waist.

I never saw him and I couldn't give any kind of actionable description to the police. He wore a ski mask and gloves. I didn't trust myself to tell them my rapist smelled of ylang-ylang and bergamot. This wasn't some quagmire date-rape situation, it was a stone-cold street attack, but I talked myself out of it. I wasn't some amateur detective, and I wasn't going to impress anyone with my theory, because I couldn't convince myself that I'd really smelled it on my attacker, or was just making something up. All of the guys in our group were really nice, they had wives back home, and nobody had given me any reason to be suspicious, and the cops and the courts would just shrug; but the company would never forget, and the next conference would leave me off the roster and the next round of efficiency lay-offs would find me with an asterisk beside my name, so…

Shigeta smiles at the fading memory we shared. "A great evolutionary sea change has occurred. Corporations are people, haven't you heard? So where does that leave people?

You're either the cells of a vast and powerful organism, or you're just bacteria..."

I look at him and see the thing inside his head, roiling and turning in a molten glow. A hermit crab in its shell, an impossibly compressed thing stuffed into the cavity where his brain once was. All at once, it comes gushing out of him to surround me. I can't recoil, I can't escape, I can't see anyone around me noticing it, because only I can see it with my other eyes, granted to me by a mentor much like the one inside him, inside me.

"Do you know why you succeeded in your interview with Wiggins?"

"He was caught up in his own image of me, but it wasn't me. It didn't affect me, but it showed how he was vulnerable . . ."

"You were able to overcome your reaction formation because of your new heightened intelligence. But you've been infected with irrational fears by another vestigial person. Don't let them sabotage you . . ."

He whispers to me like a spooked horse while his mentor communes with mine, stalks and tendrils interlocked and trembling with visions I can almost see when I blink. *A fat, jolly woman driving her Prius off a cliff so high, she has a moment to adjust the rearview mirror to check her makeup—*

"I think I'm feeling sick." I make myself wait for him to nod and for the invisible limbs all around me to retract back into his skull, before leaving the table. To the restroom, noticing the van parked out front, the bulky men smoking outside, watching me out the corner of their eyes, Megan sitting bolt upright in the back like a hooded falcon. I hope they don't see the fork in my hand.

In the ladies' room, I check myself in the mirror. I look harried, tired, sweaty, exhilarated—pretty much as you'd expect shortly after a successful convenience store robbery. I can barely see it behind my eyes, like a movie projected on a wall in broad daylight.

I wash my face in the sink, using the mercifully unscented hand soap from the Waxie dispenser, dry my hands carefully, step out of my rubber-soled shoes, and jam the tines of the fork into the electrical socket in the wall.

There's a flash that burns itself into my vision, then darkness. I can't remember where I am, what I was doing. I'm unconscious, blind, dead—no, the lights went out, somebody blew the circuit breaker; somebody's hair is on fire—

I can't move. Convulsing in a pool of my own piss, I really should've gone before… stupid… but nobody tells you how to do this online. I can't move, but I move. I see the purple, pulsing outline of my hand pass in front of my face while my numb fingers spasm on the floor tiles. For just an instant, the shock has separated me from my body like a car from its driver. Before it passes or before I die and dissipate or go wherever I'm going, I plunge the ghost of my hand into my head.

It squirms in my grasp like an octopus. It stings me and tries to wriggle free. I twist my grip and try to rip it out. The pain is so intense I almost abandon my body altogether, just to get away. A hundred venomous whips throttle my gray matter, triggering cascades of ugly memories and nightmares. Phantom taproots woven into the net of my nerves, so that pulling it out feels like ripping out my own spine through my mouth.

It nearly kills me. I don't know whether the relief I feel is endorphins or the elation of finally dying, but it's wonderful until the lights come back on and I can feel my body again.

I roll over and throw up. I look at the vomit like I should be able to see it expelled, a hagfish-man-o-war thing writhing at my feet, but it's just the salmon and rice and broccoli they served us for dinner.

Someone knocks on the door and then pushes it open.

Shigeta stands over me, shaking his head. "We're not usually this wrong about someone," he says.

He kneels and pulls back my eyelid. My body can't move beyond galvanic twitching, can't stop him as he checks my pulse, then flattens his hand on my chest, lazily sliding it to cup one breast and viciously twist the nipple. My body doesn't react. He sees this, but he doesn't see *me*.

I reach out of my body into his head and squeeze.

It convulses like a bag of scorpions, stinging and stinging to no effect. Unlike the one that was inside me, his mentor has gone corporeal, bloated taproots burrowed into his spine like a counterfeit nervous system. It can't react, because it can't accept that I can still do it, until it's too late.

Shigeta sags to the floor, bleeding from nose and ears. A plump, colorless thing like an earwig abdomen extrudes, twitching, from one tear duct. My hands reach out for him, for the wall, for the door. Sacred cows make the best hamburgers . . .

I stumble through the diner, brushing off the waitresses, and make my way outside. The two husky men turn towards me and I reach into them and tweak their cortical arousal thresholds so they simultaneously go for their guns. Each sees the man they hate more than anything in the world standing opposite him, reaching for his sidearm. They shoot each other in the face. I pat them down for keys, unlock the loading door and order Megan to get out.

She obeys, docile as a guard dog, stands where I leave her in the parking lot.

The keys unlock the shotgun mounted behind the driver's seat, and as I drive into the city, I am already planning how I will get into the corporate headquarters, how I will go from office to office, killing every mentor I can find, before I laugh at myself. This is exactly the kind of primitive, reactive thinking the Seminar was supposed to fix. I need to think as they do.

I'm so exhausted, I can barely keep my eyes open, but I no longer have to. I reach for the phone as I merge into the fast lane and type out a Craigslist ad for a management consulting service. I can feel them inside my skull, hatching and dividing and devouring. My brain is having babies. If I'm going to survive, I need followers.

No… a family.

EMERGENCE - BRUNO LOMBARDI

There's a hole in the sky where the Moon used to be.

Hold up your thumb and extend your arm as far as it'll go. See that size? That's how big the hole is.

It's there 24/7. When it's daylight, it's a black spot in an otherwise clear blue sky, like a computer screen with a big clump of dead pixels. When it's night-time, the hole is blacker than the black sky, which makes no sense but there it is. When it's cloudy or raining or whatever, the black hole still shows up, as if it's a black laser beam shining through the muck and crap and clouds. Again, it makes no sense but we're used to things making no sense these days.

It's been two days since the Moon exploded and the world came to an end.

And I'm out of medications.

Nothing makes sense anymore.

We still have electricity—but all the power plants have stopped operating. And the radio and TV and internet still work—but nobody on them says anything logical or factual or even sensible. They say the Moon exploded—but no debris can be seen and none have crashed. They say the hole is there —and yet, *not* there. They say that there is an explanation for everything—but none have come.

I stay in my apartment, the curtains drawn and sleeping with the blankets over my head.

The hole in the sky doesn't frighten me.

It's what *behind* the hole that does…

It's been four days since the Moon exploded and the world came to an end.

And I'm out of food.

My iPhone beeps. There is an alert on it—all cap letters.

It says "DO NOT LOOK AT THE MOON. UNDER NO CIRCUMSTANCES DO YOU LOOK AT THE MOON".

My iPhone beeps again. Facebook, emails, text messages, Instagram, Twitter—they're all going crazy. I have dozens—no, *hundreds*—of notifications. From friends and relatives and even strangers. They all say the same thing.

"It's a beautiful night tonight. Look outside. Come. Look outside."

I go under the covers and throw an extra blanket over my head.

Even under the layers, I can still sense it.

The hole in the sky. The…calling…from *behind* the hole.

It's been five days since the Moon exploded and the world came to an end.

I had turned on the news first thing in the morning, only to see empty news desks and empty studios and dark screens. All the stations are like that—except one. A man in a rumpled suit, sitting behind an empty desk. The lights are dimmed and I get the distinct impression that he is the only one in the studio. He's murmuring words over and over again. His speech is slurred and stuttered and he clearly has not had any sleep in days.

"The…migration…has…begun. The…migration… will…occur."

He repeats the words over and over for as long as I watch as if they are a mantra. Or a blessing.

Or a warning…

I go out. Out for the first time in five days.

My plan is to find a store or a supermarket and buy or steal some food.

I did not know what to expect when I went outside. But what I *didn't* expect was to see all the people standing. They were standing on street corners and sidewalks and driveways and balconies and rooftops and roads.

And they are all staring *upwards*.

And smiling. They're all smiling.

Meg. I see Meg. Beautiful Meg.

She's standing. And staring. I dare not follow her gaze, dare not look upwards, at the Moon.

"Meg?" I ask, my voice croaking from disuse. I wave my hand in front of her face, hoping to dispel the spell or curse that she is under. For a few seconds, there is no action, no reaction, no acknowledgement.

And then she blinks and turns and faces me, the smile still on her face. *"Look. Look at the Moon. It's a beautiful day."*

I take a step back and begin to circle behind her.

There is a cracking sound…a horrible, cracking, tearing, *ripping* sound.

Meg begins to move her head to follow me…and her head

slowly twists around, the horrible creaking and tearing sound rising higher and higher.

Her head is now at an impossible one hundred and eighty degrees. And she is still smiling.

"Look. Look at the Moon. It's a beautiful day."

And I then hear creaking and tearing sounds from all around me.

Everyone is staring at me, many with heads tilted and twisted at impossible angles. They speak in unison. As one.

"Look. Look at the Moon. It's a beautiful day."

I run home. I do not get any food.

It's been seven days since the Moon exploded and the world came to an end.

And I have not eaten in two days.

When I glance out from the window, I see all the people are still standing. And staring.

And then…

As if a switch was turned on, they turn and begin walking. But still staring upwards. Ever upwards.

The people disperse in every direction, seemingly without rhyme or reason or plan. And then, after a few moments, I get a sudden revelation. There *is* a rhyme and reason. A *pattern.* A…plan?

They are all heading for the parks.

Curiosity compels me to follow them; hunger compels me to find some food instead. In the end, hunger won.

I eat my fill of junk food and energy bars and chips and stuff armloads into my knapsack. I go to leave, to go back to my apartment, to stay there until…I'm not sure until what, to be honest. But something—mundane? emotional? supernatural? human?—*something* draws me towards the park.

They're there. Hundreds, maybe thousands of people. Standing. Smiling. *Staring*. And quiet. So, so quiet.

And then, as if a puppet master was at work, they turn and begin to move.

I hide. Ducking inside a building. I take the stairs two at a time as I rush up to the roof. The building is huge—thirty, forty stories—and I get to the roof, gasping for air, my legs on fire, my lungs aching. From up here, I can see a fair chunk of the city.

There is a tsunami of people. Like those films of army ants from nature documentaries, there are tens upon tens of thousands of people. Moving as one. Marching as one. I blink and then I notice that there are other groups spread out throughout the city. I stare in jaw-dropping shock. The whole city? Or most of it, at any rate. Surely I cannot be the only one unaffected? But then, perhaps I am…?

It takes me a few moments for me to realize that there is a pattern. A purpose. A *plan*.

There are precisely four groups. And each is marching….no…*migrating*…in one of the four cardinal points. North, south, east and west.

The ocean is directly east of the city…and I watch one-quarter of the city calmly, methodically, and unhesitantly march into the ocean.

I debate which group, if any, to follow. I have the whole city to myself now, but for how long? If the city—and presumably other cities—is being emptied, then what will happen when the last group leaves the last city? If I stay here, as King of the City, will it be a short reign? Will fire or ice come from the sky? Will the earth swallow the cities whole? Will the oceans drink its fill?

And always…always…I feel the *pull*. The pull to follow… to obey…to march. It is a *compulsion*. One that I can resist… but it's there…always there…tugging at my brain…my heart…my soul.

Follow the group going north? No, it is close to winter and just a few weeks of walking will get me into cold and snow and ice.

Follow the group going south? That is a possibility—but just a few weeks of walking will get me to the ocean again. Will they walk into the sea like their brethren?

West? Yes…westwards. There is safety…at least for now… in walking westwards.

I take my backpack and I follow the wave westwards…

It's been ten days since the Moon exploded and the world came to an end.

The waves of people are leaving from every town and city we pass. In each case, they too were following the four cardinal points. Some of the groups invariably intersect with others. When they do, there is a…parting. It is the only term that springs to mind. There is no mixing of different groups. The group marching eastwards will not interact in any shape or form with the group moving westwards. The group marching northwards will pass effortlessly through the group marching southwards. What criteria are being used? Does one being melancholy doom you to being an eastwards marching group? If you drink alcohol, do you get shuffled into the southwards group?

And why am I still unaffected? Can I really be the only one who never stared at the Moon? Who sent the text warning? Are there others like me, hidden in secret government bunkers? Or was it the last desperate act of a lone final survivor? And how can they march onwards and onwards without needing food or water or rest? Or staring unwaveringly upwards?

I have so many questions. And so few answers.

I stop at a grocery store and replenish my supplies. Unlike

them, I need to sleep and I fall, exhausted, onto a pile of coats at a department store.

I awake in the late morning, to see another group marching westwards.

I follow.

It is twelve days since the Moon exploded and the world came to an end when I see the giant spider.

My mind reels at its size. No, *her* size. I should be terrified —and yet, I feel nothing but…contentment?

She is as tall as a skyscraper and black as the darkest night.

She also has the face of a kindly old grandmother.

Spider Grandmother? The name and image tickle some faint memories from my anthropology courses in university. Ojibwa? Hopi? Navajo? A few others, I think. Many others, possibly.

A protector? A guide? A messenger? She is all these things.

She takes a position in front of my group.

And we follow.

It is twenty-one days since the Moon exploded and the world came to an end when I reach the desert.

And the group comes to a stop just before midnight.

For a moment—a very long moment—I think we are at the base of a mountain.

Then I notice that the mountain is *moving*.

It is a mass of bodies—*human bodies*—rising thousands—no, *tens* of thousands of feet—into the sky. A pyramid of bodies and limbs. The base—crushed under untold tons of weight—is a smear of blood and flesh and bone hundreds of feet thick. As my eyes stretch upwards, I see the mass of human bodies rise up into the sky.

And they are still alive. Still *alive*.

Spider Grandmother smiles a grin as huge as a stadium, teeth as huge as a house. She moves and begins to climb up the mountain of flesh and bone and dead and living.

Guiding our group. Calling our group.

Beckoning our group.

We follow.

It is twenty-four days since the Moon exploded and the world came to an end when I reach the top of the mountain of bodies.

Arms and legs and heads brush against me as I climb. When I dare look, I see smiling people. Staring upwards.

"Look. Look at the Moon. It's a beautiful day."

Spider Grandmother is at the top of the mountain. Waiting. Waiting. Waiting for me. For me.

I feel her smile. Her benevolent smile. Her caring smile.

One leg—as long as several city blocks—reaches down and touches my forehead with a delicate touch that I *should* find surprising for something so huge but I do not. The touch…

The touch imparts…thoughts. Knowledge. Purpose.

A new world awaits my children. You are the chosen few. Those that will be the descendants and stewards. Of the Fifth World. It is time. Time to leave this world. This Fourth World. The wicked and impetuous and angry and disobedient. Follow. Reach to the Moon. To the Portal. The Entrance to the New World.

And a leg reaches down at my feet.

And another leg reaches up.

And touches the Hole where the Moon had rested.

I feel the tears well up in my eyes. I understand now. Understand everything.

I climb. I climb the immense spider, using the hairs as handholds and footholds.

It is twenty-five days since the Moon exploded and the world came to an end when I reach the top of Spider Grandmother.

The Hole in the Sky awaits me.

What awaits me beyond? Hope? Oblivion? A new body? A new purpose? I know not…and care not.

And with joy in my heart, I take a step forward.

And cross beyond the Hole in the Sky…and into the Next World.

"Look. Look at the Moon. It's a beautiful day."

GENITAL FREAK - KATY MICHELLE QUINN

"The doctor is ready for you," the receptionist tells me. "Um, miss," she adds, inflecting the word questioningly.

She's lying in two parts. The doctor is not ready, doctors never are, especially not the famous crotch wizards of Price Gynecological Professionals. You wait for them, like a fangirl for a celebrity, they don't wait on you.

The receptionist's other fib is the word, *Miss.* Her tone, her southward-wandering gaze informs me that she has pegged me as a trap, a woman with something up her skirt. She'd be right, of course, but that business is none of hers.

Not to fear, hun, I won't carry this burden much farther. I will leave this place a new creation, if the doctor does his due.

It's been two years since I first perused the praises of the Price Professionals, of the frontiers they have forged between the legs of patients. Two years' hoarded papers and snipped articles pasted to the dream board hanging inside my suffocating closet. Two years it's taken to scratch together cash for the cost, one spent back alley dick at a time. Sometimes two. Two years of calling to schedule the appointment before hanging up silently, all the while thinking *what they could do for me.*

After six hundred days and as many milliliters of whiskey, I finally spoke in that voice I hate, the one that says "call me sir" no matter what words I use. Two minutes finding a time, one question before I go.

"Are you sure he can help?"

The whiskey slurs syllables.

Does she catch my meaning?

"Price Professionals is the choice of the modern women," she assures me, though I am unassured if she knows how modern I am. "Our techniques, our tools are ahead of their time."

So am I.

I hang up. *Why am I even bothering?*

I tell myself that maybe the magic of medicine has finally caught up with girls like me, force myself to forget my concerns.

Now that the day has come, I smirk off the stares of staff as the nurse leads me down the sterile gray hallway. She towers over her stilettos, broad shoulders balanced neatly over a back like a violin. It's women like her that make me anxious. Heartbeat hammering harder, I follow the nurse through one featureless door of many. She waves a hand at the stirrup-laden throne in the middle of the room, smiles slightly, and leaves without further comment. An invitation, I take it. My movements are gawky as I mount myself in the mechanism with some degree of difficulty. I spread my legs wide to fit my feet in place, my skirt-hem sliding up to snitch my secret. The air conditioning blows cold, but it is the ice of anticipation that makes me shiver as I settle in and wait. Twenty more minutes is nothing on the years I've waited for this.

A firm knock on the door.

"Are you ready."

An imperative poorly disguised as a question, tone telling me that if I am not ready after all this time, I bloody well better be. The British of the brogue and its caramelized baritone demonstrates that this is a man confident in his abilities. I run away with his words, my sex stiffening a bit at the scene I write for us.

The door opens before I can answer. A handsome man walks in, long white coat fluttering behind him like a cape. A clean part reveals his severe brow, and his eyes stick to a clipboard that holds enough pages to compose a tome.

"Miss..." the doctor says, searching for my name on the paper.

He is more man than I was expecting. My cock hardens *sans permission* and I gasp silently, scandalized by my body's audacity.

"Ah," he says. "Miss...Peck?"

As he looks up, his mouth gapes. A tall drink of water turns to a cocktail of disgust and desire as the doctor meets the thing standing between my legs. The clipboard clatters. After a moment, the doctor explores toward me, as if a sudden movement would upset this delicately balanced situation. I feel breath on my sex as he bends over to examine the anomaly up close. His small eyes engorge. He shakes his head, then snaps to attention before backing away to a socially acceptable distance.

"And you're not a man?"

I shake my head. He analyzes the rest of me, fact-checking it against my crotch.

"Then they were right," the doctor tells me. "You are an interesting case."

My cock softens at the slight.

"It's not out of your purview?" I ask him.

"Not at all, but I am not quite prepared for this," he waves a hand at my underskirt. "Back in a minute."

The doctor collects the clipboard as he gathers his composure with a parting smile. The door slams behind him, the breeze of it smacking me in the face.

What if he can't fix me?

A photo of the man who just left watches me from the wall. *Eyes like this can't lie,* his photo fibs, blue irises polished to a realistic gloss. Oceans of certainty I drown in. My confidence in the doctor reawakens, as does my erection. I unbutton my top to let the air in, nipples crystalizing in the air-conditioned chill.

A quick knock followed by the door whacking open.

The doctor clamors in as if escaping a hurricane. His Brylcreemed part has been blown into a wild nest of twigs, and he has grown a pair of glasses. His eyes dart like angry animals behind their lenses. The coat that had been so clean is now stained with patches of beige and pinpricks of crimson. Without meeting my eyes, the doctor gawks at my crotch. He seems freshly disgusted, newly desirous.

What is it with men that they can't sit with their wanting?

He creeps toward me, fingers spidering at his sides for understanding.

"How?" is all he says, eyes riding up the rest of me to ensure that I am, in fact, a woman.

His smooth accent breaks in the air like ash from a cigarette.

I clear my throat, give him an eyes-up-here look.

The doctor snaps to attention. He tosses me half an apology, eyes chasing up my stomach then down again. The confident fox that had first entered the room has been replaced, it seems, with a pathetic clone. Unenthralled, my cock begins to soften. The doctor's gaze falls with it.

"Fascinating," he says.

"What do you mean?" I ask him.

"This is a unique mutation, and it will have to be removed. Though I have never seen anything like it, I believe I can help you." His tone infests the air with possibility. "I assume that's why you came here, is it not? You're not expecting anything *routine,* I hope."

"I've been waiting for years," I tell him.

"The techniques at Price Professionals reach past the pinnacle of innovation. We employ methods that most in our field couldn't fathom. Some haven't even seen a research study. I cannot promise what the result will be, but I can promise to do things for you that no one else can," he clears his throat, "or will."

As timid as his entrance was, the small speech sparks fire in his eyes. *Eyes like this don't lie.* Confidence rekindled, I nod to show him that I am ready for whatever he must do.

"I was hoping for nothing less," I say.

"A moment," the doctor tells me.

He turns and walks out, carelessly leaving the door wide open. The wandering stares of passing staff caress me, curious at the new find. In a minute, the doctor returns clutching a blue sheet close to his chest. It clinks with the sound of frisky machinery. The nurse follows behind him loyally, her empty expression unchanged from before. The doctor crashes the contents onto a nearby counter before handing the sheet to the nurse. She holds it loosely, face painted with the vacant smile of a game show host. The pieces of steel on the counter are contorted into strange shapes. They glimmer as if they detest the dullness of the rest of the room. The doctor's fingertips brush the tools, mouth silently numbering them. He hesitates over a pair of hooked scissors, then a thing with the look of a spider's mandible, before selecting a large, beaked cone with a jagged seam down the middle and a smooth, finger-like handle. He regards its steel with a touch of lust before positioning himself between my sprawled legs. His eyes fixate on my genitals, expression overflowing with grim excitement as he nods to the nurse. She flutters the sheet over my belly, obscuring my view of the doctor and my lower half.

"Absolutely revolting."

The words bleed through the sheet, though they had been barely whispered.

"What is that?" I ask, directing my question at the nurse. Her only response is a plastic smile.

"I asked if you were ready," the doctor says. Volume raised, tone sharpened.

I could vomit my heart out.

"Yes," I tell him, breath like a breeze.

He clears his throat, then grunts. I feel the steel beak bite my taint as the doctor thrusts it into me, tearing a gash where there was only a wall. My skull fills with fireflies as the tool bores into me. Of all the times I have been penetrated, I have never felt anything this intense.

"Mutant," the doctor mutters, syllables squeezed, "radical techniques are required."

The nurse holds the sheet still and smiles blankly.

The doctor mumbles hungrily as he fucks the metal further into my body. I feel a release as blood ejaculates out of the opening. The fibers that clasp me together tear, ragged as scrap fabric. Seeking cohesion, my loose ends tie themselves to the angry beak. My body drinks the tool down, flesh fusing to steel until only the handle protrudes from me. The doctor's fingers grasp it tightly in an accidental act of submission as he tugs then twists, but the metal will not move.

"Very unusual," he says, stale brogue dumb to how unusual this is. He turns to the nurse. "Help me, please."

The nurse drops the sheet on the ground, revealing the two appendages cragging up from my crotch. One half-hard cock, unwanted, and a spear of surgical steel standing below it like a celebratory statue. The nurse and the doctor pull at the handle together, trying to rip the tool from me. I writhe in the chair as a wave of pain drowns my spine, its crash echoing in the chasms of my brain.

"Stop!" the doctor says, his first act of mercy. The two cease pulling.

I relax, until I see what the doctor is doing.

He fumbles with his belt, though this is hardly the time. The nurse looks unconcerned as she watches him unbuckle. I am about to ask what the fuck he is doing when he drops his pants, revealing oversized eggshell boxers sporting a crispy stain. He bends over and snaps them down to his ankles. Instead of genitals, the doctor is equipped with a gaping red gash, a slit cut in flesh framed by sharp lips of surgical steel. The wound seeps yellow blood, which runs down his thigh like sick semen.

I shudder at the infected maw.

"What…?" I gasp through the pain.

The doctor hears me and barks to the nurse, "The sheet!"

She grabs the sheet off the floor and flourishes it over me, again obscuring my view of anything past my belly button. Task complete, she blesses me with a placid grin. Her incisors shine with a white that overtakes my vision, blurring out shapes until everything is brightness. The fluorescents flicker, then the room falls out from under me.

When I come to, the nurse is still smiling, curtaining me off from my own body with the sheet. I feel heavy. On the other side of the sheet a shadow straddles me like an incubus.

I try to call out, but any sound I make is drowned in the squelch of wet sex.

The doctor's wound consumes my cock, seeping sick juices onto my stomach like lube. Bile bubbles in my throat.

"With biological abnormalities," the doctor narrates to no one, "a procedure can be as unexpected—and disgusting—

as the patient. A mutant problem requires a mutant solution."

The nurse smiles and nods along with his words. This is not the first time she has heard this.

"Sometimes that solution is radical, to say the least."

The shadow shifts, and gore-drenched flesh swallows my sex deeper. I feel a tickle like a hundred spider legs as our insides intertwine. *This is not the medical miracle I was hoping for.* I thrust my hips to buck him off me, but the fusion has progressed too far.

"Nurse!" the doctor calls.

The nurse drops the sheet again, holds my shoulders down. I try to push against her, to sit up and see what is happening to me, but she is too strong. The doctor slumps his weight onto me, ensuring that I am fully pinned.

"The key to our methods at Price Professionals is biological intuition," the doctor continues, as if our struggle had not happened. "Trusting your subconscious to divine the solution before your conscious mind even has the words for it. I created this tool in the spirit of experimentation," he gestures to our married crotches, "with no plans for it. But it is proving to be very effective in a case such as yours."

The nurse pushes me down to stop my struggling, smiling as she does. The doctor settles onto me, gobbling every inch of my groin into his flesh-tool. His bladed lips scrape against my skin. The doctor clenches his thighs and begins to stand. The strands of connected flesh pull at my cock until it feels as if it can't stretch further. A sound like the tearing of paper, a metallic snap. The bridge between me and the doctor severs, and I emit a small scream that recoils off the sterile walls.

"Ah," the doctor says, grinding his hips into me to ensure the cut is clean. "It appears our procedure is almost complete."

He hoists himself off me, moaning a bit with the effort. The gash that graces his front has closed, a flytrap with captured prey. A muted murmur tells me it is digesting the meal.

I see the suggestion of gore where my cock had been, vision blurred by the afterhurt. The nurse is already threading it closed with a long, curved needle. Beneath the wound, the steel handle of the beaked tool still protrudes from my body.

I didn't come here to exchange one dick for another.

"Um," is all I can manage through the searing expanse of pain.

The doctor locates his trousers and pulls them on messily, smirking at the nurse and I as if this is a necessary and usual moment of social awkwardness.

"Just one final step," he says, buckling his belt.

He reaches toward the tools on the counter and grabs the one that looks like a spider's mandible. He brandishes it and approaches me again.

The nurse smiles as she ties off the stitches.

"Lie back," the doctor says.

Out of exhaustion, I comply.

A clinking spasm like a metallic bug, then a clunk as the beak falls to the floor. A sharp-yet-fleeting pain.

"Perfect," Dr. Mantle croons into my crotch. "Alright, Miss Peck, your procedure is complete. Would you like to see?"

The nurse helps me onto my elbows, and my expression screws at the effort.

"Healing will take time," the doctor says.

The nurse smiles silently. The doctor gazes into me with the admiration a potter holds for clay.

"You see," he says, to no one in particular, "there are times not even I know what the result of a procedure will be. In this case, I believe my biological intuition has surprised us both."

Fear skitters across my face.

"For the better, that is."

For the first time since entering the room, the ice melts from the doctor's eyes. He even offers the hint of a grin before turning to the counter and rattling a silver object from a drawer. I wince as he turns around.

"I thought you said," I say, eyes spliced shut.

"Oh, we're done," he says. "Open your eyes."

They flutter open, though my gaze evades the mirror the doctor holds between my legs. The nurse smiles expectantly and speaks for the first time.

"What do you think?" she asks.

The depth of her tone is familiar to me. Too familiar.

Of course. The skyscraper height, the athletic build, the androgynous features. She is a woman like me.

I look into the mirror, seeing the manifestation of a decade-long dream grinning vertically back at me.

"It's beautiful," I tell her.

ELK: AN ORAL HISTORY OF AN ABANDONED FILM (1987) - JACK LOTHIAN

FRANCOIS EDWARDS (Producer)

Dentists. That's where all this began.

It was around '86, and I'd had some moderate success as a producer, tending towards the low budget end of the market. There had been *Red Hollows,* a slasher series in the vein of *Friday the 13th* only transposed to a Beverly Hills type neighborhood. We got a few good sequels out of that. A few other films here and there, some good, some bad, and one about a werewolf baseball team I'd rather forget.

During all this, I'd discovered a rich vein of investment from people in the dental industry. For some of them it was the perceived glamour of the movies, for others it was simple tax write-offs. I'm told that's how the first *Evil Dead* got funded as well.

They'd keep investing and I'd keep looking for properties to develop, which was how I came across a promising spec script called *Elk.* It was by a young writer, Michelle Tonte. She had this punky attitude that made me feel old and out of touch, which is always a good sign, and it felt like a notch above the usual fare I'd been producing.

Everything outside of the film, everything else that happened… I was in the dark. I didn't know about any of it. If I had, I would have never bought the script, I would never even have spoken to the dentists.

You live and learn, although not always in the right order.

MICHELLE TONTE (Screenwriter)

I was your classic struggling scriptwriter, working minimum wage jobs whilst scribbling away. I'd moved to LA from Toronto in my mid-twenties, plunging into the subculture, trying to write stories that meant something.

I'd had some problems; medical issues, bills, that kind of thing. I did a lot of ghostwriting, script polishes, brutal hours but enough to consider myself a financial success if not an artistic one.

Then I got the call from Francois about *Elk*. It came at the best and worst possible time.

FRANCOIS EDWARDS (Producer)

Michelle was kind of odd, but in a town like this, that's expected. She made it clear that she wouldn't do a re-write on the piece, but I figured that was a bridge that could easily be burnt later. She also wouldn't do lunches or face-to-face meetings. Everything was by mail or by phone, but that was fine with me. I was busy enough as it was without needing to babysit a writer. I put my production coordinator Sara on 'Michelle duty' and focused on finding a director.

SARA SCHNEIDER (Production Co-Ordinator)

I was twenty-three years old and although I had experience working on movies, drawing up schedules, juggling finance, I was probably under-qualified and over-enthusiastic. I think Francois quite liked that, this ball of energy with frizzy hair that came rocketing into the interview.

He handed me *Elk* and got me to draw up a prospective shooting schedule right there and then, based on three levels of budget,. He took a look at the first few pages and decided I was competent (and cheap) enough to be hired. That was when he casually mentioned that Walter Brezzle was circling the project.

I wasn't a huge horror buff, but of course I'd seen *The Arachnid,* which had come out earlier that year. It was a loose adaptation of some fifties monster movie, one of those rare genre films that had crossed over to the mainstream. I liked it a lot; it was all about the horror of seeing your own body slowly transformed into something both repulsive and fascinating. It was smarter than it should have been.

So naturally I assumed Francois was bullshitting me.

FRANCOIS EDWARDS (Producer)

At the time there were adverts in *Variety* announcing *Walter Brezzle's Frankenstein*—but the sense I got was that he was far fully committed to it, and had concerns about doing another adaptation of a known horror property off the back of *The Arachnid*. Hollywood is a place where they pigeonhole you, first chance they get. I think he could see a career stretching out where he'd end up doing all the old classics—*Walter Brezzle's The Blob, or Walter Brezzle's Creature from The Black Lagoon.*

That said—I'd pay good money to see that last one. Without a doubt.

I'd met Walter before at the Sitges Film Festival in Spain, so I sent him a copy of *Elk* and a note asking if this were something he'd be keen to direct and re-write as he saw fit.

Aside from his 1983 movie *Precognition* he'd had a hand in writing all his films, and I wasn't looking to change that, plus it solved the issue of Michelle's continued and almost aggressive refusal to tweak the script.

It was fortuitous timing—for many people commercial success is a drug; they have one hit, and they want another and another. Walter wasn't like that. The fact *The Arachnid* had been a box office success worked in our favor—he'd be keen to avoid the constraints of commercial filmmaking that he knew the studios would push him towards.

MICHELLE TONTE (Screenwriter)

The premise of *Elk* was relatively simple. A female doctor is losing her sight, and she tries to find a technological cure. She creates a mechanical replacement for the retina and attempts to fuse it with her own nervous system. The nerves start to become infected by it, and then it spreads to her cells. Even worse, she's infecting other people with it—through touch, through breath, through salvia.

It came from a central concept; what if a mechanical virus could infect the biological. DNA is a code, but what happens if that code gets over-written . . ?

At the time computer viruses were still relatively new; the Elk Virus had been the first major outbreak, a few years before in 1981—it infected Apple computers, and was spread via floppy disk transfer. It's why I named the script *Elk*. Just that one word alone seemed oddly foreboding.

SARA SCHNEIDER (Production Co-Ordinator)

I was in awe of Michelle. She was like the cooler older sister I never knew I wanted. Michelle had mentioned in passing that she'd had issues with her own sight, and I guessed that's where the heart of the piece came from. The script had a dark, emotional edge to it—what it meant to be mortal, and to be surrounded by machines that were meant to save your life, but would outlive your flesh.

FRANCOIS EDWARDS (Producer)

Walter responded to the immediacy of it. It was a virus movie, but a smart one. Despite all the weighty themes though, it had a popcorn heart.

JONATHAN BERNWOOD (Film Critic)

There was a wave of films in the 1980s that dealt with the speed at which technology seemed to be entering our lives —*The Terminator, Blade Runner, Videodrome, Robocop*—where we see the merging of the organic body with that of a machine. They're both a fantasy of how technology can enhance our power and a paranoid fable about the diminishing of emotion and connections to nature.

You look at our relationships with technology now and it's hard not to feel these films were onto something.

FRANCOIS EDWARDS (Producer)

Walter wanted to shoot some test footage. This was as good as it got to a commitment without papers and lawyers involved. It also meant we could use for footage to whip up a proof-of-concept to help raise some more money. Dentists only get you so far, and as yet we didn't have studio backing. Even though Walter was coming off a hit, it was still an R rated movie, and this was by no means a sure thing.

• • •

SARA SCHNEIDER (Production Co-Ordinator)

I booked some studio space in Westlake and apparently, Walter came down for a few days, along with Andre Sluchevsky *(cinematographer)* and Tony Howarth *(special effects supervisor).* I wasn't on set—Francois wanted to keep the numbers down.

MICHELLE TONTE (Screenwriter)

I wasn't told about it, but I don't think it would have mattered to me either way. Once you hand your script over, it ends up becoming someone else's property. It mutates and changes. It's not like I could have gone and visited the set anyway.

SARA SCHNEIDER (Production Co-Ordinator)

Michelle was definitely told about it. I was aware she was going through some issues at the time though. I guess we'd become friends—I tended to be the first point of contact, and we weren't that far apart in age.

We'd talk a lot on the phone at night. Sometimes she'd tell me to be quiet, and she'd make me focus and listen to the crackles and hiss on the line. I think back now, and it seems crazy, but we'd spend what felt like hours in silence, hearing the distant fizzing of electronic waves down the phone. It was a bonding experience.

I came from a small town whose idea of art was a painting of a dog by a vase of flowers. Everything seemed fresh and new. That's what I miss the most. That feeling of fascination. The unknown. I guess I didn't recognize quite how deep that ran with Michelle.

• • •

FRANCOIS EDWARDS (Producer)

The footage looked great. I'd expected Walter to go for a primitive style, something raw and scratchy, like *Eraserhead* or his own *Blood Parasite* but it was actually quite lush and rich.

It was an unscripted dream sequence where a woman wakes and moves to the mirror, only to discover that her eyes have been infected by metallic particles. When she goes to pick the fragments out, she cuts her fingers on them, and the blood that pours out is black and slick, like oil. In desperation she grabs a razor and slices through her skin, only to find machinery and wires lying beneath.

Walter said he was trying to capture the feel of Dali and the eyeball sequence in *Un Chien Andalou.* All I knew is that we had something special on our hands.

ARMAND WALSH (Film Historian)

I'm certainly skeptical as to whether Mr. Brezzle shot anything for the project. There's never been any actual record or confirmation, and Mr. Edwards has never shown this supposed footage. The only thing that comes close to a confirmation is an interview where Mr. Brezzle says he was considering a lot of options in the post-*Arachnid* period, and the interviewer brings up *Elk* and gets the response that it "may have been one of those options" which is hardly evidence.

FRANCOIS EDWARDS (Producer)

The only reason the footage has never been released is because of what occurred afterward. I don't have to defend myself, or my decisions. It certainly happened. Directors shoot test footage all the time.

One thing stuck out, early on. We were having dinner and Walter asked me if I'd ever read the Wood and Geasland book about Stewart and Cyril Marcus, the identical twin New York gynecologists. At the time I thought he was just making erudite conversation, but within a few months, it had been announced that he planned to make *The Oath of Twins*, a loose adaptation of their story. Walter sent me a very polite handwritten note explaining his reasons for choosing a different project, none of which I could disagree with.

I knew he had concerns about whether he'd covered this thematic ground before. It felt like the sort of film he'd make, which for most directors is a bonus, but he wasn't the type of artist interested in repeating himself.

Even worse, I really liked *Oath of Twins*. It wasn't *Elk* but in a lot of ways, it was far better and more unexpected than our movie would have been.

SARA SCHNEIDER (Production Co-Ordinator)

I was devastated. Francois took it in his stride though. "Nothing is until it is," he said, and so we pressed on with finding a new director.

FRANCOIS EDWARDS (Producer)

The actual quote would be 'Nothing is, until it is, and even then it quite possibly isn't.' That was kind of my mantra at the time. I wasn't upset with Walter, he'd never signed anything official, and he was kind of enough to say we could use the footage if we wanted, no need for a credit or payment. So essentially we had one solid dream sequence that played very well.

Walter also gave some very good, brief script notes. You could see the innate sense of the storyteller at work. I told Sara to take them over to Michelle, babysit her while she churned out a re-write. I was hoping to land another name director and wanted the material to be in the best shape possible. I could have hired another writer, but there was a certain tonal quality to the work that I wanted to preserve.

And despite her refusals, her contract stated she owed us one set of revisions. Don't sign on the line if you can't do the time.

SARA SCHNEIDER (Production Co-Ordinator)

I went over to her apartment.

I'm not sure I want to talk about it.

NERI COVELL (Film Professor, City College of New York)

There are a lot of people who believe the infamous Michelle Tonte video footage is a hoax, a kind of pre-viral advertising campaign to try and raise money for *Elk*. And there are those who believe that what they're seeing, in amongst the fuzz and distortion, is as real as it gets. Guerrilla marketing or genuine footage; I've never taken a firm stance on either side.

For me, it's the ambiguity that fuels the intrigue.

FRANCOIS EDWARDS (Producer)

I wish it had been us who were responsible for it, that I'd been that smart and creative. I would sleep a lot better at night if this were the case.

SARA SCHNEIDER (Production Co-Ordinator)

The door was unlocked. I'd left messages letting her know I coming, but her phone line was always engaged. Pushing it open the first that hit me was the smell. Thick, acidic, almost bitter. The place was a mess. Blinds drawn.

Trash scattered everywhere. The coffee table submerged in wires and tools.

Then I saw Michelle, slumped in the chair by the window. I thought maybe she'd had an accident, a stroke, but as I got closer, she seemed to stir, waking up.

She was covered in small silver pinpricks. I still remember how they glittered in the half-light. It was like every pore on her had been transformed into tiny stars.

Then as she moved, her whole body seemed to shiver, and thin filaments of some kind of metal pushed out through the skin. Through her neck, her arms, her shirt. She was bleeding, but the blood seemed dark and thick.

I wanted to shout at her to stay still, to stop moving, but then I saw her face. Metal threads were protruding from her eyes. They ran in a lattice across her cheek, her jawbone, into her mouth moving her jaw up and done, like she was some jerky unsure puppet.

There was a VHS camera sitting amongst the debris on the table. As Michelle stood up, I grabbed it, turned it on. I don't know why. I think it was an almost protective gesture. That if it was on film, then it couldn't harm me, couldn't be real. I don't know. The metal tips were wavering, jutting from her throat, like the antenna of insects, trying to sense something. I wasn't thinking straight.

NERI COVELL (Film Professor, City College of New York)

The camera work is shaky, and it often slips out of focus, and there's a significant amount of visual interference, not to mention the—possibly deliberate—low lighting.

A spasmodic zoom finds Michelle. She reminds me of a peacock, the way the metal fans out as she finally stands up straight. It's her face that draws the viewer in, as we realize that the metal which appears to be coming out of her skin is actually burrowing its way back inside.

We're witnessing the battle between the biological and mechanical, where the two states to co-exist. You can hear Sara on the soundtrack, she mutters "Oh God" and the camera moved back as I assume Sara does as well. For a second we see Sara's hand fumble for the phone, attempting to make a call. The image becomes swamped in static.

Michelle takes a jolting step forward, and her mouth extends—rather than opens—and you can just make out the writhing metal shards inside. She tries to say something—it sounds like *I have a garden in me*—but her voice is hard to make out, like someone trying to speak underwater. That is the true horror of the piece, where you have no idea if Michelle is a victim or willing participant in all this, and if you are listening to a human or a machine or something else entirely.

I have a garden in me.

Then she grabs the person behind the camera.

SARA SCHNEIDER (Production Co-Ordinator)

I remember picking up the phone to call Francois, screaming for help, and then Michelle was beside me, and I was looking into those eyes. Everything went quiet. The phone fell from my hands, as Michelle placed a finger on my lips.

I could feel the metal threads extending, slivering over my teeth, my tongue, down my throat. It was like a burning fire and a freezing wind at the same time. I felt connections being made that I didn't understand, across my body. I felt the emptiness disappear and I knew I was drowning, and I don't think I minded.

FRANCOIS EDWARDS (Producer)

Sara was near incomprehensible. I understood there'd be some sort of accident. I called 911 immediately.

You can read the medical reports yourself. You probably have. They found both Sara and Michelle collapsed. Michelle appeared to have gouged out her own eyes. I can't think of another way to put it. She took some kind of drill, and she forced it into one eye and then the other. Jesus. I think back to that period and the pressure I was putting her under for rewrites… I shoulder some of the blame. I won't hide from that.

Sara had obviously suffered from severe shock upon seeing this.

All the metal sci-fi bullshit, the video… there was no evidence of that.

So I don't know. I set out to make a movie and ended up with this. Sara never forgave me for not backing up her story. I didn't believe it though. I still don't. But I should have supported her. Maybe we'd still be talking if I did. I did ask for the tape to be destroyed, to protect them both, but copies leaked out anyway.

Michelle's still in a long-stay psychiatric facility. It's a nice place I'm told, out in Connecticut. It's been over thirty years now. I hope she found some peace.

MICHELLE TONTE (Screenwriter)

It started in my early teens. Dark circles in front of my vision. Two black holes hovering in front of me, growing in strength and definition over time. That's what I remember from that time; doctors, specialists, the way the word degeneration seemed to atrophy and crumble on their lips.

As long as the outer circle of nerves held fast, they said I'd retain some sight.

Then in my early twenties, those nerves curled and turned white, fading one by one.

They said I had ten years at best before I lost all sight. I was determined to try everything. A willing guinea pig, searching out any possible solution. Electrically conductive polymers, fitted on the dead ends of the nerves, to allow electrical signals to be transmitted. Pluripotent stem cells grown from the embryos of mice, blossoming behind the eyes. Bursts of electronic data and noise, to reprogram the behavior of decaying cells. It was hard to find doctors who would help, but not so hard if you have money.

You want an easy explanation. I can't give you one. Somewhere between the wires and fear, the metal and flesh, the noises down the phone lines… I felt something replicate and grow inside me. Something new. Maybe *Elk* was my attempt to control that, to understand it all.

The doctors say it was all in my head. A psychotic break. Most people passed the video off as a hoax. Sometimes I think they're right. You can't even make out that it's me on screen. It's true there were scars and incisions all over my body, places where some metal implement had pierced the skin, but the doctors believe I did that to myself, and either way you look at it, they're right.

I still watch the video, now and then. They tell me not to, but it's simple enough to find online. Is it my voice, saying how I have a garden within me? Sometimes I say yes, sometimes I say no. Both answers are equally correct.

SARA SCHNEIDER (Production Co-Ordinator)

I work in real estate now. I was in therapy for a while, but I got past it. Life goes on. I never believed the official explanation, about what I saw being a reaction to how Michelle had harmed herself. That doesn't account for the video. Maybe it's just impossible to dig out whatever truth lies underneath those grainy images.

I'm fine. I'm happy. Sometimes I look around though, see people hunched over little machines, jabbing and swiping at their screens, lost to the world around us. It makes me think about where we've ended up; biology, technology, who will end up controlling who. And maybe I see a sliver of light across my eyes, little metallic galaxies twisting and turning, only for a moment, and I wonder if I have a garden inside me too, and if it's growing, waiting, coming to bloom.

But mostly I'm just fine.

THE TAINT IS SAINTLY WITH HER WELCOME - MONA SWAN LESUEUR & FIONA MAEVE GEIST

They know my secret. They must know. Mirna Donovitz had forgotten her purse in the station locker at the end of her previous shift. When she woke up to an email from her boss asking her to come in early tonight for a "performance review," she knew her time at this job was over.

She works the overnight security shift at Penetrax. Her only approved purpose: noting deviations from the norm. The norm being nothing but the occasional dribble of coffee on her crossword puzzle or a stray crumb on her clearance badge. A badge that doesn't have her true name on it.

Tonight, there is a deviation in the flickering feed. A lone, suited figure marches down the empty corridor on monitor three. The figure reaches the bottom of monitor three and enters the top of monitor four. They take a left out of monitor four and reappear in monitor sixteen. *They're coming this way.*

The door to Mirna's station slams open. Her boss *click clacks* over to Mirna, looming over her for a beat, then throws her purse onto the Formica countertop.

"Chiram, I hope you accept we won't put on niceties like the deviants want. We know about your problem, your urges."

Mirna is stricken at the utterance of that dead name. The name that tastes like the bitter leavings of ashes in her mouth whenever she reproduces it.

"Chiram, we at Penetrax value our family. And like any family with a crisis, we have an offer for you," her boss places a Manila envelope on the counter. "We are experimenting with a drug to tame urges of the flesh. Urges like yours. We seek to eradicate glitches in the system. You'd be taking a short vacation from work, only coming in to receive your injection and do your debriefing . . . it goes without saying that this is proprietary and that you are not to discuss it with anyone."

Mirna's boss holds out his hand. Mirna hands over her badge. Her boss yanks her cosmetic mainline off the counter, smirks, then turns on the back of his heels and leaves the station. Mirna just sits in her chair and stares at the envelope. Bile rises in her throat like a glottal wave of rejection. She goes to her battered locker, yanks out her lunch cooler, and rushes to the bathroom. She sets the cooler down in the sink and looks in the mirror.

Was any of it worth it? Hiding away from family and potential friends, all for a few days of freedom from the 70s throwback dress code of suits and ties and slacks and wingtip oxfords? Those few days where she unveils herself like a butterfly breaking from chrysalis—a vibrant, brilliantly colored woman emerging from the suffocating rigidity of her work.

She takes her cooler into the farthest stall in the row and slams the door behind her. She sits on the toilet and pulls two cold steel whiskey stones from the cooler and places one in each hand. She grips them tight, and after a few seconds, bites down on the sleeve of her powder blue jacket.

The day guard must have found the purse and gone to turn it in, thinking it a stolen prize, only to find out the bitter truth when intake opened her wallet and read that awful name on her driver's license. Have they notified her family? Oh god. Is her Grandma going to call her and berate her for her *lifestyle choices*?

Mirna's hand spikes with pain. It burns away the lancing fear in her chest. She screams into her sleeve, holds on to the stones for a few more seconds, then drops the stones back into her cooler.

She returns to her desk and looks at the Manila envelope once more. She wants a life fighting for freedom, not submission. But now she must forget herself. The desire to do otherwise with her flesh. She rips open the envelope. At the top of the first page: **Testradiol 450ml**

She feels traitorous. She slams her fist on the desk and starts gathering her things. She goes to throw away her crossword puzzle, but notices it's folded differently, filling in 10-14 across: WE HAVE TO MEET, TONIGHT, 11 PM, OPTICAL VIDEO.

Ding. Plastic-wrapped, unsubtitled anime DVDs—untouched since the mid-00's—line the l-racks of OPTICAL VIDEO: a throwback to the era of video rental kept alive by obscure pornography, exploitation films, finer anime, and strange imports. An old woman sits at the front counter, sorting used console games into paper sleeves. She greets Mirna with the familiar voice of a thousand cigarettes. This woman, incidentally the owner, is one of the only people to ever accept Mirna's true self. Part of the reason why Mirna feels so comfortable spending her nights off in one of Optical Video's several crumbling viewing rooms.

The owner gestures towards a man in a forest green suit sifting through the 18+ section—kept visible so management can stop any funny business, and sufficiently closed off so no one could feign innocence walking in. Often, its swinging doors were hounded by adolescent boys seeking a peek of pert, forbidden flesh. Mirna's exclusive tastes meant she had long abandoned this section, her former haunt, with its brown paper bags whispering of release; how abnormal could she be? She isn't the one buying them.

The man turns and looks over at Mirna, summoning her with a wave of his crimson velvet gloves. Stacked before him are a dozen DVDs. He scrutinizes a cover rife with scantily-clad demon girls.

"Would this be good for my sixteen-year-old son?" he asks, holding out the DVD to Mirna. She recognizes the case: the first five episodes of a harem romance.

"Unless you want your son to think that his childhood girlfriend might try to stab him with a boxcutter in a jealous rage, I would not recommend it," Mirna rejoins with a hint of trepidation.

Mirna looks through the stack of DVDs and pulls out a contender: The cover features a well-dressed, androgynous figure posing with dual-rapiers decked out with revolver chambers above their hilts.

"This one will help him swallow a moral compass with a good dose of action." Mirna couldn't be certain she was being tested and equally uncertain she wasn't being just a touch sarcastic.

The man nods, momentarily browsing deep in thought, leers around the store, then slips the DVD into his inner coat pocket.

"I take it you're the one who sent me the note?" asks Mirna. *Did he just want me to find hentai for his son—trying to make sure he turned out normal? Was the knowledge of her personal indiscretion that widespread?*

The man ignores Mirna's inquiry, reaches into a coat pocket searching for something. He produces a receipt and gingerly places it next to the cellophane wrapped stack of DVDs. He mutters about cost and ambles away from the store. Mirna picks up the receipt. *Two-hundred for five DVDs? Yikes.* A loose disc rattles when she picks up the stack—Mirna shakes the cases until she finds the culprit: Satoshi Kon's "*Perfect Blue*".

Mirna supposes there isn't any harm in nabbing the DVDs, nor any reason to look a gift horse in the mouth. Especially if all her fundamentally wrong choices are about to be erased through innovative therapy and paid time off—anyway, they are already paid for. She grabs a diet cola and a bag of chips, then pays for six hours of viewing time.

The viewing room splashes to life with static grey as she enters. She pops open the "*Perfect Blue*" case to find a loose DVD with a cheap strip label: GLEEMAX INFORMANT ORIENTATION VIDEO. A business card with a date and a location is tucked into the insert tab of the DVD case.

Mirna sticks the DVD into the media console, cracks open her soda, and shoves a handful of chips into her mouth.

Happiness knows no limit, with Gleemax!

There is an overwhelming blur of information, infographics, and claims to be ". . . combining the forefront of transhumanist self-actualization and Neo-Reichian therapeutic intervention". The words are unfamiliar, but the DVD reassuringly proclaims one thing insistently: "you aren't alone, you don't have to be, there's a way out" and all it requires is industrial espionage and knowingly continuing with her arranged therapy while feigning compliance so Gleemax can "...innovate the fleshy potential through reverse engineering."

Mirna hums the jingle—like free jazz played on a cheap synthesizer—while waiting in the Penetrax clinic lobby.

She looks down again at the name tag the clerk gave her. **Chiram Donovitz**. Soon she'll be rid of that horrid name. Just have to go through some treatment and hand the details over to the Gleemax representative. Piece of cake, right?

"Chiram? The administer is ready for you." says the front desk attendant. The inner office door clicks, then pops open. No one is on the other side. *Automated doors.*

Mirna stands up, adjusts her tie, and walks through the door and down an expanse of drywall and speckled linoleum keeping with Penetrax's 70's aesthetics. The examination room is no different with its powder blue leather seats, and beige leather bed with nimbus white sheets.

A man wearing a powder blue coat not too dissimilar to Mirna's enters the room just as she takes a seat in a chair. Something about the man's unkempt hair and the mustard stains on his lapel help her realize how right Gleemax was about the entire operation: Penetrax is out of their element.

The man reaches into his lab coat and pulls out the syringe. Periwinkle viscous liquid moves like hair gel in the unlabeled vial. He asks Mirna to roll up their sleeve. She complies, and the drug is injected with a sting and burn. Then the interview starts.

"Chiram, we need you to relax" the unnamed proctor injecting her states, "the serum is only half of the process. The rest is what we will call a suggestive therapy."

Additional nurses in starched uniforms, faces covered in gauzy wrap, start attaching electrodes and leads to Mirna. One offers a lascivious wink that makes Mirna feel a twinge of self-hatred. "But don't worry, this will be like a vacation."

Vision blurs.

"You won't remember a thing."

Buzzing sounds fade in and out.

". . . and when you wake up, Chiram. Chiram? He's fading. Let me tell you, when you wake up, everything will be better."

Curtain draws.

"You're going to go away for a bit. But don't worry. When you hear three knocks?"

Blackout.

Wakeup.

Knock knock knock.

Mirna is soaked in sweat, tangled in sheets in some anonymous hotel room—how did she get here?

Knock knock knock

What did she agree to?

Knock knock knock

Like shrapnel blossoming in the wound, a memory unfurls with the rising pitch of a bad gramophone wind-up to a synthesized Swedish Rhapsody No. 1 . . .

***Happiness** knows no limit, with* **GLEEMAX!**

Hello Mirna, this part of your subconscious encoding is most important, do not panic, do not even think of panicking or the revolver in your pocket or what was in that syringe—the Penetrax treatment is a reverse engineered Interzone commodity—it has some side effects, but enough about that Mirna. It's time to cover Agents, Signs, and Counter-Signs.

Agents are representatives of institutions—whether ours or the enemy's. You know you are among friends when you are among our agents—you feel at home in your skin and like you could express anything without fear or judgment: that's because you can! Enemy agents make themselves known by **Innocuous Signs**—someday you'll notice your neighbor always greets you "good afternoon" even in the morning; but that is just his sundowning and nothing to be alarmed by. However, one day the pitch will be slightly off "gewd morning" the syllables stretched and mutilated—it isn't a benign tic, it's the presence of an enemy agent. Odd taps, repeated phrases, inexplicable machines, and contradictory orders are all signs that you have been contacted by an enemy agent. This is a normal part of your process, dispose of them, quickly, make your escape. Find us at our special place. Don't be late. Your new friends await you.

Remember: Disposing of Enemy Agents, like fealty to The House of Skin and

Happiness is **Mandatory.**

The off-key symphony bores into Mirna's soul. She sits up on the bed and wipes the drool off her face. Everything smells like the industrial cleaner used to cover the smell of sweat, vomit and cum. She gurgles. Oh fuck.

Knock knock knock

Mirna half disentangles herself from the sheets—looking like some ridiculous cultist who couldn't tie their robes right—and drags them like a bridal train into the nearby bathroom. The jaundiced tiles are sticky under her feet. She tries to not think about ringworm as she voids into the toilet in coughing spasms.

KNOCK KNOCK KNOCK

Everything is like a fever dream, blurred and hazy outlines and radiant heat from every part of her body—she is certain it is not room service or the maid knocking so incessantly on her chamber door.

KNOCK KNOCK KNOCK a series of door shaking kicks follow and the deadbolt rattles like a carton-a-day smoker giving up the ghost, the screws straining in the wood. Mirna, still frazzled, drags her impractical toga in a sort of half crouch, then kneels behind the bed and starts fishing through the pockets of her pants—the encoded memory said she had a revolver . . . right? Encoded memory—how goddamn absurd.

KNOCKKNOCKKNOCK

CLICK

SHIT SHIT SHIT charge handles are snapping back—where is the fucking revolver?! That's the sound of an automatic. Why are there so many silhouettes shifting outside the window? *What the fuck did I get myself into?* Mirna's mind inventories as her body's strange heat juxtaposes with the twisting cold dread deep in her bones, radiating through her stomach.

She had undergone minimal preparation for the snub-nosed .38 her job issued her, but that was a training film. Her gun was for show. *Fuck, I've never even fired the damn thing.* She unbuttons the holster, pulls the revolver out and thumbs back the hammer. Most of what she knows about guns is from television. Which brings her attention to the sickly phosphorescence illuminating the room: the TV pulses between a strange test pattern with a skull in the center of complex gradation diagrams, and blurry black and white footage of a boot being ground into a young woman's face. The screen flickers and warps. The industrial orchestra thrums and whips to the distortions. Mirna scoots in for a closer look. The woman on the screen seems to wink at her knowingly.

The next 8 seconds: Flying shells chew the door apart before tearing up the bed, sending plumes of feathers into the air and shattering the glass vase with plastic roses like a love letter. Time slows; eternity is shredded hotel room basics and zipping rounds. A dry click announces the end of a magazine, and again there is the *KNOCK KNOCK KNOCK*—a wolf blowing on a house made out of anonymous humans dozing.

Mirna stands and empties the revolver into the flash of an anonymous suit she peeps through the riddled door. She hears something clatter on the other side—her first enemy agent.

The hotel room window explodes in a hail of gunfire and rounds catch Mirna in the shoulders, legs, and stomach. She swan dives back on a tilted axis. The gun flies from her hand and—huh, despite all the gunfire, the TV is intact and playing footage of some strange ceremony where robed figures talk with a man in a fedora while centipedes crawl across the lens of the camera.

The fedora-wearing figure, dressed in a neat dun-colored suit and red velvet gloves approaches the camera and in the nasal drone of a dying door to door salesman says:

"Well Kid, yer bleeding, there's wolves at the door and you spent your wad on the first of four, bad day's luck for a rookie agent. It's fraught and nasty skullduggery the whole way down in the House of Skin. But if you know one thing: a croaker always sells you stepped-on goofballs, a William Tell trick is best performed sober and those rats feel like they got you at the advantage. Lemme tell you, Kid, you can do something tasty or die."

Whether this was the shock or cold reality doesn't register for Mirna before a second volley of gunfire explodes the television and any remaining, unobliterated hotel amenities.

Christ coming again atop the Blessed Virgin Mary in ponyplay gear, this fucking hurts. Her wounds pump blood across the carpet. Three men she hadn't put bullets in push open the remains of the door and stand in a deadly wedge—anonymous trench coats, sunglasses, boxy black guns; like extras in a beautiful gore-spattered denouement to an action film. They grin at Mirna lying behind the bed.

Her left hand unfurls and snaps open like the abomination offspring of a bloated starfish and a sea anemone. Her pseudopodial flesh tendrils disassemble the revolver piece by piece. The wooden grip drops to the ground. Mucus drips onto the barrel, hammer, firing pin, and chamber. Metal melts and bends inside the chasm of her arm. Muscle and sinew string out like spiderwebs around the shifting metal—flesh strands pull and reshape it until six barrels of flesh, bone, and metal protrude from the aperture. All the bullets within her rush out in a desperate chorus. The peculiar blast lays waste to the remainder of the room—two of the men's lives end splattered across the hotel room walls.

One agent left.

The remaining agent, sniveling in a puddle of piss and

tears, begs Mirna for his life. Of largely their own accord—Mirna at least vexed by the possibility of killing the sodden blob beseeching her for mercy—the six petals making up Mirna's appendage slurp forward elongating/stretching/twitching/wrapping around his face like a sensual and enraged octopus which suffocates his screams before crushing his head in its loving, tender embrace.

Mirna's arm undulates and twitches. It sucks the man's cerebrospinal fluid and engorges like a tick. His body contorts like a garbage bag rotting in time lapse photography while the arm debones his spine and rebuilds itself. On closer observation, Mirna's new arm feels slightly alien—prone to acting out of instinct or against her first inclination. It drips a slushy mixture of grey matter, skull fragments, and oral mucosa. The fleshy confusion between her newly reshaped arm and its newly acquired spinal column shudders, coalescing into a human arm; different than before. Mirna marvels, rubs her hands together for comparison—the new arm is soft and affirming.

Somehow it simply seems right.

Her encoded memory intones: *Now you know their center of operation within Penetrax. Go to the TV. INSERT THE DISC INTO YOUR SYSTEM.*

Mirna approaches the television stand. The DVD player sparks. All the shooting tore off the top of the player and Mirna can make out the disc on the tray underneath the chipped plastic frame. The disc remains spinning despite everything.

It will bend to your will. Take it. INSERT THE DISC INTO YOUR SYSTEM.

Mirna swipes her fingers across the top of the disc tray. Periwinkle fluid seeps out of her fingernails and vaporizes the plastic. She grabs the disc off the tray. The skull logo from the television set is embossed upon the disc.

The taint is saintly with its welcome and awaits your gentle hand. INSERT THE DISC INTO YOUR SYSTEM.

Mirna pulls down her trousers and bottoms. She pushes her package against her thigh and positions the disc underneath her taint—which unfolds with a miry snap, gaping like a ragged jaw; *holy fuck are those teeth?* Blood coats her thighs. She inserts the disc expecting pain, which never manifests. Instead, the procedure feels warm and inviting like being fisted by a loving stranger. Looking down, her gaping stomach wound is an open window that reveals her improved fingers placing the disc within her abdomen.

MORE

Her new finger idly rotates the disc—rather than a plastic buzzsaw in her gut . . . it feels good. Like the contented feverish dream of her weekends expressing her true self—now shameless with the doors torn off rather than triple-bolted, and ragged curtains so distinct from her duct taped cardboard to prevent even a glimmer into her secret pleasure/shame.

Her new hand is perfect. She wiggles her fingers to spin the disk faster. Viscera jets from her open abdominal cavity. The disk scrapes against her pelvic bone with a strangely pleasant rasp, not unlike ASMR videos. Her erect cock twitches as it spins faster and faster—faster than should be possible. The wound expands. Fragments of stomach skin drop to the ground, falling away like bad plaster as her pelvic bone quivers and lets off a wet crack.

The disc enlarges, still spinning like a saw blade and slices away within her—festooning the already dripping room with more chips of bone and sprays of viscera as it scalps her prostate. She screams like a wounded feral cat as she cums. Bone chips and organ pulp spurt from her wound-cunt and pool amidst broken glass like a monstrous afterbirth. Sharp, pleasant shocks ride her core like slagged electrical cables merging with her being. Her knees buckle and she lands on her ass atop the bed. Pelvic bone contorting to wrap itself around the disc like an enclosed record player. Pulling her hand out and looking down, the disc spins on its own.

Consume the bigots' spinal columns. They will bring you closer to your true self.

Mirna looks over at the men on the wall. Her right arm splats, opens, swirls and flails in the air, then snaps back onto their heads. Flesh and muscle contort, twitch, ripple, and bulge; vibrating before relinquishing the crumpled corpses; they slide down the wall like clotted fruit puree.

Her sleek ribbons flit about searching for sustenance. They stiffen, then dart towards the scattered guns and caress the smoking armaments—the plump, flanged ovipositor ejaculates ooze all over their lethal detritus: revolvers, rifles, magazines, bullets, and casings melt into puddles of steel, brass, and nickel slurped up in spasmodic gulps. The hue of her veins change—solid blue, to wine purple with blue hints, climaxing in a tri-tone mixture of blue, silver, and purple. Everything coalesces and forms a normal arm—save looking and feeling more like her true self.

Bring the disc player close to your heart. Envelop it with your loving arms.

Mirna greedily yanks the thrashed DVD player off its stand, snapping the cords with her eagerness. Hugging it to her chest, her arm undersides open in marvelous slits—like the gills of an exotic fish—slathering tricolor mixture over the player as the ichor continues dribbling down into her lap. Her chest quietly opens dozens of tightly knit pinholes, which the DVD player seeps into. The excess drips onto her lap and on her leg. Her ribs bend back, unfolding like a hidden, enormous second mouth that smothers the player and brings it close to her heart; then her bubbling skin seals itself.

Now, the television set, reflection of our darkest, deepest, innermost desires. Be the reflection you want to see.

Mirna's outstretched arms unfold into a confusion of dripping veins and textured pseudopods blindly proliferating and stretching towards the shattered remains of the TV.

Good thing we didn't leave a credit card to cover incidental room charges.

Her arms latch on like leeches to an inorganic nipple. They halt and arc when she tries to pull back. Her skin writhes and shakes like she's an alcoholic, then snaps the set into Mirna's face. It unfolds like a fleshy and tumorous mass impersonating an HR Giger satellite dish—her neck snapping back from impact and dramatically throwing her back into bed.

Mirna wakes up to a hotel employee shaking her shoulder. She is nude and covered in semen. *Oh, thank god. It was only a wet dream.*

"Sir, it isn't safe to be here. Please get dressed."

Mirna doesn't remember telling her hand to violently snap into his crotch. Drill fingers shred his junk until they find the base of his spinal column and tear it out. His body collapses like a water balloon puppet stuck full of needles. The spine splits and the surgical spikes sink into her legs like spears in quicksand.

Not a dream. Her legs unfurl like a monstrous flower and hungrily grasp the proffered spine. The spinal fluid seeps into her veins and swims through her body to her own spine. Mouthy toe tips noisily devour the rest of him and lap up the gummy mess from the carpet. The drained employee is idly tossed amidst the other devastated corpses. Mirna scarcely registers as she marvels at her true legs: long and muscular as a pony.

Mirna shambles across jagged glass and splintered wood towards the bathroom. She stops to extract a shard of glass that looks like a QVC knife from her sole—it gushes blood, yet she is unimpaired. There's enough mirror left to necessitate grabbing the counter to catch herself as she nearly faints. She smothers a shocked, strangled yell. Tears run down her true face. She slaps her cheeks, stares, and breaks into a smile for the first time in years. Her true self. She never thought she could see Mirna, the real Mirna, looking back at her.

An explosion, or perhaps an earthquake, rattles the bathroom. She shields her eyes from the midday sun as she steps outside. Smoke pours from vacant windows throughout the city. Fire licks at exposed points throughout. She looks around and spots a tacky fluorescent sign. Gunslinger Inn. Just outside the city limits.

Head into the city, child. Join your siblings at the Faire House of Skin. Our Lord of Red Velvet awaits you.

The asphalt is hot enough to cook the skin off feet and serve alongside a full breakfast, but she feels none of it. Naked, without a token stab at modesty, Mirna sets off towards the city. Sweat trails down her body like she stepped out of a sirocco shower and she regrets her lack of umbrella, her hand held up to blot out the pitiless sun. Not a moment too soon, it compacts and stretches thin, like the birth of a flatworm before it fans in webs with a delicate latticework of bones. Transmogrified into a succulent parasol.

Ask! Your body now bends to your every whim. Your hands will never hurt you again.

Closing in on the city; banks, churches, apartments, and office complexes are replaced with jagged corpulent spires. Open sores speckle their surfaces and ooze iridescent viscous fluids. Mirna's fingerskin umbrella steams in the sweltering sun. The sultry flesh commands: *Feed and replenish.*

A slouching figure sporting a stupid maroon hat emblazoned with arrogant ignorance fumbles towards Mirna—her boss. He is shocked gazing upon her body, moist from birth, and cannot even manage a scream before she unfolds and stampedes him like a sarcoidosistic avalanche. He slips into her undulating folds. He begs and whines. She wraps her arms around him in a crushing embrace. Bones snap and jut out. She increases the pressure. Fingers attempt and fail to grasp onto anything. Head and toes and arms and legs flail about. Frenzied pleas and senseless, idiotic burbles slip out from within her carnivorous mass.

Thank you, monster, for this wonderful gift.

A final squeak ekes out of his collapsed throat as he bursts like a rotten eggplant, drippings sizzling on the pavement as apertures within Mirna's flesh gorge themselves with a sick suck of the enveloped slurry. Wandering in an effervescent daze, Mirna's people are everywhere she looks. They wave and call out her true name. Their newly malleable flesh absorbs the kinetic energy of bullets falling upon enemy agents like adipose jello suffocating the regrettable G-men.

At the center of it all: a carnival cathedral carcass twisting like a funhouse mirror distortion adorned with neon Christmas lights. In front, the man with the fedora and red velvet gloves offers a somewhat stiff and awkward embrace:

"Well, look at you, Kid. Whatever that croaker sold you, it's done the body good. This is the program: we splatter and devour the rat bastards wherever we can find them, take over the liquifactionist machinery, make it our own. You're a Rebus of the Black Grail," he proffers Mirna a card:

Mirna Donovitz

Agent of Gleemax

Beloved of the House of Skin

She reaches for it but he immediately snatches it away. He ignites it and uses the flaming square to light two cigarettes. He passes one to her:

"Sorry, Kid, it's strictly burn after reading here; you can't teach a hammer to love nails—that dog don't hunt—and you can't find love in your heart for the enemy agents. It was tasty, Kid. You done me proud."

The dun-colored suit, fedora, and red velvet gloves peel away like the man's body is nothing but plaster encasing. The former face and outfit crumble to reveal a grubby looking woman with slick cropped hair and a leather jacket going bad at the seams. In the unchanged croaking lilt she finishes:

"What we have here is an opportunity to become part of the family, birth a new world, wear faces and cast them away as any agent would, and reveal the mutability of the skin."

They both take drags from their cigarettes. Mirna nods and looks to the future as they bear witness to the final scene transition of our world:

Secret lost signals, perverse joy and biodigital integration —factories of traumatic flesh shaping themselves into new networks of greedily caressing raw and ragged tentacles that blanket the surface of the earth. An ocean of flesh, pipes spilling forth a torrent of media milk like greened magnesia amidst skyscrapers. Like a boxer's broken teeth. Mirna realizes she's soaked thinking about it, her hands at her pelvis slick with discharge.

The Lord of Red Velvet laughs and places a hand on Mirna's shoulder.

"There'll be more of those wet dreams to come."

TYPHOID ANANYA - MADELEINE SWANN

She was tingling by the last demand that she should be raped by AIDS gorillas and left naked on the Scottish rooftop. Their hatred blistered her skin and howled through her body. "Typical immigrant sending their worst now sending infected scum sent you to destroy the west on purpose dirty bitch." She was a crucible for their burning fury. Their words echoed off the concrete tower blocks and bleak Highlands landscape. Ananya wondered if it was the same people day in and day out, or if new ones turned up each time. Perhaps they did shifts. As always, though, it was over too soon and she was alone once more, in her tiny room, staring at a secondhand laptop, surrounded by a hard bed with standard issue blue blanket, a yellow plastic cross trainer with zero resistance and a small, chunky TV. The tingles decreased each day. She'd have to up her game.

She dared her anonymous Reddit account to have changed overnight but the same old comments were left by different people. Be strong, we're here for you, blah blah blah. Her lament over her brother was inundated with selfish replies about their own relatives, rounded up or crumbled into rotting forestry. It was as boring as her unchanging view of heather and bracken from her window. A hare tore across the green, pausing madly. It stared at the new buildings for a minute before darting away, disgusted by the eyesores. Ananya hated that hare and then hated herself for it. Her pulse thudded.

"It's that time again," said a well-spoken, apologetic Englishman as he let himself in, his hazmat suit rustling as he placed a tray of swabs and needles on the table, "you know the drill." He was always pleasant to her, never rude, half smiling, always closed the door behind him instead of letting it slam, but Ananya saw the sliver of judgment in his watery, pale eyes. He never laughed with her like he did the others. His conversation, as she rolled up her sleeve and gritted her teeth against the pinprick, was limited to the weather and what he had for dinner. Ananya wanted to ignore him, wondered what he would do when faced with total resistance, or tell him she was nothing but a guinea pig to him, an anomaly, but she whispered something about looking forward to Tuesday's pie and mash. Under the plastic of his suit, he smelled of leaves and freedom. Her pulse increased and a sick, sticky sound slurped from her chest. "Looking forward to that pie and mash, aren't you?" said the Englishman, but there was no controlling it now. She groaned as the thin snake of green oil oozed slowly, painfully slowly, from her chest cavity to the scientist. "I'm sure they'd let you out in the grounds for a few minutes if I asked them," his words were rushed, as if he could still stop it. The scientist held his works aside as the ooze splurged against his front, brainlessly and uselessly searching for a hole in his suit. After a few seconds it cooled and hardened. She would peel it from the carpet and throw it away later.

"All done," he said, forcing a smile as he wiped her arm. He barely glanced down at the mess and Ananya wondered if that was part of his training or if he didn't want to risk enraging her. When he was gone, the rattle from the heater battered her ears.

She returned to her blog, Typhoid Annie. It had taken a whole wonderful day to customize her theme to piss as many people off as possible. Her picture grinned mischievously above a Halloween font of the Westernised name given to her by the papers. The red and black background invoked old horror movies. "Got a glimpse of Lee again," she'd written yesterday, "definitely saw him on the outside, probably infected him myself, who cares?" She'd only checked the comments three times and had fifteen new ones, which made twenty-seven so far, ten less than yesterday. Ananya clicked on bookmarks and opened the BBC News video of the outbreak. 100 dead in the first week, all located in Newcastle, a few thousand in the second week, thousands in the third, then millions, spreading further and further out. They'd stopped travel but it was too late. Oddly, though, it remained contained within the UK. Scenes of house windows blocked with a green substance flashed on her laptop, a reporter pushing a pub door open to film wasted corpses dangling from bile green cobwebs. Ananya daydreamed through it all she'd seen it so many times.

The window on the left wall was filled with the next tower block. She knew every mark and crumbling dent and wondered about the people in its rooms and the blemishes they'd memorised from their windows, and the people in the next building over, and the next. She forgot how many they'd built out here, grey monoliths against the bleak sky, a safe distance from society, always there to remind the rest of the UK that its occupants were once friends, lovers, partners, relatives.

A yell sent Ananya scrambling to her feet. She'd always overreacted, squealing and crying at the slightest thing, her move to England more traumatic than it was for others. She'd lost three jobs and all her friends by showing up to work but not taking that step through the front door. It wasn't just the rude supervisors, or the British men's crude jokes, or the way her colleagues spoke to her as if she were a child. There was something fundamentally wrong about this being her life. She wasn't supposed to drift through her days, barely noticed, not mattering, a person others noticed only if she was in their way. She'd tried explaining her feelings to Rabia and Aleksandra and they'd told her everyone felt like that, it was normal, you just had to get on with it. They weren't wrong, but Ananya had yelled at them, said terrible things, that they'd always been poor and were only good for this life. She'd left in shame, crying all the way to the agency over her cruelty and rage. At the next job, she'd learned to keep her mouth shut but nothing inside had changed.

She peeked through the rectangular window in the door to the corridor—Lee Campbell. She wasn't supposed to stare but couldn't stop. Suited security guards rushed to his room, their bodies holding the door open. Lee, or what she could see of him, was sprawled on his bed. Luminous green webbing smothered his corpse, tendrils stretching to the walls and ceiling. He was barely visible through the mess but Ananya saw his open mouth hanging down to his chin and his half-closed lids. His flesh bubbled and writhed and oozed. He was definitely, unquestionably, dead. He'd been here almost as long as Ananya. They'd nod to each other now and then and she felt they were friends despite never having spoken. She'd seen those on the left and right of him come and go, and now he was gone too. She covered her face with her hands, surprised at the wail leaving her mouth. The guards radioed for the duty doctor, who Ananya supposed must sit in an office all day testing samples, waiting for something to happen. Today it was a young man, sleep in his eyes and hair mussed up, going through the motions of checking for life. He filled in a form, spoke on his phone, and requested a stretcher. Tomorrow, someone from the makeshift pens would take his place or a new patient whose family could afford to skip the waiting list.

She straightened up, recognising Maggie through her hazmat suit. As Lee was scooped up by every available hand, chunks falling to the ground, the green web clinging to him and them like silly string, Ananya tapped her window, softly at first then more insistent. She swallowed each breath hard. Maggie glanced up but was waylaid by the woman in command. Maggie held up a finger to indicate she'd be a moment and Ananya's right leg swung in a dance of impatience. After a brief conversation, Maggie held up five fingers, meaning more waiting, and followed the others to the stairs.

Ananya stared at the threadbare blue carpet in the corridor. They wouldn't let Maggie return. This was another way of getting back at Typhoid Annie, The Carrier, killer of whole families for the sake of a low paid cleaning wage, never mind that it first happened in Britain. She'd spent hours scrubbing the house and the first thing the woman did when she got home was point out the marks from the mugs still on the transparent tea trays. Ananya had watched gleefully as the poison stretched to the other woman's chest, trapping her, sneaking into the mouth of her reddening face, sliding down her choking throat.

Her brother, Karun, had been the biggest surprise in all this—not a word since her trial, after everything she'd done. She'd pay rent and add up the leftover on her phone, assigning this much to his school trips and that much to his university fund. Night after night she ate lentil dahl and chickpea naan so he could go out with his friends, and now he'd cast her adrift in her new career as destroyer of the west. She was glad she'd snuck outside to the communal bins one night and thrown away that designer jumper with the green patches. He'd brought it home so proudly and she'd admired it, furious with herself for her jealousy. She had almost laughed when he scoured the flat looking for it, hoping it would teach him humility. That night, however, when she'd heard him crying in his room next door, she'd cried with him and pinched the skin on her chest until it bruised.

She stretched the muscles in her face to dispel the memory. That was why she was here, she kept giving in to ugly impulses. She unclenched her fists and checked the nail marks on her palm. She couldn't blame Karun, it couldn't be easy at university, surrounded by strangers waiting to ask about Typhoid Annie, maybe giving him a hard time for it. She just wished that someone would tell her if he was settling in OK, it didn't have to be him personally. How could he just leave her, not knowing?

Blood bubbling once more, she returned to her computer and opened a new blog post, "Lee Campbell just got dragged off by medical. Definitely dead. His guts were green as they ran out over the floor. One of the medic's shoes was smeared in it. I remember Lee. I cleaned his house on Tuesday mornings and he never offered me tea. I suppose this is payback." Once the filth and rage had leaked from her fingers onto the page she pressed send and sat back. She'd never met Lee before their incarceration but the commenters didn't care.

"Disgusting, UR SICKQ!"

"Should of stayee in your country rag bitch."

"You killed him over a cup of tea and get a nice comfy room as punishment. You should look at yourself inthe mirror."

Too soon it was over again. She clicked refresh, more comments but she barely saw them. She couldn't lose her only outlet, there would be nothing left but TV, radio and the vast silence. She couldn't go back to that. Fingers twitching, she refreshed the page, fighting to reclaim the first twinge of fear and shock. Instead, she was greeted by a single imploring sentence, "My husband is called Lee Campbell. Is he really dead? Please just let me know."

Ananya slammed her laptop shut and sat on her bed. She

was still there, chewing her nails, when Maggie stepped inside. "Can I sit down?" she indicated to the chair. Ananya shrugged. Usually, they chattered happily, Maggie being the only one who didn't look at her as though she'd emerged from a toilet. When Ananya first arrived she'd stare at the wall, wondering how to commit suicide without sharp instruments or unmonitored medication. Maggie had brought her spices with her own money, the Chelsea buns Ananya had grown fond of, and her son's old laptop. She chatted when she had a spare moment, encouraged her to download books and use the cross trainer for twenty minutes a day. Now she stared at Ananya as though her face had melted. Not you too, she thought, not you too.

"What?"

"They might be letting you out."

"What?!"

"They've made antibiotics. We'll have to test it further but it's on the cards. I mean, it's very likely." The words punched Ananya and she fell back hard against the wall. "Christ, you alright? Course, if it works, we'll arrange a new identity for you." Ananya opened her mouth to speak but couldn't. "This could be it," Maggie beamed, "this could be bloody it. A new life." She seemed confused when she didn't get the expected response. "You can go outside, make new friends, get a new job, maybe meet someone and have kids? You can forget all about this place."

"I've got no money, no home."

"They'll help you out. Within reason. Ananya, it's good news."

"Will I get a job like before?"

Maggie smiled, apparently thinking she was warming to the idea. "Absolutely, we can put you in touch with an agency."

"Ok." Ananya made her way to the window and stared at the heath as if she'd never seen it before. Maggie, sensing the conversation was over, excused herself, promising to pop by the next morning before they brought her first dose. Ananya watched the light fade, her fingers finding the old bruise patch on her chest, and squeezed until tiredness interrupted.

She checked her blog as usual in the morning, pleased to see several new comments. Perhaps there had been another news story. There it was with a google search of her name, hit after hit of papers around the world announcing her potential release and the protest in London. Almost all of them used the same photos of crowds holding signs scrawled with "Murderer," and "No to Letting Carrier Go," but Twitter showed the truth. "Filthy," they called her, "Paki," she needed to "go home" and "should be put to death." An elastic band snapped in her head. Of course . . . this was who she was. All the terrible things she'd done, it all made sense. They'd found her out. Her heart was infected, it was her fault.

She squeaked when her body shook violently. Pressing the panic button, she sat on the bed with her head down. Maggie burst through the door and embraced her.

"I told you not to look at the news," she crooned, swaying Ananya like a crying baby. Ananya still saw the pictures without looking at the laptop, their teeth gritted, faces red, like battling chimps. Some of the protesters must have travelled for miles, hours, and they were all here for her. She had never imagined so many people would know her name. She would control her pulse during testing and ditch the tablets, or vomit them up, or dig the poison out of her chest when they let her out if necessary, and then she would embrace them all.

"I don't want a new identity."

"Everything will be fine, they won't find you, we'll change your hair . . ."

"No," Ananya sat up and stared Maggie hard in the eye, "I don't want to be someone else. I don't want to hide."

"But they'll kill you, they'll hurt you . . ."

"I don't care," Ananya grinned, spreading her arms and lifting her eyes to the ceiling. "I don't care."

A FUTURE OF VIOLENCE - CHARLES AUSTIN MUIR

"Please try and focus, Dylan. We only want to ask you a few questions. Consider this an interview, okay? Not an interrogation. The guards are a standard precautionary measure. We have a lot of secrets to protect and you, young man, have become one of them. Now listen. Please, Dylan, look at me. This is important. Your, um, *pitch* was a success. Mr. Rader watched it via live stream… he wants to hear more about your product."

"But I'm really tired, ma'am."

"Hailey. Call me Hailey. I understand you must feel a bit strained. But Mr. Rader is CEO of Rader Tek Security Group. He's wealthier than all the investors you presented to combined. With functional fitness all the rage, he wants to enter the supplement industry. And he says he's never seen a better display of… functional fitness than your presentation to the panel. He'd like to know more about CytoSwol, Dylan. This is a huge opportunity for you and Swolov Technologies."

"But Dr. Abellon—"

"We've spoken with Dr. Abellon. It's *you* Mr. Rader wishes to interview right now. What do you say? Do you want to blow off one of the richest investors on the planet?"

"Well—no."

"You should know this is the first time Mr. Rader has wanted to speak to an entrepreneur since he discovered he has Parkinson's. Consider this an honor. Now before we start, do you need anything? Coffee? Tea? A bathroom break? Water? Of course. Lieutenant, please get our guest a glass of water. Okay, I'm live streaming our conversation now. Understand everything I say is on Mr. Rader's behalf. Can you tell us how you got involved with Swolov Technologies?"

"Well... I'd heard you could make money volunteering for scientific research. I'd kind of broke the bank flying to all these writers' conventions. I figured this could be a way to generate extra income without cutting too much into my writing time. I spent enough of my day sending out job applications and doing chores on my aunt's property. Anyway, I looked around on a recruitment site called *Lab Warriors*. At first, I was like, 'Yeah, I'm not going without sleep for ten days or trying some new chemo treatment.' But then I read about a clinical trial for a device that improved exercise habits. I filled out the online application and got an email from the company right away. It said I would be testing a fitness app called Swol-Vox. I went to the company headquarters the next day and met Dr. Abellon."

"Tell us about Swol-Vox."

"Hailey—can I ask you something?"

"Certainly."

"Would you mind unbuttoning your blouse a little more? Just one button."

"It's okay, Lieutenant. Our guest is only asking a question. No, I'm afraid I can't, Dylan. That sort of thing goes against my beliefs, at least under the circumstances. Please stick to the subject matter."

"Sorry. That was inappropriate."

"Let's move on. So what, in your own words, is Swol-Vox?"

"It wasn't anything like what I expected. It wasn't really a mobile device. It was... it looked like something in a David Cronenberg movie. Have you ever seen a David Cronenberg movie?"

"I don't think so. But let's put aside David Cronenberg for now. Why don't we shift our attention to your meeting with Dr. Abellon. What did she tell you to do?"

"I figured she must have developed the app. She was the strongest looking woman I'd ever seen. Like her shoulders were as wide as my last two girlfriends put together. She wore this tight, sleeveless blouse with the first two buttons undone. Oh, man. Her breasts... they had to be fake. I mean, you can't be shredded and have D cups, can you? Or—not that I'm judging..."

"Dylan, please. Stick to the subject."

"Okay. So Dr. Abellon met me in the lobby and had me sign some papers. Then she made me wait in a room in the basement. It was full of exercise equipment and shipping cartons with the logo "Cold Steel Fitness" on them. I sat in a folding chair imagining ways I could die there. I was a writer, right? I was in a situation that could be in one of my stories. I mean, no one knew where I was and my phone had died. Dr. Abellon could have strangled me with one of the chains hanging on the wall... or bludgeoned me to death with a kettlebell... or raped me with Cold Steel Fitness products. The weird thing was while I pictured these scenes, I got an erection. What with getting dumped and losing my job, I hadn't been so hard in weeks. My pelvic floor issues made it hurt like a mother. Oh, sorry... I'm freaking your guards out, aren't I?"

"You're fine, Dylan."

"Was that inappropriate?"

"No, you're describing your experience waiting for Dr. Abellon. Clearly, she aroused you and it affected your fight-or-flight response to your environment. Go on."

"Okay. So finally she came back with the app. That's really not the right word for it. It looked like—like a leech the size of Shaq's shoe. Do you have any frame of reference for that? An animatronic leech thing the size of an NBA center's shoe. It was black and shiny with ring-like segments and smelled like day-old urine. Dr. Abellon held it out to me like a newborn. 'That doesn't look like a smartwatch,' I said. I actually said that. And I'll never forget what she said next: 'The Swol-Vox unit is not something you wear... *on the outside.*' Can you believe that? 'Not something you wear on the outside.' I wish I'd come up with that."

"What exactly did the Swol-Vox unit do?"

"Dr. Abellon said it was an artificial general intelligence developed by the company's late founder, Paul Swolov. He'd wanted to create a biosoftware program containing all his knowledge of strength training and nutrition. The best part was it not only made the user an instant Swolov-level expert, but it also measured every component of the human movement system relevant to strength and muscular growth. In other words, you had Swolov's digital ghost in your head telling you what to eat, how to train, when to rest and so on... round-the-clock fitness coaching by a trainer of champions. In theory. Because the company hadn't found a test subject who could run the program."

"You mean interface with the computer?"

"It's very cyberpunk. Dr. Abellon said they had experimented with several implantees, but none of them had fully integrated Swolov's representation. Some reported having bursts of insight and memories that felt like someone else's, but these were blips—ghosts of Swolov's ghost. I was to be the last volunteer before the company sidelined the project. So we'd come to the moment of truth. Dr. Abellon turned the unit on. It wriggled in my lap. 'Don't panic,' she said. 'If you're too tense, the implant might not take. Now do you want six hundred dollars and an alpha physique, or do you enjoy being broke and average-looking?'"

"Dylan?"

"Mm?"

"You zoned out again. Try and focus. What happened during the download process?"

"It's funny. I remember very clearly right up to the moment Dr. Abellon turned on the Swol-Vox. But the actual—I only recall a couple things. One is the leech thing jumping at my face. Two is the third button on Dr. Abellon's blouse. She was leaning toward me, staring into my mouth… God, I wanted to undo that third button. But that's it. Just impressions, like I'd reverted to an infant state or something. At some point, I snapped out of my fog and things went back to normal. Dr. Abellon escorted me to the lobby. She told me I was to see her again in twelve weeks. Isn't that lame? I'd gone through a real-life Cronenberg event and fast-forwarded through the body horror."

"You might have been anesthetized as part of the procedure. Or maybe you lost your memory due to trauma."

"It's weird, though. How does a brain implant the size of Shaq's shoe fit in your mouth?"

"Well, we don't have all the answers yet, right? But you say—"

"You've really never seen a David Cronenberg movie?"

"Tell me more about the implant, Dylan. Did it 'take,' as Dr. Abellon put it? Did you converge with the simulated brain of Paul Swolov?"

"Oh, yeah. Almost immediately. When I got home, I took a nap and dreamed I lifted these immense weights. Two days later, I joined a gym and pressed my bodyweight overhead. Not that 170 pounds is immense, but I suddenly knew how to train like a pro. I knew what exercises to select, how many sets and reps, how much weight to add and how to cue each lift. I knew how many ounces of steak I would eat when I got home. And I didn't have to think about any of it. I just had to do the motions. At the same time, I felt driven by a hunger I'd never known. Suddenly I wanted to be the world's strongest human. This was not my mindset before the implant—I was a writer, remember? My thing was hitting word counts and pandering on social media. The Swol-Vox took over my life."

"So it's like you became Paul Swolov?"

"I mean, I was still me. You wouldn't have thought I was any different except for all the time I spent at the gym and making meals. I didn't even look that much bigger with a shirt on. Swolov didn't want me building size so much as mutant strength. I quit writing, though. I didn't have room in my head for anything but training. If I thought about writing, the Swol-Vox would make me review my next mesocycle or consider the best exercises for different load vectors. That kind of bummed me out, because I lost contact with all my friends. I became like this robotic, super strong weightlifting monk."

"Dr. Abellon must have been ecstatic, though."

"She was. She kept up with me through email. She knew I was becoming a thing on the Internet with gym members posting my lifts on YouTube. She called me in three weeks before I had to see her again. She said I was ready for the next phase of the clinical trial. That caught me off guard. She'd never mentioned a second phase of the study. The company was developing a supplement called CytoSwol. The formula was supposed to enhance power and suppress protein degradation for quicker recovery. Dr. Abellon said Swolov had wanted to support everyday people engaged in trendy, but harmful, exercise. She said my rapid subjection to extreme stress made me perfect for testing the product. If CytoSwol could help me, it could benefit your fitness warrior wannabes."

"Did it?"

"More than steroids, in my opinion. And no funky side effects. I trained harder, heavier, more often and with better motor control than ever. But here's the best part: *My pelvic pain went away*. Three days after I took the first pill. I'm sure women have it way worse than men, but male pelvic floor syndrome *sucks*. Your butthole feels tight, your balls throb, the tip of your penis hurts and your pubic bone aches so bad you can't sleep. At least that was my experience of it ever since my mom died when I was in high school. Doctors said it had to do with stress and would heal if I learned to relax. Right. When I worked out, I just gritted my teeth through it. But now I could train without my junk seizing up. I was crazy strong with a happy pelvis. Can you guess what happens when a gym rat with a constantly sore dick gets a happy pelvis?"

"You got erections while training?"

"Not exactly. But I was horny as a sixteen-year-old. I would watch a woman doing Bulgarian split squats and feel hot like when I wanted to undo Dr. Abellon's blouse button. The Swol-Vox didn't appreciate me getting worked up all the time. The moment it sensed my arousal, it would make my calf seize up or give me blinding visions of white light. It got so vindictive I gave up thinking about women. Swolov's cyber-ghost redirected my passion into the workouts."

"CytoSwol sounds like quite a supplement."

"Sexualizing the weights was the Swol-Vox's idea of managing my second puberty, so to speak. I know this sounds weird, Hailey, but because of the implant my battles in the gym became even fiercer expressions of desire than intercourse. No one else existed anymore, just me savagely making love to a steel shaft with knurl marks so sharp they could scrape your shin to the bone. Sometimes I gave too much, and blood sprayed from my nose. God, that turned me on. The torn calluses... the floor covered in chalk mixed with nosebleed and sweat... the bar's whip as I forced it off the mats... the weight was like a woman I could never get intimate enough with. A woman I loved so much that I'd have to split her apart to merge with her essence. You know, I've had the thought sometimes, one of those reptilian ideas that lacks any social grace, when I'm going down on a girl that if I were to—"

"We get the picture, Dylan, thank you. Did you tell Dr. Abellon about this emotional side effect of the supplement?"

"No. I'm not even sure she would have cared at that point. As far as she was concerned, CytoSwol was a success and we needed to raise funds for it. The company wanted financial leverage to make the supplement go worldwide. A month after I took the first pill, Dr. Abellon arranged the meeting with the investment group. Here's something funny, Hailey. Last night, I went into my bathroom and caught this whiff like when you walk down an alley that's been used as a trough urinal. I did my business and turned to the sink. There it was—the leech thing sitting next to my Lubriderm. Don't think I hadn't wondered what had happened to it ever since my first visit with Dr. Abellon. At 3 a.m. on my bathroom vanity, it didn't look so hideous anymore. I even felt reassured by it, like it might have some medicinal value. I had the impression it wanted to communicate with me. I scooted as far back as I could and got down on one knee. I kept my hands in front of my face in case I misjudged its intentions. A gob of yellow goo shot out of the leech thing's head sucker. The goo separated into streams that flowed up my arms into my eyes, ears, nose, and mouth. Unlike the first implant, Swol-Vox 2.0 spoke inside my head: 'Pain is weakness leaving the body.'"

"It quoted a Marine Corps saying?"

"I'm kidding. It said, '*You will know when it's time.*'"

"And is that why you went off script with the investors? Because the voice told you it was time?"

"Hailey, can we not..."

"Please, Dylan. Your answer is crucial to Mr. Rader's final decision about investing. Tell us what precipitated your actions at the end of your pitch to the panel."

"All right. So everything was going great. I'd gone through my strongman act to show how effective the supplement could be. The investors were impressed. They also seemed surprised that I spoke so knowledgeably about business. I should have waited for someone to make me an offer. But I wanted to show them *more*. I called for more weight on the barbell. I pulled a thousand pounds. Afterward, one of the panelists asked if I needed a doctor and I realized my nasal blood vessels had burst from the exertion. The warm, metallic fluid washing over my tongue... oh, man. That's when I knew it was time. This wasn't just about raising funds anymore or putting on a circus with the weights—this was about all of us in the room. A transcendental experience. A union of flesh, bone, and iron. I wanted to *merge* us all in a brutally sensual act of loving violence. That was the only way I knew how to love anymore. And I loved those people, Hailey. The way they bore witness to my strength. How they admired me covered in sweat, blood, and chalk, my fingers torn and stinging with ammonia. The space between us made me furious and yet elated—the battle of love was on. I grabbed the table in front of the investors and threw it over their heads. They jumped in their seats but laughed, thinking it was part of the performance. Then I grabbed the man nearest me, lifted him overhead and slammed him to the floor. One step closer to ultimate union. Now, I realize from your position in the control room how horrific the turn of events must have looked. But I want to believe on some level those men and women shared my obsession, my determination to destroy the barriers between us. Their bodies were like Dr. Abellon's third blouse button—they stood in the way of what we needed to become one. So I tore the investors apart. I pounded them into puddles. I broke them on the wheel of steel and iron. You saw the footage, right? You must have seen the smile on my face. And the smiles, at the briefest of moments, on theirs as they snapped and popped and showered me in red spray? I know what the social norm says about what I did, but I tell you we were connected in a way only a martyr knows with their god."

"Mm. Yes. Thank you, Dylan. It took courage and insight to share your experience with us. We simply needed to understand your motivation for... expressing yourself to the investors so intimately before Mr. Rader does business with you. That way, we can redirect your more cosmic urges."

"What do you mean?"

"We want to buy Swolov Technologies. And we want to hire you as brand ambassador. Mr. Rader can make you a star, Dylan. You'll have sponsors, a private jet, a lucrative YouTube channel. TV spots, maybe movie opportunities. We'll need to alter your appearance and change your identity because of your criminal actions, but you're worth it. You've truly impressed us. Mr. Rader says he has never known anyone with a stronger connection between brain and body."

"I'm blown away. A bit confused, though. What does Mr. Rader mean by my 'connection between brain and body?'"

"He believes the neurobiological mechanism behind your muscular enhancement will withstand a correction of the myths you've created about yourself. You need to know the truth about Swolov Technologies if you're to be your best self moving forward."

"Myths—"

"Please, Dylan, don't take the word as a judgment. No one can deny the strength you've built. It's just that you developed it by means other than what you thought. In a way it pains me to tell you this, but... *there is no Swol-Vox*. It was a wonderfully elaborate story, though."

"No—you're lying."

"When you visited Dr. Abellon the first time, rather than equip you with a fitness app she hypnotized you to absorb information faster. In that altered state, you were seated in a room with a television playing hours of Paul Swolov's video lectures. Because you were attracted to Dr. Abellon and wanted to impress her, your subconscious mind responded to the problem of information retention by concocting a covert narrative powered by your creative influences. Think about it... this explains the rather odious, visceral imagery in your origin story. And why you of all people would be the only guinea pig to succeed with the implant. For your mutation to have meaning, you needed to play the role of the Chosen One. There is also the question of why a company that could implant an AI in a human brain would waste the technology on a mediocre supplement."

"You're saying CytoSwol didn't heal my pelvic floor syndrome?"

"Once again, Dr. Abellon hypnotized you to believe in the supplement's benefits before you took the first dose. And once again, your writer's subconscious mind crafted a secret story that upgraded your already extraordinary power and repaired your pelvic floor. CytoSwol has potential, Dylan, but it's just a pill. You alone can take credit for your transformation. That willing brain of yours."

"In other words, I became one of the world's strongest and horniest humans because of a David Cronenberg Placebo Effect? That's stupid."

"As I mentioned before, we've spoken with Dr. Abellon. While you were being decontaminated. When we told her what you did to the investors—and more importantly, what we want to do with her company as a result—she gave us some illuminating facts about the state of Swolov Technologies when you applied for the clinical trial. She also faxed over several corroborative documents. The company was failing. Swolov was a genius by anyone's reckoning, but he couldn't handle money. When he died, he was well past his zenith as a strength guru and had not only estranged colleagues with his increasingly unorthodox ideas, he had ventured into the financially hazardous arena of entrepreneurial invention. Among his diverse interests were accelerated learning and nutritional supplements. The clinical trial was the management's desperate attempt to combine both in hopes of making a quick buck. They wanted to produce a spokesmodel who would make CytoSwol appear to work as effectively as a steroid precursor. Only your progress, starting with the fabricated implant which you never mentioned to anyone, far exceeded their expectations. And what's more, as the company was too ignorant to factor in, you complicated matters with your personal baggage. Now, however, thanks to your confession, we understand what this consists of: Your history of sexual disconnect due to chronic pelvic pain. Mr. Rader wants to assure you we will use that knowledge for everyone's safety when our Rader-Swolov subsidiary puts the supplement on the market."

"This—this is a lot to process."

"Unfortunately, you don't have time to digest what I've told you. You murdered six people. Please don't take this as a threat, but if you refuse Mr. Rader's business our only alternative is to turn you into police. Let me remind you we can make you rich and famous."

"But… you don't want a brand ambassador. You want a puppet."

"That's your inner dramatist framing the situation again, Dylan. Which is why you're desirable to us. Only we want you to *live* the stories instead of writing them."

"Like I've supposedly been doing since I first saw Dr. Abellon? How do I even know you're telling me the truth? Why should I trust you?"

"Considering your horror background, do you really believe you owe your initial strength gains to biosoftware implanted by a cybernetic leech? Yes, it's true, we will adjust your personality for promotional purposes using Dr. Abellon's hypnosis methods. But in return, you'll accumulate a vast store of riches and experience. You'll also attain strength beyond what is considered possible by modern sports science. You should be pleased to know we have big plans for you, Dylan... building awareness of CytoSwol is only the start."

"But if you decide what stories I'm going to live, how will I know what's real? How do I know *you're* real? You could be part of my delusion."

"How about if I played back the video of your presentation? Would that be real enough for you? I'm not being snarky. This is serious. We want you on our team. And we need your wholehearted commitment to ensure your continued response to hypnosis. Now I understand you must be overwhelmed, not to mention exhausted. I wish we could make your transition easier. But let's get to the bottom line—would you turn down Mr. Rader's offer for multiple life sentences in a maximum-security prison?"

"There may be a third option."

"We're open to discussion."

"Well, Mr. Rader is right about my brain-body connection. Despite everything you've told me, I'm still feeling the David Cronenberg Placebo Effect. It's helped me recharge all the time we've been talking. Not only that, Swol-Vox 2.0 is telling me it's time again. Whether or not the implants exist, I feel a miracle happening inside me. My skin is as tough as steel. My nerves burn with the fury of six people screaming against their return to dust. I'm walking out of here, Hailey. That's the third option. And you better not try to stop me."

"Lieutenant, stand down. Please, Dylan, this conversation is going in a dangerous direction. You haven't even listened to the terms of Mr. Rader's proposal."

"Pardon my language, but fuck Mr. Rader's proposal. Go ahead, let your guards raise their weapons at me. If they fire,

I'll merge with them like I did with the investors. Then I'll go for you, Hailey—starting with your third blouse button."

"Damn it. Lieutenant, Mr. Rader approves the use of lethal force according to your discretion. Dylan, this is your last chance…"

Please try and focus, Dylan.

"But I'm really tired."

You need to stay awake. I'm scanning the network for an indoor building map so I can get you out of here.

"I've screwed up big time, haven't I?"

You acted in self-defense. You warned them.

"Do you think they knew that I loved them?"

Doubtful. It certainly won't look that way to whoever watches the video footage. But enough about the interview people. Our main concern is getting out of here. Wait—that mechanic by the service elevator. Shove him into the elevator and crush his throat or something. Then morph yourself to look like him. You bulletproofed yourself, right? You can shift your appearance to pass yourself off as Mr. Lumberjack Beard over there.

"Hmm… I guess even if someone caught me on a security camera no one would figure out what we were up to in time. We *could* make that work."

It's our best shot. All right. I found the floor plans to this place. Go over there and do your merging thing. Keep it clean, though—we don't want to have to wash up again or make a mess of the guy's clothes. Then all we've got to do is take the stairs and get out at the service entrance.

"I'm on it. Man, this is going to be great. We can steal a car and look for David Cronenberg next."

Negative, *Dylan. Leave Mr. Cronenberg alone. He's a highly public figure and an artist, for God's sake. One of the best who's worked in multiple genres. You're still an artist of sorts.*

"So? I love David Cronenberg. And I can do anything I want now."

I'm not letting you go after David Cronenberg.

"Well, a star from one of his movies, then. James Woods? Jennifer Jason Leigh? Jeff Goldblum? Who's still around? Come on, S-V 2.0. You said it yourself—it's time."

ORIFICIALLY COMPROMISED - RYAN HARDING

I.

Porter returned from work to find Ella in the lobby of their apartment building, sticking push-pins into a notice on the bulletin board—a quaint carryover feature for those residents who didn't "do the internet," though he knew she herself did. She lived two doors down from him in 1511. They had exchanged pleasantries in the elevator, something he strenuously avoided with everyone else when possible.

For her, he made an exception.

Perfume filled his head as he drew nearer, something jasmine-scented.

Ella stood a few inches shorter than him. Late thirties; brown hair parted in the middle which fell past her shoulders, gold-rimmed glasses. She always wore business professional attire with skirts and dresses that promised to slide up past her knees if she sat down. No ring.

She brightened in recognition. "Hi."

"Hey, Ella. Emergency meeting?" he joked.

"No, but something important," she said. "Or I think it is."

Porter agreed, and read the flyer aloud to see what exactly he agreed with. "EphemaSpect presents Dr. Braedon Obrist, author of *Transitory Bodies: Anatomy in the Digital Age*, Friday, August 15 at the Keller Center…our changing reality and the threat of InterphaZ."

Ella looked at him expectantly.

"InterphaZ?" he repeated.

"You know of them, don't you?"

He nodded. "I've seen the name around." Not untrue, and he had her to thank for that.

"Mega conglomerate. Medical research and technology, social media, weapons systems, foreign interests, you name it, they're in it."

Porter made the sign of the cross with his fingers. "Social media, now there's an evil if I ever heard one."

Ella offered an indulgent smile. "Yes, they have a video chat site to meet new people." She leaned in conspiratorially. "I lasted about five minutes before I'd seen enough dicks to last me a lifetime."

He laughed, deciding not to ask her familiarity with certain other InterphaZ products. They'd kept their prior conversations PG-rated, but now she had ventured their first profanity, a most special occasion. Knowing she relied on the tram system also provided him the ideal opening.

"Sounds like there's a lot I need to hear about InterphaZ and this other…" He pointed to the flyer, searching his thoughts for an impressive word. When none came, he settled for, "Stuff. So you're definitely going to this on Friday?"

"Eight o'clock, if InterphaZ doesn't shut it down first. You should come."

He nodded like he'd only just begun to seriously consider the idea. "You know where this Keller Center is? I could drive us, if you like."

II.

Porter cautioned himself against expectations in the interim days. Ella clearly didn't consider it a date, as there had been no discussion of plans outside Dr. Obrist. He started to give her his number in the lobby and she waved him off, saying just knock on her door Friday at seven. He'd have to hope she liked his company enough to consider doing something another time that didn't involve a self-proclaimed technological prophet in the role of cockblocker.

Porter picked her up on the dot, if that could be said of walking down the hallway to knock on 1511. She answered in a sleeveless dark blue dress he hadn't seen before with a jacketless hardcover in hand, slipping through a narrow clearance and closing the door behind her in a practiced fluid motion. Inquisitive meowing bled through the other side.

Nola, the Persian cat.

Porter complimented the dress as she locked up, inhaling jasmine and relishing the allure of Ella's smooth legs and the carefully painted toes revealed by single strap heels. She thanked him without looking at him or acknowledging his own wardrobe, a white button-up shirt and black slacks he'd actually ironed for the occasion.

The humble beginnings of their deeper rapport from Wednesday weren't easily fortified. She talked plenty on the way but more at him than with him and rarely about herself, mostly Dr. Obrist.

"Such a brilliant, brilliant man. I bought his book." She held up the hardcover where he now saw *Transitory Bodies* in gold letters on the spine. "I hope I can get it signed. It's just articles from his blog, they're all online, but I had to have it. Have you read any of them?"

"Not all of them just yet." Or any of them.

"Aren't they fascinating? The way technology has not only changed our lives, but our bodies too, our psychology. I keep thinking about a child who recreated his father as an avatar for a boxing game where the other player ruined him. And the boy sobbed uncontrollably because, in his undeveloped mind, he'd just seen his father beaten right in front of his eyes."

Porter turned his snort into a believable cough.

"These weren't traumas a generation ago, but now the mindscapes of these children will be reshaped in ways we've never seen by new confusions of experience. That's just one facet of this."

He nodded, thinking, *Maybe don't put a controller in the little bastard's grubby paws until he knows how to use the block button.*

He dared to say, "I see why that would interest you. You told me you were in therapy, didn't you?" He laughed. "As a profession, I mean."

She'd never told him that and seemed puzzled that he knew but shrugged it off. "I'm a counselor, yes. I work with women who have histories of horrible trauma. I moved here to work with the Raglan Group. I don't think you told me what you do."

He indeed told her when she first moved in, hoping she'd share the same. "I'm IT at the Somafree building. Basic troubleshooting, but we also write programs for the website and go through the grind to test them. So, if you get a virus or anything like that, feel free to ask for my help."

Ella laughed humorlessly. "It's changing our language, too, isn't it?" She patted his arm. "Well, thank you, I'll keep you in mind when I have a virus. I bet if I ever do, it will be called InterphaZ."

III.

Hoping to score some points, Porter dropped her off in front of the Keller Center while he drove off to find a parking spot and regroup. He'd spent more time with her in the past twenty minutes than the last six weeks combined but if anything, he felt closer to Braedon Obrist after that. He'd known little about him, beyond being mouthpiece and research director for EphemaSpect, a rival to InterphaZ positing themselves as some gluten-free alternative to corporation dominance. Now he knew about the eye-glazing articles too, which somehow earned Obrist enough cachet to assure an audience for even local speaking engagements like this one, making the most of his fifteen news cycles of fame.

Porter found Ella in the atrium introducing herself to a couple of fellow guzzlers of the Obrist Kool-Aid named Hart and Rose Trellan (recognizable by their shared copy of *Transitory Bodies*). She gave them only a first name, though of course he knew the last too—InterphaZ introduced her to him as Ella Geller.

"This is Porter," she said upon his arrival. "He's from the same building."

They shook his hand but he quickly found himself sidelined with nothing to contribute to their Obrist discussion. They waited to place their electronic devices and keys in plastic containers before walking through the metal detectors. Handheld scanners traced anyone who failed the first pass. Someone commented this was standard procedure at all the doctor's engagements.

Ella made him sit with the Trellans once inside the auditorium, and soon it was time for the man of the hour…an hour Porter glumly suspected would last the rest of the night.

IV.

Dr. Braedon Obrist took the stage to enthusiastic applause, an average-looking man at best (in Porter's assessment) closing in on fifty years old. All that deep thinking evidently cost him some hair follicles too.

Ella leaned forward in her seat, smiling more radiantly than she had any point in the previous hour. Porter made a note to look up *Transitory Bodies* at home; there had to be some one-star-reviews to enjoy.

"The next pivotal stages of our evolution will be quantified by technological innovations. The latest have already dictated our diminished attention spans, where even as we are more connected, we also become more disconnected from our world and each other…from our own identities."

Several heads nodded with murmurs of agreement, including the seat to Porter's left.

"We tailor ourselves more than ever to an ideal of how we hope to be perceived digitally. It is becoming more important than the reality of this room, of everything beyond it. Someday soon we could see a new variation of identity theft which changes who we are even to ourselves; a future InterphaZ may lead us to."

Mutters of condemnation for the hated entity spread through the audience.

"While the claims are unsubstantiated, some believe InterphaZ's medical implants are a Trojan horse for nanotechnology—additional implants of mysterious purpose. To track the recipient? To manufacture disease their products would be needed to address? Something unthinkably worse? Even their so-called line of pleasure enhancements—"

VenEros…isn't that right, Ella?

"—records and stores the measurements of its users, male and female. This is no secret, either…what they call the Interdex is a selling point for their brand."

Porter's mouth went dry. Ella's face went flush.

"With so many streams of income, there is no shortage of policies they'd love to influence for their benefit. How comfortable can we be with these unethical and anatomically unsound practices from such a powerful company?"

V.

Dr. Obrist finally wrapped the speech up an hour later, though he could have surely stroked that InterphaZ hate-boner until the audience went home and the janitors were sweeping up the aisles. Another hour of Q&A followed with Obrist offering the floor to Ella at one point, who gushed over his book and asked if she would have the chance to get it signed. Unfortunately, he replied yes, so later Porter had to tag along as Ella shoved her way against the tide to the stage. A decent line had formed by the time they made it up, but they didn't have a long wait. A security entourage stood close at hand.

As Obrist's pen scrawled across a page of her book, Ella turned to Porter to say, "Do you think you could get the car? I really need to talk to him for a minute." She swiveled back to Obrist to reiterate, "Just a minute, I promise."

Following this disappointing dismissal, Porter exited stage left to play valet. She really must not have taken long because she stood waiting outside when he pulled up, reading the inscription in *Transitory Bodies* like a schoolgirl poring over yearbook signatures. He wondered what it said.

INTERPHAZ SUCKS! HAVE A NEAT SUMMER. BRAEDON "THE PROPHET" OBRIST.

They switched roles on the way back where he talked more, trying to draw her out but Ella gave autopilot replies and stared pensively out the window as if replaying sound-bites from Dr. Obrist to drown him out. She'd recorded several minutes on her phone and maybe had a selfie of him now, too. If that were the case, Porter would surely see it on one of her social media accounts later.

In the elevator back up to their floor, he noticed a business card sticking from *Transitory Bodies* like a bookmark, enough for him to see handwritten print reading *obrist1@*. Personal email?

As they stepped out on their floor, Ella patted his arm and said, "Thank you so much for the ride tonight, Porter. I hope you're glad you went with me."

"Oh, of course." Looking at her, he even kind of believed himself. "It was a real eye-opener."

"Brilliant, brilliant man. He's giving another talk next week, if you're up to it."

Somehow Porter held his smile. "Sure, if I don't get stuck testing one of those program launches or something." But he had a strong feeling he'd miss out, whether his company had one scheduled or not.

"Great! Let me know." She waved as she walked away from him, calling back, "Good night."

"Night," he echoed and stood still a moment to watch her arrive at her door—the same spot where he'd seen the package from InterphaZ last week.

VI.

At that time he'd known only her first name. So when he spotted a package propped against her door that Tuesday afternoon, he "dropped" his keys to take a closer look at the address label.

From Interphaz VenEros, for Ella Geller.

The full name led him to a Facebook page and various networks connected to it. Her pictures were not so revealing, sadly—selfies tended to favor the same angle, rarely full-bodied—but he still relished a deeper look than the one provided by their hallway and elevator banalities. She liked her Persian cat Nola, wine ("redder the better"), binge-watching, and freedom from the burdens of a relationship ("intentionally, ecstatically single!").

Much as he wanted her, he found it easy to imagine needless complications arising from their proximity, to say nothing of the stigmata if he creeped her out with his interest in the first place—admittedly the likeliest scenario.

Still, Porter had identified a few potential bombs in his time and done nothing to defuse or evacuate the situation, opting instead for further study. True to form, he researched InterphaZ VenEros and discovered with growing excitement, of both figurative and literal sorts, that they involved "personal pleasure enhancements." A different brand handled fairly simplistic vibrators and compact instruments; VenEros did the exotic, invasive stuff exclusively. Knowing she'd bought something new for this express purpose and would probably trial it that very night escalated his idle fantasy to a more obsessive level.

Before the Obrist talk, he hadn't considered a satisfying alternative until the doctor apprised Porter of one tonight in the zest to besmirch his pals at InterphaZ. Now he had that and an opportunity to support their competitor out of good old-fashioned spite.

VII.

The oSheath: This pleasure enhancer from InterphaZ will change your life! Simply plug the corrugated sleeve into your USB port and let it do the work for you! Adaptable polyamalgamatic fibers conform to your erection while a self-moisturizing membranogel lining simulates the feel of TRUE INTERCOURSE. Easily detachable reservoir piece for convenient cleaning. Easy come, easy go! Complimentary 16 oz bottle of Depuramase sterilizing agent with every order. PLUS: All registered oSheath users will have access to the

Interdex. Submit image files of your crush and the Interdex will apply its highly advanced algorithms to recreate her inner contours in your oSheath. If she happens to be a customer of the InterphaZ VenEros line, you are guaranteed an exact replica! (Click HERE for a list of confirmed celebrity and adult entertainment endorsements.) It's not reality…it's better!

USER REVIEWS

Camvale: Amazing! U won't know the deferens!

DarrylR: its like a dualshock controller for your d**k 5 stars cant stop using.

VIII.

The oSheath arrived late Monday afternoon. Porter hurried home from Somafree to wait for the delivery guy and prevent anyone from making the same connection to him that he had of Ella. That was fine for her, but a guy purchasing some kind of space-age jack-off sleeve, well, there was no salvaging that humiliation. He'd have to move out.

"Porter Drazanian?"

"Yes."

"Sign here please."

Moments later he slipped the oSheath cable into a USB slot and his computer installed the drivers. The device possessed a pod-like appearance, thickest in its covering of black ridges at the middle which diminished toward a trapezoidal apex like a biomechanoid outline of the intended organ —ridges that could adjust accordion-like to accommodate varying girths. The oversized entry slot underneath would automatically adapt to the user's base. Porter impatiently clicked his way through the copyright, registration, and user agreement screens. He had made his peace with the notion of the sleeve adding him to the Interdex database while he exploited it to experience Ella's exquisitely recreated contours. It made a solitary pursuit uncomfortably global, but you couldn't jump in the water without getting wet. He doubted anyone would program some malleable VenEros dildo in his mold, then laugh and call a Johnny Wadd-ible pronto when they found him lacking.

He imagined Ella trying him out of some strange (and remote) curiosity, but she probably gave her VenEros apparatus up for Lent in her anti-InterphaZ hysteria. Perhaps she only learned the Interdex feature after the fact and stumbled on Dr. Obrist's accusations of their unethicality in her outrage. Such medicine had to go down easier than failure to read the fine print.

With the oSheath in place on him (disconcertingly unlifelike after all the hype and a hundred fifty bucks), Porter performed a drag and drop operation to supply the Interdex one of Ella's selfies. Facial recognition could correlate it with her online profiles and registration info. In seconds the sheath stirred to life, the clearance around his organ vanishing as the inner sleeve conformed. He wasn't so impressed so far, could definitely tell the "deferens"—

Then the sleeve cinched around him solidly, and he would have sworn its interior had been replaced by living flesh… flesh with escalating, dripping heat. It squeezed and shuddered along his length the way Ella undoubtedly would, riding him. He found her picture from Friday (she had indeed tweeted a selfie with Obrist which he retweeted, and Hart and Rose "hearted'), groaning as he fought to minimize the JPEG so Obrist didn't get to horn in on the fantasy. He had to hurry, totally bereft now of the cognitive ability required to click the InterphaZ icon and find a slower vibration setting. Maybe he should have run the tutorial after all. The tight wet grip sealed him, simulated her clamping him with her inner walls in frenzied abandon. Her picture smiled at him, pleased by his invigoration.

In less than a minute he jolted in the chair as if electrocuted, then sought the complimentary Depuramase bottle.

IX.

By Friday morning he found himself in need of a different doctor than Obrist, and begged for an emergency appointment.

"I think I have something," he said, somewhat unnecessarily given the evidence on display. The professionalism of the windowless room, papered-over exam table, and posters for mental health ("Do you remember the last time you were truly yourself?") and diabetes awareness couldn't entirely alleviate his discomfort.

As if it would stop Dr. Vinokur from crouching down for a closer look, Porter amended, "Yes, I have something."

She palpated him through surgical gloves.

"It's not what it looks like," he said.

"No? You didn't have one of those illegal operations in another country, did you?"

"I just mean…it's not a *disease.*"

"Don't you want me to be the judge of that? Or in your indelicate way are you just trying to say your affliction is not of a sexual origin?

Porter's face burned. "Right. That."

"Is there a family history of skin disorders you haven't mentioned? Maybe an undocumented latex allergy?"

"No. I break out in hives from aspirin, but…" He left it unfinished rather than say, *I haven't fucked a handful of crushed pills lately*

She pulled his member upright to examine the undersurface. The "affliction" encircled the whole organ in a spiral of raised flesh, as though a large heated corkscrew burned its pattern along his member. Except it didn't hurt and the device responsible inflicted the opposite of pain. She could be forgiven if she thought it intentional; it looked that way.

It began like a contact or heat rash, but by Thursday night evolved to this disconcerting sight.

"What aren't you telling me, Mr. Drazanian?"

Porter sighed. "I used something," he said. "For...gratification."

Dr. Vinokur raised a palm. "I need to know...did this coincide with use of an InterphaZ product?"

He considered lying, but meekly said, "Yes...the oSheath."

*It was like a DualShock controller for my d**k...I really* couldn't *stop using. Even after Saran wrapping my junk to keep the membranostuff from directly contacting skin, it* still *felt like heaven.*

"I'm not going to be able to help you."

"What are you talking about?"

"I mean I'm not *allowed.* I'm not licensed. I think your device may have introduced an untold number of implants into your system."

Porter blanched. "Implants? From a *sex toy*? That's ridiculous, they can't do anything like that!"

"It's InterphaZ. They can do anything you authorize."

"But I never consented to anything like that!"

Dr. Vinokur looked at him sympathetically. "It would seem nano implantation is the new fine print of user agreements. You'll need to be referred to an InterphaZ-approved provider if you want to pursue this... but I wouldn't trust them not to simply initiate more implants."

Porter stood there dumbfounded, lacking the wherewithal to pull up his pants.

"I fear that in the years to come, Mr. Drazanian, orificial integrity may be compromised in ways we can't begin to imagine."

X.

Porter knew of parasitic fish which entered the urethra. Microscopic nanotechnology would have an easier time if it could somehow be programmed to lie dormant in its own protective seal of membranogel until the catalyst of use for an invasion. Could the InterphaZ tech track him now or manipulate him to illness? Would this feeling of infection become a genuine disease process? His body no longer seemed his own.

He sat in the parking lot, searching the phenomenon on his smartphone. There weren't many alleged cases, and the only ones anybody credited were from medical procedures. InterphaZ steadfastly denied any implant accusations about their specialty products, dismissing the damning user agreement verbiage as "content error." They insinuated the complaints came from hoaxers seeking an easy payday.

This info was available to him and Ella all along, but you didn't know what you didn't know, especially with access to too much in the first place. Insidious details could creep past undetected like…

Nano implants.

No way Porter could face a shift at Somafree. He called out for the rest of the day and drove back home. At some point on the way, his thoughts shifted back to Ella.

The puzzle pieces all fell into place. Defecting from InterphaZ support so soon after her purchase, her admiration for Dr. Obrist and needing to talk to him alone, a retweet about his new exposé on InterphaZ—she'd been a victim of the implants too.

XI.

He walked to 1511 from the elevator, not expecting her to be there but hoping she would in the wake of his revelation.

They could commiserate about their condition, a disease support group without an actual disease, at least not yet…the Orificially Compromised.

Ella answered after all. He hadn't considered how he would explain what he had to say—the language was still new to him, the implications largely unexamined, her involvement mere speculation—but she stood aside and urgently beckoned.

Desire enveloped Porter instantaneously, the full body seal equivalent to the rapture triggered by his first use of the oSheath. Sex had been nowhere near his thoughts but overwhelmed him anyway. She looked exciting in a cream skirt and jacket with a black top, though that wasn't why; the inferno seemed born of nothing and everything.

More incredibly, he saw the same need mirrored in Ella's face. She'd shown no hint of it before but now she reached for him, tilting her chin up to lock her mouth to his, slipping her tongue through his parted lips. She melded their bodies together, nudging her groin against him. Her warmth seeped through the fabric to find where he'd become rigid as he crossed the threshold.

This only furthered the illusion of the day's dream-like impossibility. He'd wanted this since she moved in.

Ella led him to the living room section of the open floor plan to a black leather couch where she slipped out of her heels and scooted all the way to the far end, undoing the single button of her jacket at waist level. She braced herself long enough to slide her fingers under the hem of her skirt and pull it up to her waist. The silk cream fabric of her underwear whispered down her thighs.

Porter fumbled with his pants to offer her the same access, even as he said, "I don't think I can. I'm…"

He started to say *infected* but she waved him off. "Yes, you can, with me. I know you can." She spread her feet apart on the cushion, knees out, and between them, he saw he'd been correct about her. Where she wanted him inside her, there were indentions in the membrane like the furrows of a cone-shaped drill, sure to match the ridges encompassing his sex. Had this eventually become her template in the Interdex after implants, with the oSheath shaping him into the ideal fit?

She helped drag his pants down and guide his erection inside, paying no mind to its new mold. The connection brought startled gasps from them both as their contours alternated between friction and symmetry. Where entry would have been a grand sum experience previously, their new flesh consolidated to create deeper levels of immersion; a pleasure the equal of the need.

Ella soon pushed him to an upright sitting position and settled onto him, grinding up and down with greater urgency. The oSheath had trained him for this in a way. She finished just ahead of him after a minute, clamping tighter and bringing him along. He seemed to ignite inside her.

She soon unseated herself and stood up, smoothing her wrinkled clothes. Porter tucked himself away. He still didn't want to look at what became of him.

Nola meowed inquisitively in the recesses of the apartment, safe from the incursion of strangers.

The spell had passed. Did the implants allow InterphaZ to manipulate their pheromones to trigger this meltdown? Did his and Ella's close proximity activate them?

"I know about the implants," he huffed, still breathless.

She nodded, rebuttoning her jacket. "I'm in contact with Dr. Obrist. He wants EphemaSpect to create nano antibodies for them to purify us."

"Do you know what they're even for?"

Ella paused as if seeking a specific word. It went unfound. Porter jumped as her stomach and chest exploded, shredding the fabric of her shirt in numerous places like hot shrapnel from a bomb. Moist tissue clumps spattered the couch, borne on a gust strong enough to stir his hair. The button from her jacket struck him in the forehead and bounced away. Blood spattered his face. A misshapen mound of organs burst from the blown cavity. Ella slumped to the ground, glassy eyes fixed on Porter from the floor.

He bolted up from the couch, mouth agape, bloody fragments dropping from his hair as his head swiveled to find cover from what could only happen within. He finally stopped and looked down at himself reluctantly, waiting to see and hear his own detonation.

Instead, he heard Ella.

"Porter." Or a halting approximation of it. Her body remained motionless except for a fluttering in her throat—not a pulse—and the slightest shift of lips and tongue, ventriloquist like. "You have to go all the way through it, Porter...all the way through it to the end. Assemble the weapon. Eliminate Braedon Obrist."

XII.

Determination to complete his mission drove him, as irresistible as the previous display of desire.

He arrived at the Keller Center by seven, showered and casually dressed, wanting to assure himself a front row seat. He crossed the metal detector without incident, holding a copy of *Transitory Bodies,* which didn't completely shut. No one noticed. He spotted Hart and Rose but didn't acknowledge them, and once admitted he commandeered an aisle seat in the middle section.

When he cracked it open, the cover of the book shielded the instrument sequestered in its hollowed out pages from the people to his left. They wouldn't have known what it was if they did see it, though.

Dr. Obrist emerged to enthusiastic applause once more. When Porter stood, others followed his example for a full-fledged standing ovation. The gun made from Ella's organs felt slippery in his hand, its body formed from the ruin of her pancreas, like a melted corncob, and the grip a conglomeration of her kidneys. A spleen remnant formed its trigger. Porter squeezed it, unsure of the ammunition, only the certainty whatever implants he'd exchanged with Ella would assure the function of the apparatus.

Obrist's delight over his reception quickly dissolved into distress at the sight of Porter extending the impossible contraption. It retained its form enough to allow proper aim, and when Obrist flinched, he knew he'd hit the target. Security converged from both sides. He fired at them too, and although nothing resulted from it, someone with a clear line shot him as if he wielded a pistol.

Screams around him.

Porter sank to the ground, bleeding out from a bullet in his chest. Obrist stood far above on the stage, puzzling over the sequence. As if the revelation—

InterphaZ

—took physical shape in Obrist's mind, his head abruptly exploded in a shower of blood, bone, and brain fragments which seemed to suspend in the air for multiple seconds like lazy dust particles in a sunbeam. A vibrant assassination worthy of JFK, though less "back and to the left" than back, forward, left, right, and all points between.

Porter turned the Ella-gun toward his own head and squeezed the spleen tip once, twice. The second time, the whole thing seemed to melt like taffy in his fingers. Empty.

Horror dawned on a security team member's face, and a delayed gut-shot manifested itself literally as a bouquet of entrails erupted from his belly in a heap on the floor. Someone else raised a hand to the Fates, imploring a stop to something that had no end.

Porter smiled and waited for his turn.

LIMBS - ALEX SMITH

Maddie drew air through the regulator into her lungs. The red milk's weight made breathing labored and shallow. The red milk was in her armpits, between her buttocks. It swirled in the canals of her ears. They'd given her nose-plugs, but it found its way into her nostrils, stung at her sinuses. She daren't open her eyes, as the milk might burn her tear ducts. The red milk was in every part of her. It bonded with her. Learned her.

They wouldn't have scheduled a reunification date until Maddie had proven herself. In preparation for immersion, Maddie had learned to meditate in sweltering heat and frigid white cold. She flatulated and she wept, though she never moved, her remaining arm limp in her lap, her legs akimbo. She let the urine and feces drain out of her without so much as a shortened breath. She laughed and rejoiced when they finally assigned her a reunification date. She circled the limits of the compound in celebration, nodded to the white-shirted guards at the high fences, completed longer and longer walking meditations with ease. She fasted for 72 hours prior to her date, sipping fish broth to stave off hunger pangs, until they had retrieved her from her bunk, and led her to the milk tanks.

Now, suspended in the red milk, Maddie couldn't know how long it had been. It may have been near a day. It had certainly been hours. She was hungry and thirsty, near hallucinatory in her deprived state. She released all desires and pain into the milk and waited for her limb to return.

Then came the tingling sensation at Maddie's stump. The red milk flitted its tongue at the peach-colored mound of flesh at her right shoulder, examining the absence. It tingled, almost burned, where the arm had been torn away. It *had* to be working.

"Don't move when it comes," Lucas had told her of the reunification. They'd been sitting in the inner garden. The azaleas were alive with sparrows. Her date was fast approaching. "The reunification is a tentative process for the limb, too. It's a reconstitution of two wills. You'll feel good, Maddie. But you won't feel just good. You might feel, well, invaded. Let it all wash over you."

Lucas was the first to reunite with his phantom limbs. He was a double amputee, his arms disintegrated while trying to defuse an IED at the foot of the Sinjar mountains. Since finding the red milk, Lucas had risen their compound up from the remains of a large, abandoned orchard. Over the years he'd grown the reunification into an exclusive process only he knew the secrets of. There were people who believed in him, people who didn't, and people who resented him for what he knew, who hated him for hoarding his secrets.

"I know I'm not supposed to say anything," Maddie said. "To doubt. But it didn't work for Glen," she said. "I mean. Three days he was in those tanks."

"It worked for me," Lucas said. Maddie felt the pressure of his phantom fingers on her lips, then a hand cupping one of her breasts. "For every Glen, there is a Lucas. Or a Maddie."

She let her head sink, brushing away at his touch, finding only air. "But it almost killed Glen. For what? Starvation. Dehydration. The risk of drowning?"

"Glen wasn't ready. His impatience and anger owned him. Glen ran away. You're ready. It'll find you, Maddie. It will."

She went on floating there, remembering the image of Glen's contorted features on the day they dragged him from the milk tank. Licks of red peeled off of his arms and stumps as he fought. He'd left soon after, though his shadow remained, disrupted her clarity even then.

She wanted to open her eyes to the crimson. She wanted to rip the regulator out of her mouth and scream for it to join with her. She'd occasionally felt the phantom pain after the accident. It was like her right arm was still there, itching, tingling, burning. It wanted to grab for her, to *do* for her. It was there, yet it was gone. Now it flicked about in the milk beside her, lapping at her stump, learning her all over again. She would have it back if it would just, fucking, commit.

She felt its presence at her neck, her ears, her swimming cap, her eyelids. It slithered over her chest and down her belly, its touch matching her pulse. She exhaled into the regulator, attempted to dispel the agitation that came with her visitor. She needed to be willing and pliant, never forceful or impatient. So, she breathed with the sense of it lingering near her stump, tentatively rubbing against the silken skin there.

The penetration began as a calculated series of stabbing pricks at her stump. Each pang climbed the shoulder, webbed over her collarbone, her neck. Then it was in her mind, singeing at her brain stem.

She saw bolts of flickering light. She tasted salt, then sweet, then metal. It was entwining with every nerve, tendon and blood vessel.

Maddie tried to breathe through the pain, releasing globs of it with each exhalation, but it wasn't enough. She urgently wanted to free herself from the breathing apparatus, to abort the reunification and escape. But she couldn't pull the rebreather away—she'd drown then and there. She flapped her way to the top hatch, rapped on the solid iron once with her knuckle.

There was no answer.

Maddie whipped her naked body back and forth through the thickened red, making muddied, blubbering waves of noise. She banged on the hatch twice, a third time. The pain at her stump worsened, traveled through her body in throbs of agony. She began to convulse. Her thrashing arm caught the umbilical, tore the rebreather from her mouth.

She screamed bubbles in the milk, its unctuous, chalky taste pressing at the back of her throat. There were thick sounds of metal on metal, and the hatch shifted. A ray of light turned the dim crimson bright pink, and Maddie saw shards of green paint mushrooming off at the seal of the hatch. Then the iron bowed and curled. Another ray of light broke through.

She felt the metal yielding, yet she wasn't touching it—not with her own flesh and blood. It was her phantom. Her new digits clasped at the vault's edge, pried at it. She heard frenzied footsteps on her tank. The others were intervening, but they were too late. Her lungs were flaming, her body sucking in on itself. She was drowning.

Maddie felt the metal squeezing through her new fingers. The slight bend in the door tore fully open and swung backward. She linked her elbow over the lip of the tank and pulled herself into the open air. Finally, she breathed.

"You found it," Lucas said. His voice was honied, firm, and alien. "Broke the damn door, but you found it."

She cleared the milk from her eyes, saw him standing at the iron grating looking down at her. There he was wearing his blue jumpsuit, lumps of curly blond hair pushed behind his ears. His inner circle surrounded him, their eyes alight in approbation.

She'd been so far away. Now she was in the green-tiled basement. Now she was alive.

"I found it," she said. "I fucking found it."

Days later Maddie sat at a reclaimed wood table in an old aluminum folding chair. Rain occasionally peppered the long windows of the compound, pines swaying wildly in the far-off hills. A Ferrero Rocher sat across from her wrapped in golden foil in its espresso-brown cup. Maddie focused on the candy. She was covered in a film of sweat, bangs glued to her forehead.

"Go ahead," Lucas prompted from behind her. He'd come and gone during the hours, leading his classes and guiding mass sittings in the tents that specked the compound. This time when he returned he smelled of rain. "It waits for your signal."

"I can't feel it," Maddie said. "It was there. The phantom. Now it's gone."

Ever since she'd crashed open the door, she hadn't felt it. Couldn't feel *with* it. Couldn't touch, grasp, rub.

"I don't get it," she said.

"Stop trying to get it and be it," Lucas said.

She closed her eyes, tried to relax every muscle as Lucas had taught her, to melt into herself. Then, she opened her eyes, tried to send her consciousness through her shoulder, into her stump, and then into her returned limb. But it was as if the shoulder was an impenetrable membrane—like she couldn't reach through the stump and into the limb. Nonetheless, the stump pulsed and moved. Tendons and joints shifted beneath her skin.

"There you go," he said softly, but the experience for her was tenuous.

Maddie brought her attention fully to the Ferrero Rocher.

She willed everything toward it. It didn't even tremble. She slammed the table, crying out. She felt the pressure of Lucas' invisible limb massaging her shoulders, like dozens of rippling fingers dancing on her skin.

"Don't," she said.

She felt the fingers roll away.

Lucas said, "We should sit."

"I'm begging you—no more sitting. No more meditating and breathing walks and no more believing. It didn't work, Lucas. I shouldn't be here anymore."

"You mangled a cast iron door, Maddie," Lucas said. "The reunification is forever, an unbreakable fusion. It's there." She felt him touching her again. "You know what I think?"

She exhaled through pursed lips, let herself lean into him. "What?"

"You're thinking too much."

The Ferrero Rocher lifted into the air, golden rapper tearing away. She relaxed further into him, and there was his erection beneath his jumpsuit. He was unabashed, had been since her sister first dropped her at the compound. Maddie was indifferent to him sexually, though her curiosity had been seeping forward. They all slept with him. That was the word around the compound. Why did she have to be any different?

She felt the candy touch her lips, took a bite.

"Let's walk," Lucas said.

They made love under one of the tents on the outskirts of the compound. Maddie straddled him, rocked back and forth. Rain poured around them in curtains of blue noise. She felt his limbs on her breasts, her neck. His fingers kissed her, all while he lay back, jumpsuit sewn over the stumps at his shoulders. It was exhilarating—the flowing rain, the sensation of him inside of her, the ghosts of his limbs caressing her skin.

The pleasure mounted and she arched backward. Beside her knee, the Tyvek ripped open to expose the matted grass beneath. The grass tore away, exposing the mud. It was her phantom, grabbing at the mud. She closed her eyes, felt the wet earth pressing between her spindly new fingers. She felt the drops of rain that had broken through the tent landing on the ghost of her forearm, felt Lucas's chest and neck.

She looked down at her stump, saw it throbbing, the withered muscles terminating in the pink soft flexed and relaxed. Flexed, relaxed. "It's back!" she said, laughing. She dug her new fingers deep into the earth, threw a clump of mud at the ceiling of the tent.

"See," Lucas said. Blobs of dirty water dotted his forehead and chest. "...Thinking too much."

Weeks later, Maddie walked the limits of the compound's orchard. With her new limb, she plucked free a glimmering Granny Smith apple, cupped it lightly. She brandished it before her eyes, floating it there. She bit in, intuiting and avoiding her new fingers without thinking. It was tart, near-perfect with its juicy, granular texture. She hadn't felt fully healed until then, that easy moment in the orchard. She was a master of her phantom.

She had tried everything since the accident. Prosthetics caused unrelenting aches mere hours after their fastening. Mirror therapy was a revelation until it wasn't. In psychotherapy, she was encouraged to mourn the loss of her right arm as if she was mourning a death, or a freedom she hadn't known she'd had until it was gone. In physical therapy, she was encouraged to feel that she remained free, and that what seemed like a loss was only another mountain to summit.

Boyfriends came and went. Some were confused by her incompleteness, turned off, made guilty by her struggle. Others were turned on by the absence. She cast them out along with the sickness they made her feel. Some didn't seem to care at all, but that insouciance lacked something, too.

Maddie's sister once told her that she was the worst person in the world to lose a limb. Maddie was the kind of person who couldn't let anything go. She was experienced by others as vaguely authoritarian and moderately athletic. This plus stump was an awful mix.

The absence was unbearable to her, the recovery unforgiving and interminable. Worse still was the phantom pain—an itchy tingling or a sharp ache at her stump, a sense of reaching where the appendage no longer was. It wasn't livable, she'd decided, and so her mind traveled to darker places.

Then Maddie heard about the compound, about Lucas. Her sister promised her that it was a mirage, and a rather insane one. The videos were fakes, the red milk just another brand of snake oil. The government would break them apart, or someone else would. But a drunken hope returned to her, one she hadn't had in years. She had been determined to go. And she went.

Now, in the reunion of forever-purposed neuronal bunches to her phantom limb, there was no longer any pain. Maddie was whole again. Beyond whole. She took another bite of the Granny Smith from her new arm, relishing its freshness. She smiled at a couple strolling by in the opposite direction, juice drooling out of her grin. Gazing at the compound, she felt a mist of ennui about her—that all was good and fine, and the loneliness that accompanied that feeling. Then she looked off at the fences that demarcated the compound and the lividus clouds above. She wondered what it would be like when she went back out there.

There was a flash near the fences. The bright of it burnt stars into her eyes. Something whistled past her ear and *popped*. She scanned the orchard, sparkles dotting her vision. There, amid curling smoke and rising ash, was a gaping tear in the fencing. Four figures dressed in black rushed the fence holding…what were they holding? More whistling and pops stung her ears. Wood dust and leaves rained onto her. She smelled sour apples blown open.

She dropped to her knees, covered her head, grimacing at the noises. She pressed her cheek to the ground and watched the fence.

"What was that?" The woman standing nearby asked her partner. They looked in all directions, waiting to understand.

"Get down!" Maddie screamed.

The man said, "What the *hell*?"

The back of the woman's head tore off into shards of bone and purple ichor, hair floating up as if flashed by a blow-dryer. She collapsed.

"Oh, oh fuck!" He hunched over her, searching her face for signs of life.

Maddie dared to raise her head higher. She scanned the limits of the orchard and the fencing beyond. Dozens of shadowed figures raced from the tree line toward the compound. Some flung flash grenades toward guard posts. Others fired at the fencing and into the orchard. The campus guards moved to cover, fired from kneeling positions. The intruders dropped, clutching at wounds and twisting in the damp leaves, or going limp. Maddie's stomach sank. Her mind going fizzy as she watched, perplexed by the scene. The shadows kept coming, rushing the fencing, and the guards backed further away. Just as guard reinforcements arrived in white Jeeps, the intruders had reached the limits of the compound, began climbing unguarded stretches of fencing. Some were successful, dropping over the other side and disappearing into the apple trees.

Maddie had to get away. She turned, bear-crawled toward the main building, felt her new arm dragging her along with ferocious speed as the bullets whistled past her. Lungs on fire, she passed dark, motionless humps on the ground—what she could only think were bodies—as she cut through the tents of the forward camp. She passed other, living, groaning humps: people gripping at themselves, trying to hold themselves in.

She bashed into someone near the end of the tenting. It was Lucas. She felt his hands around her shoulders. A rifle was slung behind his back. Behind him, at the limits of the orchard, she saw the soot-colored figures pouring in through the breach. There were at least a dozen of them filtering into the orchard.

"Keep going," he said.

"But what's—"

"Keep going!"

Just as she reached the concrete walls of the main building, a pane of glass shattered above her. Glass rained down, catching in her hair. She stumbled to her feet again, pushed forward, feeling along the wall.

"Stop," a voice said from behind her.

Maddie turned, saw a woman pointing a machine gun at her. Her ebony hair was pulled into a tight bun at the top of her head, and she wore baggy, ill-fitting fatigues. Her face was painted black. She raised her weapon and aimed down its sight.

"Please," Maddie pleaded through shallow gulps of air.

"Take me to the tanks," the woman said.

Maddie frowned and nodded resignedly, but when she turned and opened the front door the woman fired a shot into the air.

"If you use that fucking *thing* around me again, you're done."

Maddie darted her eyes around the door, not understanding until she realized she'd opened the door with her phantom limb. She was suddenly hyperaware—embarrassed, even—by this woman's contempt for her revelation.

"Okay," Maddie whimpered. She let the door swing closed and pulled it open again with her flesh and bone arm.

Alicia was in the foyer, rolling her wheelchair toward the

two, eyes wide. She said, "Maddie? Oh, Maddie, you're alright!" Then she saw the raven-haired woman, bit her lip, inched backward.

"I'm fine," Maddie whispered.

"Get back," the woman said.

They crossed the cafeteria, the interior barracks, and then the main hall.

"How far?"

"It's down here," Maddie said, leading her to the cement stairs at the back of the hall.

Something hacked away at her mind as they walked. Her new friends were so blithely focused on their unifications: meditating, fasting, celebrating. There was nothing political, nothing dogmatic about them. How could these people hate them so much? She was ashamed of her ignorance.

"Wh-why?" Maddie asked.

The woman said nothing.

They descended, entered the green-tiled halls, and reached the ancient pool room.

Each of the three reunification tanks were 15 feet high, shaped like eggs with a hatch on top. Dots of milk oozed from their viewing portholes in rusty pink strands that collected in cracks in the concrete floor. Maddie's tank was at the far left. Its now-deformed hatch leaned against the base of the vat awaiting re-attachment.

The woman paced around the tanks, scowling. "This is where it happens?"

"Yes," Maddie said, limping behind. "Mine was just weeks ago-"

"Where does Lucas keep them?"

"Them?"

She swung the gun around, smacking Maddie above the eye.

"The things, bitch! Where does he keep the things?"

Maddie clutched her temple. "Th-they're with us," she

said. She pulled her hand away, saw blood on her fingers. "W-we fill into them. It's a reconstitution."

She curled a lip in revulsion.

"I-I promise you—it's a reunification. I can feel it."

"An art school dropout made your arm grow back? You believe that?"

But Lucas was ex-army and never went to school, Maddie thought. It didn't matter. Maddie nodded anyway, tears dropping from the tip of her nose.

"It's an infection," the woman said. She leveled her gun at Maddie's head pressing her finger behind the trigger guard.

"Please!"

"You're infected."

The woman's jaw gaped open. Her brow furrowed into knots, and her eyes widened in surprise. Her arm began to vibrate, gun quivering at the tip of her finger.

"Gha-gha-k," she choked. The gun wrenched free, flew into the shadows.

Her jaw opened further. Tiny webs of blood sprouted at her cheeks like veins on a peach, and then her lower jaw ripped away, exposing rows of teeth, her quivering uvula, and ropes of flesh and sinew remaining at the base of her neck. Maddie felt it all, the bones cracking under the immense strength of her phantom, the flesh of the jaw tearing apart like celery between her new fingers. The woman collapsed, eyes stricken with surprise, mouth spurting onto her black fatigues, going purple in the red-green light.

Maddie's stump throbbed in rapid expansions and contractions as the limb vibrated ecstatically. But she wasn't in control. She hadn't decided to do it. It was—what was it—a reflex?

Maddie dropped to her knees as the woman went on shuddering. The red milk near the vats pooled with her blood. It crept to the woman's jaw, examined the absence there. Then the woman was still, and the red milk drained away from her. The smell of urine pricked Maddie's nostrils. Tears shook from the wells of Maddie's eyes as she slid to her bottom. Her mind swam with sickening thoughts and scents. She rolled to her side and vomited.

A moment later she tried to clamber to her feet, but slipped in muck and reeled back, flesh hand slapping the leg of the corpse as she fell. She tore her arm away from the body, cupped it against herself. Then she curled into a ball, her perceptions flattening into a dread-lined numbness.

Jack's baritone voice called for her an hour later. She didn't respond. Soon his hulking form emerged from behind one of the tanks, empty eye sockets peering into her.

"Maddie," he said. He gasped, presumably at the corpse. "Oh god…it's over, Maddie. We got them. Are you hurt?"

"I'm alright," she said. "Just help me."

He took her by the pit of her arm, lifted her to her feet. They climbed the stairs from the pool room up to the basement, treading slowly.

"What were you doing down there?"

"She wanted to see the tanks," Maddie said.

They neared a make-shift triage near the foyer. The smell of fire and flesh was everywhere. Jack said, "They're identifying the people. The bodies."

"How could this happen?"

He didn't answer, but it was a damn good question, one tugging at her gut, one that only invited more questions. Lucas always insisted the only threat they faced was those who lived in the far reaches of the pine barrens. The region was addicted to meth, the drug having sucked away their humanity. The natives resented them not because they understood the properties of the pink lichen, but because Lucas' people believed in something at all. These people weren't hillbillies. These were extremists, their hate rooted in some jealous belief of their own.

"Where's Lucas?" Maddie asked.

Jack pressed his lips together and hitched his shoulders. "He's not taking it well, Maddie. No one is, but he—I mean, we're like children to him. What do you expect?"

"Where?"

He was in the dining hall, raving. The inner circle—three of them remained alive, though filthy and wounded—leaned against the walls, light green tiles climbing behind their backs. Two others—hangers-on edging their way into the fold—sat in contemplative positions on ashen plastic chairs, eyes webbed in red. The windows were fully black, pines having sucked away any of the sunlight hours ago.

"How could they?" Lucas said.

He must have had an inkling, Maddie thought.

A plate levitated into the air, swooshed off into a wall, and shattered.

Maddie crossed her arms. Lucas suddenly seemed aware of the others, shooting looks over his shoulders from his hunched position before them. He straightened his posture, drew giant breaths and exhaled, dots of snot spraying from his nose as he attempted to *kata* himself into tranquility.

"I won't blame myself."

"That's right," one of the others said.

"For *us* to doubt ourselves. That's what they want. But it's fucking them. Their jealousy. Their chaos. They want to stop me. I won't be stopped."

He said he was going for a walk and exited the room. Soon after, Micah broke the silence, launched into planning their next steps. Maddie slipped out.

The compound's tiny medical staff was overwhelmed. Emergency medical teams from the outside would be slow to arrive, and in the meantime, the foyer was converted to a triage area. Mattresses were pulled from the interior dorms and now lined the entrance walls. First aid dwindled until shirts and pants were torn into bandages. Stumps pulsed as phantoms worked in concert with flesh and bone to tend the congregation. Maddie watched Kathryn float between the wounded, offering comforting words and red Solo cups filled with weak bug juice. They'd gone from a commune to a broken camp in a matter of hours.

Maddie ventured out to the tents, hoping she'd find him. Lucas—who he was, what he stood for—was hollow to her, a husk. He'd been a shadow all along. True bodhisattvas—the ones Lucas had undoubtedly aped—found the fortitude to "sit" amid war and the threat of cultural extinction. Lucas had plunged into despair, lost all composure at the first true struggle. Lucas wouldn't have been copying the true bodhisattvas anyway. He'd have gotten it from the Zen-heads, who'd have gotten it from the New Agers—a derivative of a derivative.

She found him skulking among the wreckage, caught his eye. His face was that of a cornered stray hoarding stolen food. He turned his attention back to the tents. A pole rocked forward, drawing a swatch of singed black nylon into the air. As it absently swayed Maddie couldn't help but think of the woman's hair floating in blood. Watching Lucas work with his limbs had inspired awe only hours ago. Now it was easy to tamp down her sense of wonder in the wake of the smells. Iron, gun smoke, opened bodies.

"I so wanted this," she said. "I didn't care how." She rubbed her chin, waiting. "What are they?"

"What do you mean?" he asked absently.

She raised her phantom into the air. "How does it work?"

"Is it important?" he finally said. "I mean. Robert. Born without legs. Now walking. Does it matter?"

"I get to decide if it matters."

The tentpole dropped. "Fine. I'll show you," he said.

"Show me?"

He approached her. "Yes," Lucas said. "It's time you knew."

She felt his invisible fingers interlocking with her phantom limb. There was the sensation of millions of insects scurrying up her arm, followed by explosions of light pricking the backs of her eyes. Her perception transmuted into something wider.

There was Lucas. Battered tents and smoldering mudbanks surrounded him. A single apple tree burned in the distance. Further off she saw guards repairing fences, and the dull magenta wash of police lights shifting through the pines.

There was something else that Maddie only understood as black light—diamondized stacks of energy, shifting before her, all real, all hidden between the folds of her sight. It was beyond electricity, beyond organic matter. It was something else. Lucas watched her solemnly, and she let her eyes drop from his and down to his limbs. There they were, perceptible like some hologrammatic material. The black light bent around them.

They were *things*. Tendrilled, furry vines flitting left and right, reaching and touching and groping at the black. Maddie followed indents in the vines to tiny, insectoid eyes. Dark, black, steel discs jittering in their sockets, soaking everything in. Connected to Lucas' limbs was her own phantom. It was a different shade of dark, nearer purple, if she could label the color at all, and less furry—more naked. Younger, almost. Its tendrils knotted into Lucas' in a lustful exchange. She followed the thing back to her stump, where she saw her phantom's veins linked at thousands of her nerve-endings. The flesh of her stump palpitated in concert with the movements of the phantoms.

Tears rolled down her eyes as she gritted her teeth. "What are they?"

"Animals," Lucas said. "Much smarter than us, I know." He smiled at this. "Stay calm."

"I-," she said then trailed off.

"I wanted it so bad, Maddie. Then I learned to listen. And they found me." He gasped. "Listen! It knows its parents. Senses its lineage."

She heard Lucas' limbs—their faint, chant-like whines. In

some sweet sort of harmony, her phantom sang along in an infantile strain. It droned through her cortex, made her numb and wet.

"Now let yourself feel it."

Maddie closed her eyes as the sensations pulsed through her body, and the black vision took full hold. She convulsed, locks of sweaty hair vibrating on her cheeks, just as she had in the tanks. She teetered there, between orgasm and terror, while all else became a fog. Her gift was exacting, boundless. Her phantom wasn't her arm. It was, as Lucas said, an animal, smarter—and better—than she was. It was perfection, and Maddie loved its song more than anything she'd ever loved.

A NEW MOTHER'S GUIDE TO RAISING AN ABOMINATION - GWENDOLYN KISTE

Your new bundle of joy is almost here. Keep track of the days, because this will be the most exciting time of your life.

It starts with the wings of houseflies. Dozens of them, scattered everywhere in your home. On the cutting board in the kitchen, stuck to the bathroom wallpaper, resting neatly on your pillow as if placed there by a gentle hand.

There are no bodies or legs or bulging eyeballs. Only the disembodied wings, delicate as tiny swatches of wedding lace.

"We'll call an exterminator," your husband says, and sweeps them into the trash.

You clasp your hands in front of you and nod, but when the next wings appear, you make sure he never sees them. Tucked away in the secret compartment of your vintage jewelry box, you keep the wings safe. They're your secret, these strange treasures left in the house just for you.

At night, when your husband is sleeping, you examine them in the glow of the nightlight. How beautiful they are.

As though in agreement, the thing that lives in your belly kicks and coos. You pretend not to feel it, pretend not to know what it means, but it's already been three weeks since you've first felt the stirring within you. That longing you can't define, an unease you can't shake.

You shouldn't be so afraid. This pregnancy was planned, right down to the day, with red circles drawn on the calendar, and your basal temperature taken each morning. This was what you wanted. That's what you keep telling yourself. You wonder if it's still true.

"I'm pregnant," you finally tell your husband the next morning, and he smiles and claps his hands and twirls you around like you're a maudlin couple in a dated rom-com whose happy ending you never did believe.

Another wing waits for you next to the coffeemaker. You slip it into your pocket, never letting your husband see. You won't let anyone see what you really are.

Prepare a bag for the hospital. A comb, a camera, a crucifix. You can never be sure exactly what you might need.

The thing in your belly escapes the womb an hour before midnight.

It all goes according to plan at first. Your water breaks, and your husband rushes you to the community hospital, just like the two of you have been practicing for months.

"I can't believe it's time," he says, and you nod and tighten your hands into fists.

The two of you are the perfect couple. Everyone says so. It's easy enough to think, with you beaming in all the wedding pictures, your bright smile never quite cracking around the edges. You wear happiness like a disguise.

But tonight, you can't hide. When you won't dilate, the doctors open you up, their pale scrubs drenched in red, their metal implements tearing your flesh.

"Something's wrong," someone says, and you try to speak, try to find out what's happening to you and your baby, but in the din of the surgical suite, your voice evaporates like mist.

As streams of frothy liquid pour from you like a fountain, the doctors grab clippers and sutures and a two-bladed speculum. No one asks how you're doing. They probably figure they don't need to. You're still screaming, so that means you're still alive, and as far as the doctor and the nurses and your husband are concerned, that's good enough. They're more worried about the thing that's inside you.

"What is it?" a physician's assistant asks, but no one answers. A strange flutter within you, like an irregular heart-beat, and everyone in the room edges closer.

Your husband gapes at the place between your legs. He no longer sees you. Right now, all he can see is what you've created.

"Why does its skin look like that?" His eyes go gray and distant and scared. "And why is it making that noise?"

He's not the only one bothered. A couple of nurses clap their hands over their ears, and the anesthesiologist weeps quietly next to a table of gleaming forceps. You don't know why it troubles them so much. It sounds like the sweetest lullaby to you.

That's the only comfort you have. The operating table slick with red, you wonder how you can lose so much blood without losing consciousness. You also wonder in the hours and days to come, what else you'll lose.

A final tearing of your flesh and an emphatic snip-snip of a tangled umbilical cord, and you're officially a mother.

Through filmy eyes, you gaze at the infant, draped in downy scales, with a pair of lacy wings dripping with colorless afterbirth.

"It's a girl," the doctor says, his voice splitting in two, and as your head lulls back and the room tilts around you, you've never been more afraid.

The early weeks of your baby's life might be challenging. Remember: this is normal. Everything is normal.

Two days after you bring your daughter home from the hospital, the dead things start arriving at your doorstep.

A pile of mice with their tails tied in slimy bows.

Rats with twisted faces and intestines drooping from their bloated bellies.

Red-wing blackbirds, their silky feathers plucked out and placed in the shape of fairy rings around them.

And those are only the ones you can identify. Some of the things are no more than splintered bone or matted fur.

For the first week, you're convinced someone is killing them. A deranged neighbor perhaps, or a member of a new religion that's formed for the occasion of worshipping your strange daughter. But no, that's not it. These animals are just giving up and dying on their own. They're too tired to be bothered with living anymore, especially in a world like this. A world that's produced a baby more unknown than human.

You almost envy the dead things for that, how simple it is for them to escape. You wish you could get out so easily.

Your husband does his best not to notice. On his way out the door to work, briefcase in hand, he steps over the garden variety of rot that's waiting there next to the morning paper.

"See you tonight," he says.

You wave goodbye and watch him leave. It's your job to clean up the mess. You might not have done anything wrong —or at least not done it on purpose—but everybody knows that when a monster is born, the mother is the one punished for it. You cradled the creature in your womb, after all. Really, you should have known better.

After the oozing decay is deposited in the neighbor's trashcan—a sparrow this time, or what was left of it anyhow —you bundle up your daughter in a onesie that doesn't fit around her scales and wings, and you take her to her first checkup across town.

At the clinic, you cradle her in your lap and try to read a magazine article about a reality star you never heard of. The other mothers inch away from you, clutching their babies tighter.

"They say it's happening all over," the nurses whisper to each other behind the front desk, but when you look up at them, they stop speaking and just blink back at you. Of course, you don't need them to explain. You've seen the nightly news.

All over. Girls like your daughter are being born across the country, maybe even around the world. Birthing monsters must be the latest trend, like helicopter parenting.

In the doorway, someone calls your name, and you walk across the waiting room, past all those wide-eyed mothers with their wingless newborns wrapped in little pastel blankets.

Alone in a narrow, bleach-stinking room, you wait for the results of another blood test.

"Inconclusive," the nurses tell you. "Again."

"I'm sorry," you say and hope your contrition is enough. The doctors had agreed to let you take your daughter home after a week in quarantine showed no obvious contagion, but that doesn't mean you get to keep her. You have to prove to them they can trust you. Otherwise, it's off to a lab where they can study her. *Fix* her.

"Next week, we'll try again," they say. "Don't be late."

As you exit the way you came in, your daughter flutters in your arms, and you grasp her tighter, your hands smoothing her back. The front door isn't even closed behind you before the other mothers and the nurses start to speculate about her, their whispers like thorns in your back. You'd think they'd be hoarse from the gossip by now.

You fix pot roast that night, your husband's favorite, but he doesn't speak all through dinner, not even to ask you to pass the salt or to find out how the checkup went. You don't say anything either. You just push your green beans around the plate with the bent tines of your fork and pretend you're someone else.

Nearby, in her high chair, your daughter parts her gray lips and emits that strange noise, her own lullaby in a key she invented. Your skin buzzes pleasantly, and you almost sing along with her, but then your husband stares up at her, fear churning behind his eyes, and you think better of it.

The two of you were the perfect couple. Everyone said so. But he was expecting what all men like him expect: a happy wife, a normal daughter. He never signed on for this.

After dark, you lock the nursery door, sealing in your progeny as though her bedroom is a coffin. Not that you ever really escape. All night, you dream of her—what she is, what she'll become—the waking nightmare of your life seeping in at every edge. The way her claws will grow and thicken and rend flesh. Her throaty laugh when she'll fly over those doctors and neighbors and complete strangers who gape and gossip and never understand.

Even when you bolt awake, sweat drenching your body, you can still hear their screams.

With your husband asleep next to you, you crawl from your bed and open your jewelry box. There are so many lacy wings inside that they overflow onto the dresser and cascade to the floor.

Breathing deep, you remind yourself that your daughter hasn't done those terrible things yet, and you can't blame her for what hasn't happened. She's still so small. It will be years before you'll have to worry.

You're also wrong.

Dealing with the needs of an infant is difficult, but as every parent soon learns, they grow up too fast. You'll miss these days, so treasure them while they last.

She blossoms overnight, far quicker than an ordinary child, but then nobody ever dared to say your daughter was ordinary.

You rouse one morning to discover a cocoon plastered to her bedroom walls. Your husband grabs a shovel from the garage to scrape it away, not caring that your daughter is still inside, but you get upstairs first.

"Leave her alone," you whisper, your body blocking the doorway to the nursery. "Besides, removing it might only make it worse."

Not that you can fathom how anything could be worse than this.

When she emerges that evening before supper, you almost can't recognize her. She's outgrown her skin, sloughing off the past, her bones twisting and contorting and stretching anew. In hours, she's grown what should have taken her five years. She still looks otherworldly, those wings of hers broadening, her skin thick like plated armor. But somewhere behind the eyes, she looks a little like you too.

Your husband doesn't say this, doesn't accuse you, at least not aloud. The way he won't look at you or touch you any longer is more than accusation enough.

The doctors, as always, are of no help. They can't tell you why your daughter sprouted up overnight. They can't tell you anything. You tell yourself that's okay. You're starting to get used to the not knowing. It's almost comforting.

It's summer now, with barbeques and Fourth of July sparklers and colorful swimsuits you don't wear anymore. At a backyard soirée where your family is invited as the spectacle of the day, your daughter moves quicker than the eye. Here and there and back again, her gaze the color of motor oil.

"Have you thought about other options?" one of the mothers says, as they all gather around you at the picnic table, so close they nearly smother you.

"Options?" You stare at their plastered-on smiles. "Like what?"

They don't answer. Instead, they let the truth settle heavier on you than the summer humidity.

Let the doctors fix her. Let the doctors *have* her.

It would be for the best, their pitying gazes insist.

Your chest constricts, and you search for your husband, for an ally, but even when you spot him, standing with the other fathers around the Weber grill, you realize you're more alone than ever. He stares back at you, everything about him gone cold. Maybe he asked these mothers to talk to you. Maybe considering "other options" is what he wants too.

Your teeth clench, holding in a sob, and you glance away from him, only to see her there across the yard, sequestered from the other children. All alone, your daughter twirls in circles, the grass turning to ash at her feet, her thin wings catching the air and nearly lifting her off the ground. She babbles her ethereal nonsense, while overhead, a starling exhales its death knell and plummets into the punchbowl.

A mother screams, and then another, and a father too, but not you. You just smile at your daughter. You envy her a little too.

That evening back at home, after the lights are out, you creep down the hall and crack open the nursery door. Tonight, you won't hold her back. If your daughter wants to flutter about on her own, then who are you to argue?

You nestle in bed, a gulf of crumpled sheets separating you and your husband, and for the first time since you became a mother, you sleep a dreamless sleep.

No matter how hard you try or how many books you read, not everyone will agree with your parenting style, so prepare yourself for constructive criticism.

The television flicks on at all times of day, the talking heads on the screen with their daily messages of doom. As the number of strange daughters born across the country ticks higher, dead things keep appearing everywhere. They're in your house too. No longer content on the doorstep, the rot makes its way inside now, oozing on the carpet. Knotted tails of animals you can't name. Feathers riddled with mites. Fly wings like confetti scattered across the carpet.

"We can't live like this," your husband says, his jaw clenched.

That night, you awaken to a cold bed and a scuffle down the hall. You stumble to the nursery. There he is, his rough hands grasped around her throat, his knuckles white and tightening around her, even as she only grins back at him.

You stand frozen in the doorway, not even breathing. A good mother would scream, would run toward them, would pry him away from the child any way that she could. A good mother would also underestimate her own daughter, believing every little girl needs to be rescued.

Fortunately, you're not a very good mother.

"Have fun, baby," you say, and close the door behind you, just as she raises up those claws, and your husband starts to scream.

In the morning, there's no proof he was ever there. Not a drop of blood or a clump of hair or even a bone shard brushed away into the corner like dust. You taught your daughter to put away her toys when she's finished with them, and she listens to her mother.

"He went out for cigarettes and never came back," you say when the sheriff comes looking for him, and then you say nothing else. They can't prove it was her, and you certainly won't be the one to turn her over to the police. But your word alone won't satisfy them.

"We know what she did," the other mothers hiss in your ear, as you stand in line at the grocery checkout.

With a steady hand, you place your items on the conveyor belt. A pound of ground beef.

"You can't pretend forever."

Three cans of chicken liver pâté.

"We'll stop her one way or another."

A jar of split pig's feet.

"We know what she is. We know what you've created."

Your brown paper bags in hand, you turn away from them and rush off to the parking lot where your daughter waits for you in the car, her long fingers tapping an arcane message on the glass. A message you're convinced somebody somewhere can hear. Perhaps many somebodies.

Through the front window of the store, the other mothers watch you go. They think you're afraid, and maybe you are a little, but more than anything, you drive off quickly because you want to hide the grin that won't leave your lips.

Sometimes, your new family will outgrow your old home. At that time, relocating might be the only reasonable option.

You leave in the middle of the night, abandoning what little remains of your life.

"Where will we go?" your daughter asks in a humming voice only you can decipher.

"I'm not sure," you say, but that's all right. She already knows the way.

"Keep going," she whispers, gazing out the car window. "Until the highway ends."

You follow her directions until you find it. A compound tucked away in a desolate forest, right at the end of a county highway, like she said.

A man is waiting at the front door of a derelict lodge, as though he's been expecting you. You swear you've seen him before, on a trashy daytime talk show or a late-night infomercial, his hair slicked back. But then again, all New Age masters with silver tongues and dollar signs glinting in their eyes look the same.

"Welcome," he says, and that's when you realize you're not alone here. Peeking out of all the windows and behind the trees are the mothers like you along with their daughters, the ones you've heard the world whisper about.

Before you can stop her, your daughter rushes to the other girls, and instantly, they join as one, a clique of the unknown, dozens of them, almost too many to count in the dark. Together for the first time, they grasp each other's long hands and take flight. It's a dizzying display, all of them in the air, darting back and forth, their colorless bodies smearing across the sky. When they land, their feet burn a perimeter around the property, the trees twisting in grotesque shapes overhead, branches turning to ash in the girls' presence.

The lawn glistens beneath you, and at first, you think it's fresh dew. Then the moonlight shifts, and you see that the shimmer is from thousands of disembodied fly wings.

"You'll be safe here," the man says, and you wonder what he knows of the word, but you don't argue. You're just glad your daughter is not so alone.

Still, you know why he's happy to take you in. It's because he thinks he's running the show. Men like him always think they're in control. They're so often wrong.

"I can lead you to glory," he says and tries to bend all the daughters under his rule. He does his best to straighten their wings and tell them where to fly, when to sleep, how to summon the dead things to them. They shrug him off, uninterested in cowing to the cult he's desperate to craft in his own honor.

"This isn't the way, girls," he tells them, but they don't listen, not now that they have each other.

So he does the only thing he can think of. He betrays them. He summons everyone he can—their former doctors and the sheriffs and the neighbors always at the ready with a torch and a grudge. The world's been looking for them, and he knows it.

As figures bear down on the house, their voices close enough to prickle your skin, you awaken your daughter in her bed.

"We have to run again, baby," you whisper, but she beams back at you.

"No, we don't," she says, and it finally occurs to you that this was always part of the plan. Everyone in one place, all of those who thought the girls should be fixed, exiled, suffocated. Here on your daughters' terms, now that they're together and strong and ready.

The invaders assemble on the lawn, and the girls meet them there, your would-be leader at the forefront.

"You had your chance to listen to me," he says to your daughters, but one of the mothers shakes her head and draws the blinds. None of you wants to hear another word from him. Gathered in a circle in the living room, you spend the rest of the evening playing different card games. Rummy and War and Patience. You win three hands.

Outside, there's a symphony of chaos and pleas and the cracking of bone, but with the shadowy outlines of your daughters buzzing merrily past the blood-streaked windows, you just smile.

It's become so easy to ignore the screams.

Sometimes, all the advice in the world won't help. Sometimes, you have to let your child figure it out for herself.

In the morning, it's quiet on the compound, and you discover the phones have gone dead. Of course, you don't mind. There's no one left out in the world you want to talk to.

As the other mothers murmur in their sleep, you go outside with your coffee. There are no bones on the lawn. No people either. There will never be new people arriving here again. The girls make sure of it. You wonder if the town you left behind is still there, or if on your daughter's command, it's decayed away into nothing, the same as all the trees past the perimeter. While annihilation is a nice thought, they're probably still out there, those other mothers with their wingless children, wandering the grocery store aisles, their eyes vacant, never seeing anything. Certainly not seeing you.

But they're no matter now. This is where you belong, a

place no one will ever go hungry, not so long as the dead things keep appearing on your doorstep. Rabbits with their throats torn out. Deer that skin themselves. The scent of rot no longer bothers you. Maybe you've grown accustomed to it, or maybe it's grown accustomed to you.

Smiling, you kneel in the grass and scoop up a handful of housefly wings. Then with your daughter fluttering past, giggling, you let the wings cascade back to the earth, falling one by one from your palm, like withered rose petals.

As the sun sneaks up through the ashen trees, you listen to your daughter, and all the other daughters too, singing their strange lullabies to the sky. And at last, when you're ready, you part your lips and join in, the final voice in a chorus that rumbles through the earth and turns the universe to dust.

THE HUMAN CLAY - BRENDAN VIDITO

Liam Hedland knew the streets like a palmist knows the lines of a hand. His knowledge was especially keen where the more dangerous parts of town were concerned. He was intimately familiar with every shadow and alleyway, every tenement and drug den. And that awareness provided him with the advantage he needed as a trafficker of illicit biological material. Organs, both synthetic and natural. Infectious agents. Potent pheromones. Implants. The biohazard cooler in the back seat of his delivery van always contained one or more of these items, ready for transport to high-paying clientele and underground medical organizations.

It was the only job in a long line of odd jobs that was suited to his disability. He was able to remain seated for extended periods, avoiding the use of his legs—which grew rigid and painful after limited intervals of movement. In a way, the delivery van was part of his treatment. The necessity to remain behind the wheel acted as a form of passive rehabilitation, supplementing his daily dose of painkillers and anti-inflammatory drugs. It was a glorified wheelchair, a steel and leather extension of his damaged body.

Now, as he drove through the streets sheltered in the

warm, soft embrace of the painkillers, Liam considered tonight's destination: the home of his boss, the famed geneticist and criminal kingpin, Anton Halverson. Running his fingers over the steering wheel and narrowing his eyes against the glow of the streetlamps, Liam wondered why Anton had called him over at this hour. It was the second time he had been summoned directly to Anton's home, where he lived with his wife and three children. On the previous occasion, he'd been given the most important and dangerous assignment of his career—a delivery that ended with Anton's closest associate, Kane, taking a bullet to the throat.

They'd been less than a block away from the delivery point—Kane riding in the passenger seat with a shotgun on his lap—when a person on a motorcycle pulled up beside them and fired a pistol through the window. The biker wore a helmet with a black, mirrored visor. Doubtless, they were attempting to steal the cooler in the back seat. As far as Liam knew, it contained some form of biological weapon. That was the reason Kane was riding along.

As soon as the bullet pierced the side window, Liam stomped the gas pedal and weaved through traffic as the motorcycle growled in pursuit. Eventually, he managed to escape, using his knowledge of the streets to his advantage. The feat, however, did little to alleviate his sense of failure. His boss had outlined a specific route, and Liam had deviated from it, presuming he knew a more efficient course. In a way, he was responsible for Kane's death.

The incident had troubled Liam greatly. He doubled his dose of painkillers, losing himself in a netherworld of dulled edges and swirling grey mist. Whenever his mind drifted, he remembered the way the glass spider-webbed around the bullet. The groan and wet gurgle that escaped Kane's mouth as the bullet pierced his throat. And, above all else, his own reflection, pale and blood-flecked in the rear-view mirror. He feared punishment from Anton, anticipated it with every knock on the door, every phone call, but it never came.

Waiting at a stoplight, Liam dreaded to think what the eminent geneticist had in mind for tonight's house call. Was his employment with Anton Halverson about to end? Had his punishment finally arrived? Or was he in store for something totally unexpected?

After several minutes and an endless string of traffic lights, Liam reached the suburban hills overlooking the city. Massive homes flanked immaculate streets and well-lit sidewalks. A few late-night wanderers moved like sleepwalkers through the dusk, walking dogs or heading toward unknown destinations. Watching them as his cab rolled slowly down the street, Liam realized he felt like a stranger to these people —an altogether different species.

When he reflected on his appearance, he didn't see the slight paunch or the atrophied stalks of his legs. Instead, there was the rusted contours of his cab, the worn treads on the wheels, the scratches and finger-smudges on the windows. He liked to think of himself as the brain or beating heart of a much larger, mechanical organism—vital but anonymous. For so long, his body had betrayed him, denied him even the most basic human needs—from sexual inability to occasional bouts of incontinence—that he favored an existence that melded his defective flesh with reliable machinery. It made his biological shortcomings a little more bearable.

The sight of Anton's home pulled Liam out of his reverie. He pulled up along the sidewalk outside the gate. Visible through the gilded, wrought iron bars, was a paved driveway lined with solar-powered lights. At its terminus stood a French Normandy mansion, its windows hemorrhaging a serene yellow glow.

As Liam stared, the gates opened abruptly with a grating sound. At the end of the path, the door to the mansion, nothing more than a black square at this distance, was replaced by that familiar wash of golden light. And within it, framed by its brilliance, was a tall dark shape. The shape moved slowly toward the gate like a figure in a nightmare. Liam watched, as though in a trance as the shadow grew larger, more sharply defined. Then a clunking sound, followed by the chime of the door alarm, made him jump in his seat.

The passenger door opened and Anton slid into the seat. He wore a slimming grey suit that matched the shade of his combed-back hair and trimmed beard. His eyes were pale blue, and he had a kind, thin, effeminate face—enhanced no doubt by plastic surgery—reminiscent of an angel from a Renaissance painting. He clapped a hand on Liam's shoulder and squeezed.

"It's been too long," he said through his teeth. "How've you been?"

His smile was contagious. Despite his apprehension, Liam felt the muscles at the corners of his mouth loosen and rise. "I'm okay," he said, voice flattened by the pain pills. "You know, same shit."

"How're you feeling?"

Liam blinked at him, knowing Anton saw the glossy sheen in his eyes, the pallor of his skin. Anton pursed his lips and nodded, completing the silent exchange. Their relationship ran deeper than superior and employee. They understood and respected one another. Now and again, communication could be achieved through physical expression alone.

Liam shifted into drive, made a U-turn and started down the street. Once he reached the first set of lights he turned to Anton and asked, "Where are we going?"

Anton pointed vaguely at the windshield. "Head toward the borough. Morovian Place, know it?"

"Yeah." Liam dragged the word out slowly, summoning a mental image of the area—rundown commercial buildings, broken asphalt, faded graffiti and reclaiming weeds. A nearly forgotten corner of a decaying, volatile neighborhood. Did anyone live there besides derelicts and habitual drug users? As far as Liam knew, it was practically abandoned, a domain of shadows and starving rats.

A flutter of anxiety pierced the fog of the painkillers. Liam's fingers twitched and drummed the wheel. "What's on Morovian Place?"

Anton tilted his seat back and stretched out his legs. He heaved a sigh that filled the cab with the scent of peppermint. "I realized I never thanked you for your assistance in the whole Kane affair." Liam flinched at the name. "Seeing him die couldn't have been easy. But despite that, you successfully completed the assignment. And, for that, I owe you my thanks."

Liam blinked. Was he hearing him correctly? Was Anton actually thanking him for safely delivering the weapon, even though Kane bled out in the passenger seat? He decided not to question Anton's assessment of the situation. He allowed the news to wash over him.

"Is there a five-star restaurant on Morovian I don't know about?"

Anton barked a short laugh. "Can you imagine?" he said, then shook his head. "No. There's something much better."

The seat complained under his weight as he angled his body to further face Liam. The driver glanced briefly in his direction, saw the light of the city play in a kaleidoscope across his angular face.

"Your condition," Anton said. "I remember you telling me it presents you with limitations. Especially of the sexual variety."

Bitter, embarrassed laughter spilled from Liam's throat.

"You know that?" he said. "How fucked up was I when I told you?"

"That's irrelevant," Anton replied. "As you know, my

passion and vocation are human genetics. I see in you a problem I want to fix, or at the very least, address to a point where your life becomes a little more accessible."

Liam frowned, not knowing where this line of reasoning was heading. "What are you implying? What's on Morovian?"

"My brothel," Anton said with a half smile. "A playground of flesh and metal."

Their destination had once served as a gynecology clinic. The building was square and dilapidated, its grey brick stained by rivulets of dark crimson where rust had leaked down from the rain gutter. Sagging wooden steps ascended to the front door, which was flanked by wide, blacked-out windows. The place gave the impression of a long-neglected mausoleum, still and silent.

Liam brought the cab around the building to the rear parking lot. A sputtering lamp beside the fire door fitfully illuminated two figures. A man was on his knees, while a woman stood facing him, pointing a gun at his forehead.

"What the hell is going on?" Anton said, watching from the passenger window.

Liam eased on the brake and cranked the gearshift into park. Anton stepped out, long graceful strides carrying him toward the man and the woman. Liam fumbled the keys out of the ignition, clumsily stuffed them into his pocket. He opened the door and paused. Warm wind caressed his face and rustled the dirty napkins stuffed into the cup holder.

A feeling of naked vulnerability overcame him. His heart was a fist, tight in his chest. With a tender motion, he ran his fingers along the fabric of the driver's seat, taking in its aura of comfort and familiarity. Stepping out of the cab always brought with it a vague anxiety. It was like shedding an article of warm clothing and stepping out into treacherous weather. The sensation held Liam in its grip for several moments, as it always did, then he heaved a deep sigh and exited the vehicle.

His legs, too thin for the jeans that enclosed them, wobbled unsteadily on the cracked asphalt. He took a limping step forward, then another, shambling in clumsy pursuit of Anton. As always, Liam was acutely aware of how his knees bent inward, giving his gait the fragile jerkiness of an injured bird. He willed the image from his mind, gritting his teeth in frustration, and labored forward. He instead decided to focus on what was taking place before him.

"Carrie," Anton called out. "Everything under control?"

Carrie darted her foxfire-green eyes in his direction. She had a pointed, elfin face, an upturned nose, and shoulder-length blonde hair. Her charcoal grey work suit was rumpled as though from a struggle, and as he approached, Liam could see—clearly outlined in the glow of the streetlights—the downward curve of her breasts, sheened with perspiration, a hint of eroticism in this tableau of confusion and potential violence.

With her free hand, she languidly pushed several stray locks of hair from her eyes, keeping the gun trained on the man's forehead. He was middle-aged. His lips were pulled away from his gums and his eyes rolled like he was a cow on the path toward slaughter. He was also, Liam now realized, wearing nothing but ill-fitting underwear.

"Everything is fine, Dr. Halverson," Carrie said. Her voice was high, but devoid of inflection. "This gentleman disobeyed the rules of the house. Apparently, my words of warning weren't enough. I had to use other means to entice him out of the building."

Anton stepped up beside Carrie, examined the man before her coldly, and then turned his gaze to the weapon clasped between Carrie's manicured fingers. "Is that what I think it is?"

"Yes," Carrie said.

Anton nodded toward the man. "What do you plan to do with him?"

"He's certainly not coming back here."

Liam joined them, peering between their shoulders at the man. He met Liam's gaze and flung out his hands in a gesture of supplication. "This is a huge misunderstanding. I won't breathe a word about this to anyone. I have no reason—"

The gun in Carrie's hand popped—a hydraulic thud followed by a wet hissing sound. The man's head snapped back. His eyes fluttered. His mouth opened and closed in a series of silent gasps. Instead of a bullet hole, a raised black lump the size of a grape marked his forehead. As Liam watched, dark veins spread out from the lump, twisting under his skin as they stretched across his face like a tar-soaked spider web. Throughout this process, he remained mute and unmoving, his eyes glazed. Then, abruptly, his fore-head erupted into balloons of putrid, cancerous flesh. The jagged edges of his shattered skull thrust outward through a corona of bruised and bleeding skin. Tainted lymphatic fluid gushed from the wound in steady streams. Melanomas clouded and cracked his eyeballs with purple, distended veins. With a loud crunch, the tumors in his forehead expanded throughout the remainder of his head. His gums blackened and his teeth oozed from their sockets, tinkling against the asphalt. His tongue expanded, filling the cavity of his mouth. He let out one final, strangled gasp before slumping sideways, his legs twitching feebly.

"Jesus Christ," Liam said. "What did you do to him?"

Carrie said, "I made him malleable."

Without turning her gaze away from the dead man, she lifted the gun demonstratively. It was roughly the same size as a 9mm pistol, though the edges of its barrel were wide and rounded. The metal gleamed like polished steel. It gave off a faint odor of decomposition.

"This is a highly coveted tool. We lost one of our greatest men transporting it some weeks ago." Was she talking about Kane? She had to be. "A single projectile spreads a voracious cancer throughout the body in seconds," Carrie went on. "It also makes the flesh more…expressive. Transforms it into clay that can be kneaded by inspired hands."

She turned to face Liam. Held out her free hand. Liam stared at her fingers for a beat, visualizing them working a lump of wet clay, before finally shaking.

"Why did you kill him?"

Carrie shrugged. "He was dangerous." Her nearly bioluminescent eyes flicked to the collar of her button-up shirt, where the fabric was stretched to reveal the swell of her cleavage. "And he touched me."

Anton placed a hand on each of their shoulders. "Liam, meet Carrie, one of my biotechnicians and the den mother of this establishment."

"Pleasure," Carrie said. "And, Dr. Halverson, I'm a sculptor, not a biotechnician."

Anton nodded. "Of course." He smiled apologetically. "Shall we go inside?"

Carrie watched each man turn. "Good idea. Dr. Halverson, bring the body in with you."

The interior of the brothel defied Liam's mundane expectations.

A chorus of moans and screams, blended with wet sucking sounds, played over speakers mounted on the walls. The light fixtures on the ceiling were long and conical. They shed a crimson radiance over the space. The marble floor was made up of dizzying swirls of black and white, like a melted chessboard. A grainy hologram shone on the wall opposite the back door. It comprised a disembodied face, huge and Oz-like, with androgynous features and a perversely grinning smile. Liam thought he saw it move: a twitch of the eyeball or crease of the brow, but it could have been his overwrought imagination.

To either side of the hologram, video screens had been mounted to the walls. They showcased close-ups of genitals in act of union; lips pressed against one another, and fingers boring into orifices. All these high-definition loops were intercut with extreme close-ups of worms wriggling in their own slime and maggots feasting on decomposing flesh. As Liam stared transfixed, both types of images became indistinguishable.

When he finally managed to look away, he noticed the mural on the ceiling. The artist had rendered, with a touch of madness no doubt, Adam and Eve's story from Genesis. The first scene depicted Satan—horned, cleft-hooved, and with exaggerated genitals—communing with the first man and woman. The second had them eating the forbidden fruit, which covered their faces and fingers in blood-red nectar. The subsequent tableaux showed Adam and Eve fucking in various positions, culminating in Adam eating the womb out of Eve. A pale, dying Eve participated as well, taking a tentative bite from her reproductive organ.

"Beautiful, isn't it?" Carrie said. "The paint is made entirely from biological material."

With Carrie in the lead, they entered a room the size of a small banquet hall, dimly lit by red pot lights. The walls were painted black and lined with an array of pedestals and rolling gurneys. On each sat a shape wrapped in shadow. They moved feebly, hinting at some form of life or automation.

Liam scanned the room with trepidation clawing up his spine. The three of them stood in the doorway. Crimson light bathed Anton's face, distorting his divine features into something demonic. He said, "Liam suffers from a wasting disease that has made him unable to participate in sexual activity."

"Anton, come on," Liam cut in, heat rising in his cheeks.

Anton held out a restraining hand.

"It's fine. You're among friends."

"There's nothing to be ashamed or embarrassed about," Carrie said.

She gripped Liam's hand and threaded her long, thin fingers through his.

"Dr. Halverson only wants to help you," she continued, guiding him to the nearest gurney. The pot light overhead flared to greater brilliance, illuminating the thing writhing on its starched sheets. "This place is unique. We can break through your impotence."

It was a woman's torso devoid of head and limbs. The stumps were smooth and pale with scar tissue. Its skin was porcelain, unblemished and inviting to the touch. A light growth of pubic hair framed a delicately sculpted vulva. The torso undulated in an erotic wave, the muscles of its abdomen tensing and releasing in rippling spasms.

"Touch her," Carrie said, gently taking Liam's wrist and guiding his hand toward the thing on the gurney.

He was resistant at first, but as soon as the warmth from the torso's flesh reached his fingertips, he relented. She was incomparably soft. It was like stroking a breath of summer wind. The torso shuddered, gooseflesh spreading over its curves and folds. A thin steam of clear lubricating fluid oozed from its vaginal opening.

"You made this," Liam said. It was less of a question, more an awe-stricken statement.

"She is one piece in a gallery full of my art," Carrie replied, fanning out her arm in a gesture that encompassed the room.

"And people come here to—" Liam started, and then fell silent, a frown creasing his forehead. "I don't know how this place will help me." He glanced at Anton, then back at Carrie. "I haven't been intimate...I haven't been *able* to be intimate since this happened to me." He gestured sharply from his waist down to his old, battered shoes.

Carrie touched him on the shoulder and guided him to the pedestal beside the gurney. The light overhead grew brighter, dousing them in a sanguine glow. It took Liam a moment to process what he was seeing, his brain struggling to draw disparate elements together into a coherent whole, seeking patterns. It appeared to be a mound of intricately layered flesh, an exotic flower of labial and scrotal tissue threaded with filaments of metal. Liam stared, hands dangling at his sides as the thing heaved with a vaguely respiratory movement.

"There's something here for everyone," Carrie said. "I have found a way to abbreviate the human form to a purely sexual organism. These creations possess antibodies strong enough to combat any infection or disease. Their sole purpose is pleasure, free of guilt or worry."

"I still don't understand how that will help me," Liam said.

Anton injected his voice into the conversation. "You need to show him the thing downstairs."

Silence prevailed for a moment. Carrie and Anton exchanged glances, appearing to come to an understanding, and then both focused their attention on Liam again.

"Do you care to see?" Carrie asked.

"I don't know what's going on," Liam said and looked pleadingly at Anton. "Why did you bring me here?"

"To help you," Anton said without hesitation.

Liam shook his head, confused and overwhelmed. Whatever vague expectation he had upon entering the brothel was rapidly evaporating in a mist of anxious uncertainty. Had Anton been telling the truth? Did he truly intend to show Liam a good time as a token of his appreciation, or was something more sinister in the process of unfolding? Whatever the case, Liam knew better than to panic or question his superiors, especially someone with the influence and cold pragmatism of Anton Halverson. And besides, the two were more than employer and employee; they were friends, were they not?

"Don't be alarmed," Anton said, easily deciphering the look on Liam's face. "This is something you want to see."

The basement was a maze of boxes and defunct office equipment. Carrie pressed a button at the bottom of the staircase and a row of tube lights flickered into existence. Despite the disorder, the room was well kept: the floor swept and polished, every surface unmarked by dust. The air even smelled faintly of disinfectant and pine needles.

Liam passed a hand over the top of one of the many boxes stacked throughout the room. The words "CERBERUS BIOTRONICS" were printed across the side. He assumed it was the name of one Anton's suppliers—a purveyor of black-market pharmaceuticals and biotechnology.

"It's through here," Carrie said, indicating a walled-off portion of the room. A steel door marked "Do Not Enter" stood out against the pallid drywall, which ended halfway to the ceiling. Beyond, orange light painted the walls and a huge, amorphous shadow stirred with movement. Liam strained his ears and caught the sound of breathing, heavy and phlegm soaked.

He took a step back, flicked his gaze toward Anton, who smiled.

"It's one of Carrie's sculptures. There's nothing to fear."

Carrie extended her hand and twisted the handle with agonizing slowness. Liam's pulse pounded in his ears, sweat trickled down his back. The door finally opened, and he nearly choked on the breath he was holding when he saw the thing on the floor sitting in a puddle of semen and excrement.

It had the body of a man, hairless and pot-bellied. Its chest sagged, pendulous breasts hanging halfway to a stitched navel. Disproportionately large thighs shimmered with a thin coating of seminal fluid. Its lower extremities were a dysfunctional marriage of human feet and cloven hooves. Black keratin burst out from between half-formed toes and split the soles into uneven halves, making anything other than crawling impossible. A corkscrew-shaped organ trailed on the floor between its knees. It was half a foot long and raw from excessive friction.

Its head, however, was the most grotesque feature of all. It didn't belong on the shoulders of a man, but the bloated, humped body of a pig. Glassy, black eyes rolled in their sockets, a sickle of white visible along the edges. With an inquisitive grunt, it raised its snout and scented the air. Mucus trickled from its pulsating nostrils. It took in the three visitors and blinked dumbly, its lips quivering away from disturbingly human teeth.

"What happened to him?" Liam said, his voice unsteady and weak.

"He wanted a deeper communion with his own sexuality. He approached me with a request of enhancement. I've performed such procedures before, but this time I wanted to attempt something unique."

The swine creature lifted its head and unleashed a guttural scream. Liam flinched.

"In extreme cases, a boar is capable of having an orgasm that can last up to thirty minutes. Imagine it, an orgasm that sends you into a prolonged state of euphoria, a sexual high seemingly without end. Once this epiphany struck me, it was only a matter of putting my sculpting skills to use. You see… sapiens and swine aren't very different on a genetic level. The clay of their flesh blends nicely together."

"Why are you showing me this?" Liam asked, though an answer was already forming in his mind. He had assumed correctly when he received the summons from Anton earlier that night. His punishment had finally arrived.

Anton clapped his shoulders and squeezed. "Liam, I respect you deeply. And I want to ensure that your life is complete." The usual placid cast of his face melted into an expression that combined both sadness and regret. "What you allowed to happen to Kane was unforgivable. Had you been anyone else, I would have ended your life the moment the news reached my ears. But you're a close friend. So, I decided you wouldn't be punished. I want nothing but happiness for you. And my expertise has allowed me to give you something your condition has denied."

Liam thought of running, but his legs were too weak to accomplish the task. Instead, he grasped Anton's hand on his shoulder and squeezed, like a lover seeking comfort. The guilt and anxiety that had been roiling inside him for the past few weeks was finally beginning to slough away, replaced by a sense of resignation…of peace.

"I understand," he said, his voice cracking. "I appreciate everything you've done for me."

Anton nodded. "It'll be quick."

A loud pop behind him. Something slammed into his back. There was a sudden pressure, a cold burning sensation. He collapsed into Anton's waiting arms.

"Thank you," Anton said into his ear. He pushed him and he stumbled boneless into the room with the swine creature. Anton and Carrie stood framed in the doorway, the latter holding the tumor gun in a lazy grip. It exuded a faint stench of decay. Liam closed his eyes and dreamed as the cancer invaded his body, turning him to clay.

He lay on a plain of raw, bleeding flesh. All around him stood cairns constructed of bone and fragments of rusted metal. The sky was the color of an open wound. Thunder sent shock-waves through the atmosphere. At length, Liam became aware of a wet, shuffling sound. It steadily grew louder, approaching from every direction. He rolled his head to one side. A swine creature pulled its body across the fleshy landscape, dragging useless legs behind it. Liam scanned the rest of the perimeter and confirmed he was surrounded by a score of such creatures, crawling toward his prone, cancer-ridden body. Grunts and screams filled the air.

"You're a eunuch who dreamed of carnal pleasure," said a voice. "And now, you're awake."

Liam lifted his head. Kane stood at his feet completely naked, his body streaked with crimson. The wound in his neck pumped a steady stream of dark arterial blood.

"I'm so sorry," Liam said.

Kane shook his head. "Leave that all behind you."

The swine creatures were close enough that Liam could feel their breath against his skin. They leaned in as one and sank their teeth into his arms and legs. He closed his eyes expecting agony, but he had lost all awareness of his physical body. Gone were the imperfections, the inequities, and the pain. Everything was warm and weightless, and soon, wave after orgasmic wave crashed into his being, flooding him with an overwhelming rush of never-before-experienced sensation. He screamed, drowning out the tearing and chewing sounds of the swine creatures. His orgasm grew exponentially, swallowing, digesting, and dissolving him into protoplasm of pure, raw euphoria. Finally, his evolution complete, he opened his eyes.

And awoke into a realm of endless pleasure.

REBORN OF ASH - SAM RICHARD

"I know it hurts, Travis, but I want you to explore your grief as deeply as you can. When we truly stare inward at ourselves, within the eye of the storm that is grief, we come out the other side having done what few others dare to do. People avoid this because they think the pain is too much because our reality has become too awful and full of sorrow to bear—and it has—but the only way through is through. Now breathe deeply.

"I want you to focus your mind's eye on the pitch-black pit of pain inside your heart; the empty place where the wound still hemorrhages black blood. Inside that fissure, we will find your wife; we will find her free from the pain of your grief. Your memories of her will no longer be distorted by the shock and trauma of finding her body. You will remember her without the sorrow and the unending loneliness. Do you understand, Travis?"

"I . . . I think so." Tears spilled from his glassy, reddened eyes.

"Good. This will hurt, but it is nothing compared to the pain you have already been through. Look at me, Travis."

"I don't think I can do this, Dr. Ewing. It's fucking agony. I just want her back, man. Our daughter . . . my daughter has to grow up without a fucking mother. What the fuck is that? You said you'd help, but I only feel worse. I can't. I can't…"

"Travis, look into my eyes, it is going to be ok. Everyone in this room loves and supports you. We're all here for you; all here with you. You want to remember Sarah without sifting through all this pain, right? You want to be able to tell Abby about her mother without shattering like cheap glass under the weight of her name. This is how you do that. It will hurt. I know it already hurts so, so much. I know everyone in your life has already said their platitudes and niceties, their offers to help that always seem to fall through when you need them. I know how you feel isolated in your grief, isolated from your family and friends, from your job and your community. Isolated from your daughter. I know how you feel isolated from yourself, feeling only the pain, trauma, and numbness, but nothing else. Continually surrounded by grief.

"You are here because you chose to be. And I am here because you asked; because you asked for help. Asked for a release from this grief. A release from the memory of Sara's body dangling from a rafter in your garage. I am here to help release you from it. But I can't do it for you. I can only guide you to it. I need you to trust me; to listen to me; to do as I say. Only then will you be relieved of your suffering. Will you do that? Will you trust me?"

"I . . . I . . . yes."

"Good, now breathe. Return to that place, the black spot within the wound in your heart; your soul. Breathe through the sorrow and the misery, Travis. Look into the seething darkness with your mind's eye. See the vision of Sara, hanging from the noose. Yes, breathe. It's ok, Travis. We are all with you. And, unlike the outside world, we've all experienced the same brutality as you. No one will judge you, we all want the same thing for you. Everyone is here with you.

Can you feel them, Travis? In this room, we are all here for you.

"It's ok, let your body tremble if it must, but clear your mind of everything else and sit in that horrible place. I know your brain is firing fight or flight responses. I know that you feel like you are on the verge of a PTSD breakdown, and that is ok, Travis. Just sit with it. If tears arrive, just let them flow. Take it all in and breathe through it. Don't think about anything else. Listen to my words.

"Yes, Travis. Now, looking at the body of your beloved wife, I want you to rewind the tape in your mind. Don't rewind it so you go out the door, but rewind it as though the past is happening around you but without your inclusion. You are like a fly on the wall.

"This will be the worst part, I promise you. We are all still here. We are behind you.

"Watch as her dying gasp plays in reverse, giving way to new breath. Watch as her face changes from pale blue, to rich purple, to red, and back to pink. Look at how her still body slowly begins to swing more and more before her jerk upwards, back onto the stool that tips up from the ground to meet her once kicking feet. The way she gently loosens the noose, exhales sharply, and then pulls it off of her neck and over her head. The way she climbs down the stool, pulls the noose down from the rafters and picks up the stool, carrying both into the house, back into the kitchen.

"Rewind the tape, Travis, before you went to work that day. And before the fight, that previous night, bring it back to the last time you were happy together. The last time you saw her smile. There is a place, a memory, before the infidelity, the shame, the guilt; before her suicide. You need to find it. It is within that memory that the true version of her, untainted by grief and pain, lives within you. Do you see that place? Can you find her? Now bring her through the crevice in your heart. Carry her, as you knew her, through the hole with you. Do you have her, Travis? Is she with you?!"

The waiting room felt sterile and stuffy at the same time. I wondered what I was doing there. I should have stayed at home, stayed in bed another day, another week—fuck—maybe another month. But I had missed the first day and it was already paid for. I couldn't keep running from the pain.

"Mr. Daniels?" the receptionist's voice was firm but calming, spoken with the authority and wisdom of a teacher. I approached the cut-out window, resting my elbow on the small countertop, and told her my spiel, "Daniel, no 's'—it happens all the time—you can call me Mark." She was gracious about it, her eyes kind and tender. I got the feeling she had been through her share of hardships as well, that she knew how painful life could be and went out of her way to be kind to hurting people. Fuck if I know, though. In widowhood, I think we want everyone else to also have horrible trauma, maybe that way we won't feel so alone.

While I was lost in thought, she passed my paperwork over to Dr. Ewing who had just entered the small room. Looking up, I recognized him immediately from the videos on the Luctus Foundation website. His thinning hair betrayed the youth in his face, a scattered beard of stubble running across it. His intense, wide-set brown eyes felt out of balance with his perpetually tightly pursed lips. I couldn't help but think they looked like a sideways asshole. It made him look like he had something to hide and the stress had gotten to him; though that thought fell away as soon as he started speaking.

"Come this way, Mr. Daniel, and I'll take you into our briefing room."

"Please, call me Mark, I'm not into that formal stuff."

"Of course."

We walked in silence through a drab hallway with a smattering of small meeting rooms on either side. The lights were off inside each sparsely furnished room. Word was that the institute was still in its pilot program and was hoping to ramp up to greater numbers of patients in treatment. I had been accepted into the 3rd cohort. I felt lucky.

Dr. Ewing led me to a room at the end of the hall and motioned me inside. It looked like all the others, a desk and a few chairs, a lamp, and some brochures in acrylic holders. It smelled of lemon-scented floor cleaner and bleach. We both took a seat.

"Now I have gone over your transcripts and your application, but I like to get a sense of a patient's story in their own words. Please, tell me why you're here with us at The Luctus Foundation..."

I went over it, again, as I had so many times, stopping to feel the lifeless weight of Sadie's cold hand in my own as I spoke about coming home from work three months ago and finding my wife of 6 years dead on our kitchen floor. My words felt emotionless and robotic, as though—through having told this same sequence of events time and time again —the words no longer held any emotion for me. And maybe that was true. I couldn't tell anymore.

He sat and nodded his head with my words, his eyes equally tired and compassionate. I told him about the autopsy results. Brain hemorrhage would be the official cause of death. I went through it all, the cremation, the funeral, my inability to spread her ashes. I told him about how lost I felt. How alone. I told him about the suicidal ideation and the therapy; about hearing about the institute through my mother-in-law, if I should even call her that anymore. What do your in-laws become when your spouse dies?

After all that, I told him how I couldn't leave my house the previous day, the day my treatment was supposed to start with the rest of my cohort. There was panic, anxiety, grief built up over months. The thought of sharing in a group made me feel like I was choking.

Dr. Ewing understood. Several other patients felt that same way. I hadn't been the only one to miss the first day. He reassured me that it was ok to be anxious. That Luctus was a safe place and they would do everything they could to take care of me. He also told me that I had to work for it. That it wouldn't be easy, that transcendence only came through suffering.

Pointing to my bags, he asked, "You brought her with you, correct—Sadie, I mean?" to which I answered yes.

I wasn't sure why, but part of the application requirements included that you still have your late partner's cremains, and that you bring them to the treatment center. I was puzzled by it, but part of the therapy was for widows who couldn't part with their late spouse's remains, and I certainly fit the bill.

With that, he escorted me to my room, where I dropped off my bags, and he instructed me to bring her remains with me, to meet the others.

We entered a large meeting hall. It felt like a church. Honey-oak wood covered the walls and crawled up to the ceiling with sharp, clean accents. There was a stage at one end of the expansive room. It echoed as I introduced myself to four other widows and widowers. These would be my cohorts.

I apologized for my delay, for my absence the previous day. They sympathized. A woman who introduced herself as Lisa said she had done the same thing. Her smile was warm but tired. She had strawberry-blonde hair and looked straight out of the 70s, despite being in her mid-thirties.

Her husband had died in a car accident. A truck ran a red light and rolled over his car, shattering his spine and rupturing several of his internal organs. It had only been two months. She carried herself like a ghost, not exactly in this world but not in another, either. A feeling I knew all too well.

Another woman with dull-green eyes, who called herself Ami, led me to a table that had four urns sitting on it. My arms had grown tired under Sadie's ashen weight. As gently as I could, I placed it with the others. They formed a pentagon.

Ami told me about her late-wife, dead only two-and-a-half months from a heart attack at 37. She had been a chemist. She did yoga and was a vegetarian, a marathon runner even. It didn't make any sense. Despite her obvious sorrow and shock, Ami had a chipper way about her, energetic and warm.

Her eyes were burnt red from months of tears. I could feel the same in mine.

The two of us walked back to the group, it was like we were already old friends. This is what meeting fellow widows and widowers is like. You tell them about the worst day of your life—and they tell you theirs—all before you mention your career, the weather, that movie you want to see, a new restaurant you ate at recently. You are bonded in misery. You feel at home and no one finds it strange but the outside world.

Everyone else had taken their seats. I sat down next to a short, muscled man named Travis. His eyes looked chapped from salty-tears and his voice was hoarse. I couldn't tell if it was a bottle of whiskey and pack-a-day habit or all the crying. He reached out for a handshake, his hand was smooth and uncalloused. Looking up at the vaulted, wooden ceiling, he said his wife had hung herself. He didn't say anything more, but his look told me all I needed to know. It was probably more recent than anyone else in the room; he was still blaming himself.

The chairs were in a semi-circle facing the stage where Dr. Ewing stood, all but one of them taken. Dr. Ewing started to talk about our treatment when a door opened and another woman walked in. She was short and had pitch-black hair. She had a beaming smile that somehow felt unified with the exhausted look of pain in her eyes. She apologized and took the final seat.

"All right, now that we're all here, I want to take a moment to bring Mark and Lisa up to speed with where we're going and what we've done so far. I also want to thank Travis for being so brave yesterday exploring his grief in front of us all.

"It won't be easy, but you'll all be doing that, both in one-on-one sessions with me and also in front of the group. It's important that we all see each other going through the process and sharing in each other's sorrow. It sounds strange, but it will help form a bond between you all that will become extremely important as the next couple of weeks pass.

"Your unification as a group, your ability to hone in on each other's emotional states and love for each other's late-person is tantamount to making this treatment work smoothly. You have to be able to understand each other and work together. I know it sounds strange, but with one of the two other cohorts, we were able to skim the surface of emotional integration as a collective; and getting to that elusive place brings wonderful healing.

"We picked you all because your psychological profiles indicate that you'll work well together, that you'll be able to gel. We here at the Luctus Foundation believe that you are the best hope we have at figuring out how to help others heal, by first guiding you all on your own personal, and also collective, healing journeys.

"Well, it looks like dinner is about to be served here in a few minutes, so I'll leave you to it. And, since you're all here now, I'll give you the evening to get to know each other in a more casual setting before we start the real work in the morning."

With that, Dr. Ewing was off the stage and across the room

before I had a chance to ask even a single question. I guess it was my own fault for being a day late. That first night we ate together and then sat in the same meeting room, which would come to unofficially be known as 'The Chapel.'

The woman who had entered the meeting late, Julia, and I got to talking. Her boyfriend of fifteen years, Ian, had died of pancreatic cancer about a year ago, making her much farther out than anyone else in the group. She had a quick wit and a mischievous, youthful smile despite being in her mid-fifties. She was in the first of Ewing's cohorts and had integrated into the Luctus Foundation as an aide. Her experience was meant to help guide us from within. I liked her right away.

As that evening went on, I found myself liking them all.

It felt strange to be in a room that felt so church-like, talking with other widows and widowers; we should have been in a bar with drinks in our hands. We swapped stories about our late-people, some sad, some hilarious, all with so much love. There was a moment where I was overwhelmed by it all. Five strangers in a room for an evening who now knew each other probably better than friends we'd had for years because we were tied together by the most horrible circumstances. The growing refrain was: no one else gets it.

I heard horror stories of vindictive in-laws, shitty friends, and compassionless family. Oddly, it made me feel better about my lot in loss. My friends and family had been amazing, my in-laws and I were still family. There had been people close to me who had inadvertently said dumb shit here and there, but nothing malicious.

Travis' parents tried to get parental rights over his daughter, Abby, after Sarah hung herself, claiming that it was his fault and he was an unfit parent. They didn't win, but he no longer had a relationship with them. His face became crimson as he talked, his voice more hoarse than ever.

Julia got kicked out of the home she had lived in with Ian, as they weren't married and he had bought it before they met. She paid 15 years of house payments with him only for his family to take it away from her. It was a craftsman-style that they had fixed up together, room by room. Her voice trembled with rage and exhaustion as she told us the story.

They all had horror stories compounded on top of the tragedies that brought us together.

I hurt for them. I hurt for us all.

Exhausted emotionally by the end of the first night, I retreated to my small room. The bed was hard and lumpy, but I managed to get some sleep, though less so the following couple of weeks.

The therapy sessions were brutal emotionally and physically draining. Dr. Ewing had us exploring the moment we found our person or the moment they died in front of us. In Julia's case, Ian had died in her arms at the hospital. I think we all cried when she had her first 'social' session, as Ewing came to call them. I know I did.

In one-on-ones, we dug more into the nature of our grief and the relationships we had with our person—or at least that's what mine were like. Folks didn't talk much of the one-on-ones publically.

My sessions often revolved around the state of shock that I had been unable to shake, the way my mind always crawled back to the moment of finding her body and the dead touch of her cold skin. That moment was still so real and present in my mind. The trauma and despair, unending. We talked about mourning all the parts of who Sadie was. Mourning the death of a spouse, of a partner, is so multi-faceted. She was my best friend, my companion, my support system, my lover, my wife. I had to learn to mourn these parts as separate aspects of grief. It was horrible.

My sleep got worse, my body dragging behind me everywhere I went. A tightness grew in my chest and I worried I was going to burn myself out, or worse. But I knew I had to keep pushing through and make the therapy work. There was no turning back.

Every day we each had a one-on-one, group therapy, and then after dinner, Ewing would deliver a sermon, for lack of a better word, before the social session.

He talked a lot about collective pain and shared memory, about breaking down the walls between us on a psychological level. On the third week, he brought up manifestations of love.

"As we've begun to unlock your hearts of the pain, suffering, and trauma of loss, we are reshaping your bodies and minds to become something different, something new. Every time you explore the moment of death or revelation, you build a bridge inward, towards the pure memory of your person, free of the sorrow you've attached to them.

"Each of you has done a wonderful job, even exceeding what we hoped from this group. Tonight is going to be a little different. You have all come so far and pushed yourselves in ways that I know has been extraordinarily painful and difficult, but also rewarding. Transcendence through suffering is a very real thing, and you've all suffered terribly.

The room was cold. My chest hurt.

"Now it is time for some transcendence. Julia, please come up here."

Julia joined Ewing on the small stage. I hadn't noticed until she was in front of us, but she was wearing a dark red robe cinched at the waist, which she slipped off her shoulders. She had nothing on underneath. The ceiling lights cast shadows in her collarbones.

At the center of her chest, on top of her solar plexus, was a fleshy mass. About the size of a fist, it jostled stiffly under her skin as she moved.

We all stared at it in confusion.

As when I found Sadie dead, time slowed and the world took on an irreal sheen. I had no words with which to ask the question, "What is this?" only the answer that it both couldn't be real and also was.

An uncomfortable silence filled the room. I wasn't sure if it was awe or horror, shock or surprise. Before anyone could ask any questions, Dr. Ewing spoke.

"You have all been building a bridge between your emotions, your memory of your late-person, and your flesh. Julia has done this before and has become quite good at it. For the rest of you, it may take a little more time. I didn't want to alarm any of you if and when you start sprouting your own psychic organ; your *fructus cordis*, if you will."

I saw the glint of the knife and before I had time to register what was happening, Julia was cutting down along the length of the mass. Clear pink fluid and dark blood poured down her hand and onto the floor, becoming a makeshift shadow beneath her small frame.

It had the sensation of a dream, but I knew it wasn't. Just as when Sadie died, things were far too linear to be anything but shockingly real.

Julia then tore the skin apart, pulling a pink clump out of her chest. It looked firm in her hand, solid. All of us watched, with unblinking eyes, as she licked it clean. By the time she was done, her face and mouth were smeared with blood and translucent pink fluids. But the object she had grown inside herself was now closer to an ivory white, stamped with reddened fingerprints. With hands covered in stiffening blood that slowly dripped off her elbows, she held it out for us all to see.

It looked like a human heart.

A human heart formed out of bone or ivory or tooth.

The sound of blood hitting the pool beneath her echoed through the chapel like a solemn prayer.

"I know that can't have been pleasant to watch, but please listen to what I am going to tell you. The heart Julia just grew is actually for Ian. It is what will make him whole again. I know it sounds crazy, but I need you to understand this."

I sat in a daze, unsure of what was happening. Was this whole thing an elaborate ruse? Did a psychic surgeon just promise to bring Sadie back? I was waiting for the shakedown to come. Was this stage magic at its most exploitative and tragic? I couldn't make heads or tails of what I had just seen, of what I had felt. It was like the wind had been squeezed from my lungs.

Travis stormed out of the room in a red-faced panic. I can't say I blamed him. But I couldn't will myself out of my chair. I needed to see what happened next. I needed to know.

My hand was sweaty and constricted, I realized Lisa was clutching it tightly, her eyes fixed on Julia. All our eyes were fixed on Julia.

She walked over to the table and picked up Ian's cremains; the flaps of skin between her breasts hung open like curtains, flopping with each step she took. Setting him down in the center of the small stage, she untied her robe, letting it fall around her, landing like a melting crescent moon. Her nudity aroused something in me beyond the sexual and my skin grew tight with goosebumps in anticipation of what would come next.

Removing the lid, she squatted over the urn and began to pleasure herself with her fingers, running them across her labia and over her clit. Her erotic song echoed through the room like wedding bells and before too long she was orgasming, pushing her wet fluids out, into the open urn.

Arousal and fascination sunk into me while terror and confusion held me in their arms.

Ewing then spoke as a small cloud of ash billowed from the urn. He was visibly erect.

"It takes orgone energy, the new organ, and sexual fluids to create our refreshed visions of our loved ones. And focus; there must be focus. The energies are heightened when others are in an aroused state, which is why it is best done before the group. Now that you've been exposed to those energies, soon each of you will begin to feel the *fructus cordis* growing in your chests, and you will once again see your beloved."

Just as he stopped talking, gritty liquid overflowed from the smoking urn.

A thin, grey arm shot out, planting its hand on the stage, leaving trails of dark ash sprouting off it. A mix of liquid and solid spilled out from the urn, attached to the arm. The oblong shape crawled along the floor toward Julia, solidifying as it moved.

She touched its head, now full of thick, stringy hair that moved as one organism. The limbs grew darker as they hardened, gaining more pronunciation in their detail. The torso did the same, shifting and gaining substance, firmness. The thing rose from its belly on fresh legs and hugged Julia; an embrace of lovers divided by time and sea.

I was crying, clutching the tightness in my chest where a small lump had formed. I could hear others as well. Ami's wailing cut into my mind as I watched Julia and Ian become one again.

Ewing stood, frozen by awe or fear or pride.

Still intertwined with Julia, the thing turned and looked at us. Its hollow eyes betrayed the contentment and love on its face. The dark grey skin reminded me of the remains of Pompeii seen at night. There was a subtle hissing sound as if it were trying to speak. A haze of ash blew from the struggling lips as its rubbery, dry tongue clicked between jagged, stone teeth, but words never formed.

Their embrace lingered. Julia's hands pressed into the thing, bits of ash and dust crumbling under the pressure. With straining ears, I could hear her mantra repeated over and over and over, "I love you and I'm sorry. I love you and I'm sorry. I love you and I'm sorry."

My heart beat with the rhythm of the words and tears streamed down my face.

He began to crack and splinter, parts of him crumbling to the ground. With her love in her arms, Julia once again felt him disintegrate in spite of her love for him, until all that was left was a pile of ash on the floor of the stage, her silent tears falling into them and being absorbed by the cinder.

No one spoke a word.

Exhausted from grief and shock, I went to my room.

Sleep evaded me, as I lay in my bed focusing all my energy into my heart, thinking about what I had just seen. I focused on Sadie; on my love for her. On what life was like before she died. On how happy we were together. I thought about seeing her again.

Pushing those warm feelings through my solar plexus. I imagined the small lump in the center of my chest growing tenfold. Eventually, a semi-sleep overtook me; I could no longer resist.

It was like a fever of grief, exhaustion, confusion, and hope.

When I awoke the next morning, my chest felt tight and tender. I looked down, unsurprised to see the mass fully developed under my inflamed, red skin. Heat radiated outward from the center of the unnatural growth and I was shivering through cold sweats.

I had no other choice but to go to the dining room and get a knife. When I walked into the chapel, I saw the others, all of whom also had knives in their hands. Dr. Ewing was pacing on the stage.

Less a doctor than a carnival-barker, he turned and asked, "So, who's next."

Sadie's urn sat ominously on the table with all the others. I had to see her again.

I grabbed her cremains.

And I cut her new heart from my chest.

AFTERWORD

SAM RICHARD & BRENDAN VIDITO

The seed of this project was planted several years ago, during our first meeting at BizarroCon 2016. We had only known each other for a few hours, talking enthusiastically about everything from J.G. Ballard to body horror. The conversation then steered toward themed anthologies. We remarked how it was strange that no one had released a David Cronenberg tribute anthology. Just a few years earlier, the 'other' David had his turn with *In Heaven Everything is Fine* edited by Cameron Pierce. Drunk on booze and the creative pheromones swirling through the air at BizarroCon, we agreed that—if ever given the chance—we would work on the project together. And, as evidenced by the book you now hold in your hands, that drunken fantasy became reality.

Nearly three years later, we decided the time was right to start working on the anthology. Sam brought his experience and knowledge from editing/co-editing three previous Weirdpunk Books projects, *Zombie Punks Fuck Off, Hybrid Moments: A Literary Tribute to the Misfits,* and *Blood for You: A Literary Tribute to GG Allin,* while Brendan—having only written short fiction—was about to take his first stab at being an editor. But nothing prepared us for the sheer flood of submissions. Once the deadline hit, our inbox contained 200 stories, more than double that of previous Weirdpunk open calls. Sam did the math, and if the average sub was 4,000 words, we read through approximately 800,000 words worth of stories to decide on the eighteen you just read. That's more words than the goddamn Bible!

Needless to say it was an exhaustive and time-consuming process. We snuck in some reading at work, and when we should have been sleeping, all while juggling our various individual projects. Throughout this process, we messaged back and forth, sharing our opinions and experiences with the stories, and we don't want to throw shade at anyone who subbed (in fact, thank you if you did!), but we are unable to deny the fact that at least some of the subs we got seemed to only have knowledge of Cronenberg through that episode of *Rick & Morty*, which was a bit disheartening.

Though we received a stack of great pieces of fiction, we wanted stories that tackled Cronenberg's many themes and ideas and made them fresh, contemporary, and horrifyingly relevant. Whether we're talking about humanity intersecting with technology in frightening and surreal ways, an individual fighting against becoming one with a mass-organism, bodies twisted into strange new forms, shadowy organizations pulling the character's strings, interesting takes on new age gurus and psychotherapy cults, philosophical and psychological subtexts, and characters—either knowingly or unknowingly—headed towards transcendence, it is our belief that these eighteen stories capture that evasive quality known only as Cronenbergian. But, in the end, we'll let you be the judge of that. We hope you enjoyed reading this anthology as much as we enjoyed editing it.

Before we go, however, we want to extend a few words of appreciation. First, we would like to thank David Cronenberg himself, for continuing to inspire us with his ideas and eclectic filmography. If you happen to find, or perhaps read, this book, please don't get mad at us—but if you do, would it be cool if we used your anger as a blurb for the book? But seriously, thank you! Secondly, we would like to send our sincerest gratitude to the incomparable Kathe Koja for her work on the introduction. Your fiction is without peer and like Cronenberg you have inspired us, and so many others, with your talent and creative daring. Of course we also need to extend out deepest thanks to the contributing authors, who all wrote such brilliant and engaging stories that we were forced to make this book 10,000 words longer than initially planned. Y'all killed it. We also need to thank Michael Bukowski and Sarah Seember Huisken for faithfully bringing to life the spirit and visceral gut punch Cronenberg's aesthetic for the front and back cover; as well as Jim Agpalza, for sending us the amazing interior mugwump illustration. And finally, we would like to thank YOU the reader for picking up the book and supporting the many writers herein. You make our psychoplasmic polyps throb with ecstasy and joy. Long Live the New Flesh!

ABOUT THE AUTHORS

SARA CENTURY is a writer, artist, podcaster, and comic creator, which you can read more about at www.saracentury.-com. She got her start in media working for Toronto's CIVIC-TV and is eagerly awaiting the development of her very own external womb.

BRIAN EVENSON is the author of over a dozen books of fiction, including mostly recently *Song for the Unraveling of the World*. He teaches at CalArts and lives in Los Angeles. His first Cronenberg was *Scanners,* which he saw in a drive-in when he was in high school. He's never been the same since—he's pretty sure someone else came back from the drive-in instead of him.

FIONA MAEVE GEIST spent her teen years glued to the exquisite body horror of Cronenberg and never lost that love. She is a former academic, present editor and her critical work has appeared in *Lamplight Quarterly* and *Lovecraftian Proceedings* and her fiction has appeared in *Ashes & Entropy* and *Vastarian*. She primarily works in pen and paper roleplaying games, tweets as @coilingoracle and lives in WXXT country where she cultivates neuroses and her friendship with her cat.

CODY GOODFELLOW has written eight novels and five collections. He also wrote, co-produced and scored the short Lovecraftian hygiene films *Stay At Home Dad* and *Baby Got Bass,* which can be viewed on YouTube. He is a cofounder of

Perilous Press, an occasional micropublisher of modern cosmic horror, and the editor of *Forbidden Futures,* a quarterly hyperpulp zine featuring art by Mike Dubisch. A lifelong devotee of Cronenberg's work ever since he was dropped off at the multiplex to see Popeye and snuck into *Scanners* instead, he is still obsessively seeking a typewriter that dispenses hallucinogenics when it likes what you wrote.

RYAN HARDING is the author of *Genital Grinder* and coauthor of *Header 3* (with Edward Lee), *Reincarnage* (Jason Taverner), and *1000 Severed Dicks* (Matt Shaw). He is a 3-time Splatterpunk Award nominee and 2-time winner (*Header 3* and "The Seacretor"). The sequel to *Reincarnage* and a new collection will be released in 2020 through Section 31. He maintains Cronenberg's run of sci-fi/horror cinema from *Shivers* through *eXistenZ* is unsurpassed. He has been a devotee since VHS was the only format to own *Videodrome,* which along with *Rabid* and *The Fly* are his top 3 Cronenberg films.

EMMA ALICE JOHNSON writes stories and books and zines. She lifts weights and eats ice cream. Having had her skull completely disassembled a couple of times, she feels like she could really teach that ol' Cronenbum a thing or two about body horror. She lives in Minneapolis by the lakes.

GWENDOLYN KISTE is the Bram Stoker Award-winning author of *The Rust Maidens,* from Trepidatio Publishing; *And Her Smile Will Untether the Universe,* from JournalStone; and the dark fantasy novella, *Pretty Marys All in a Row,* from Broken Eye Books. Her short fiction has appeared in *Nightmare Magazine, Shimmer, Black Static, Daily Science Fiction, Interzone, LampLight,* and *Three-Lobed Burning Eye,* among others. Her discovery of David Cronenberg's work during her teens and college years has left her with an insatiable adoration for all things body horror. Find Gwendolyn and her grotesquely beautiful stories at gwendolynkiste.com

MONA SWAN LESUEUR is an author, performer, and theatre director/dramaturg from Scottsdale, Arizona. When they are not busy creating/collaborating, they like to eat sushi, watch weird films, play roleplaying games, and explore/photograph abandoned locations. Their favorite David Cronenberg films are *Videodrome, Scanners,* and *Crash.*

BRUNO LOMBARDI was born in Montreal in 1968. He has had a rather distressing tendency to be a weirdness magnet for much of his adult life. He currently lives in Ottawa and works as a civil servant for the Canadian government, as well as being a slave to his cat Mynx. He has a number of writing credits including a novel *Snake Oil,* and stories in *Weirdbook* and other anthologies. His first introduction to David Cronenberg was at the ripe old age of ten, when he saw *Shivers*—with his initial reaction being 'What the fuck was that?'—a mantra that has followed much of life since then.

JACK LOTHIAN is a screenwriter for film and television and is currently showrunner on the HBO / Cinemax series *Strike Back.* He's had short fiction published in a number of anthologies and magazines, and his graphic novel *Tomorrow,* illustrated by Garry Mac, was nominated for a 2018 British Fantasy Award. His first Cronenberg was *Rabid,* thanks to Alex Cox's wonderful Moviedrome series, and it put him off experimental surgery and garbage trucks for life.

CHARLES AUSTIN MUIR is the author of *This Is a Horror Book* and *Bodybuilding Spider Rangers.* His stories have appeared in horror anthologies like *Peel Back the Skin, Dark Visions Volume One,* and *Year's Best Hardcore Horror Vol. 1.* His favorite David Cronenberg movie is *Videodrome.* It gave him permission to embrace his television, literally. "Don't keep me waiting," Caroline Ingalls told him one day before he stuck his head into the television screen and sucked on her huge teeth. He went on to become a regular on *Little House on the Prairie,* including the notorious clown rape episode.

C.M. MULLER lives in St. Paul, Minnesota with his wife and two sons. His tales have appeared in *Shadows & Tall Trees, Vastarien, Weirdbook,* and a host of other venues. As editor and publisher, he is responsible for the annual anthology series *Nightscript,* as well as *Twice-Told: A Collection of Doubles,* a themed anthology featuring 22 unique visions of the doppelgänger. His debut collection of stories, *Hidden Folk,* was released in late 2018. A long-time admirer of David Cronenberg, he counts *Videodrome* as one of his favorite films. For more information, please visit: www.chthonicmatter.wordpress.com

KATY MICHELLE QUINN is a queer punk who writes sappy, sapphic weirdo horror. As a transgender woman, body horror is a part of everyday life, and she appreciates the work of David Cronenberg because of its obsession with the transformation of the body into new and unexpected forms. Currently, Katy lives in the forests of Olympia with her partner and cats. Her first novella *Winnie* was released by Eraserhead Press in 2018.

LEO X. ROBERTSON is a Scottish process engineer and writer, currently living in Stavanger, Norway. He has work published in *Weirdpunk Books' Zombie Punks Fuck Off* anthology, *Flame Tree Press' Urban Crime* anthology, *Pulp Literature* and others. His favorite Cronenberg movie is *Maps to the Stars*. He knows it isn't quintessential Cronenberg, but Bruce Wagner wrote it, and he's one of the greats.

ALEX SMITH is the author of *HIVE,* a novella tracing a fragmented couple's descent into the child-laden bowels of a building in Queens. Alex's fiction has appeared in *Theaker's Quarterly Fiction, Octopus Magazine,* and the Muzzleland Press anthology *Terror in 16-bits.* His favorite Cronenberg film is *Videodrome.*

MAX D. STANTON is an academic, writer, and morbid oddball who hails from the gritty land of Philadelphia. His stories have appeared in publications including *Vastarien, Hinnom Magazine, Sanitarium,* and the *Corporate Cthulhu* and *We Shall Be Monsters* anthologies. He is currently at work on his first novel. Stanton was introduced to Cronenberg's films in college and they have stuck with him ever since, like a brain infection imbuing him with incurable notions of horrific transcendence and grotesque beauty.

MADELEINE SWANN's connected collection of stories, *Fortune Box,* was published by Eraserhead Press, her second novella by Strangehouse Books, and her first was part of the New Bizarro Author Series. Her short stories have appeared on various podcasts and anthologies and can be found at madeleineswann.com.

ABOUT THE EDITORS

SAM RICHARD is the owner of Weirdpunk Books and is the editor of *Zombie Punks Fuck Off,* and co-editor of *Hybrid Moments: A Literary Tribute to the Misfits*. His debut short story collection, *To Wallow in Ash & Other Sorrows,* came out in fall of 2019, and his writing has appeared in such varied publications as *Strange Stories of the Sea, Breaking Bizarro, Strange Behaviors, Dark Moon Digest,* and many others. His first brush with Cronenberg comes in hazy memories of seeing the infamous head-exploding scene from *Scanners* on illegally descrambled cable as a child. He's fairly certain it rewired his brain. Recently a widower, he slowly rots in Minneapolis, MN with his dog Nero.

BRENDAN VIDITO is the author of the Splatterpunk Award-nominated collection of body horror stories, *Nightmares in Ecstasy* (CLASH Books). His work has appeared in several magazines and anthologies, including *Tragedy Queens: Stories Inspired by Lana Del Rey and Sylvia Plath, Past Indiscretions: The Very Best of Splatterpunk Zine, Dead Bait 4,* and *Pluto in Furs.* When he was a teenager, he watched *The Brood* and *Videodrome* during a post-surgical, morphine-fuelled haze and Cronenberg has been a major influence on his writing ever since. He lives in Sudbury, Ontario. You can visit him at brendanvidito.com.

CPSIA information can be obtained
at www.ICGtesting.com
Printed in the USA
BVHW032118131219
566648BV00001B/71/P

9 781951 658007